OPERATOR

by
David Vinjamuri

ISBN: 0985775602
EAN: 9780985775605
LCCN: 2012942193
ThirdWay
Pleasantville, NY

For S.K. and Spenser, his namesake.

Prologue -

Wednesday

She almost misses the child: a small, frail thing trembling in the rain. The pale young woman hasn't come looking for anyone, but only to right the trashcan. She was grading a stack of essays when she heard the metallic clatter outside her window. Seeing that it was the neighbor's can and not hers, she was tempted to ignore the spill. But it is not in the woman's constitution to let a thing go un-righted, and so she ventured outside in a bright yellow raincoat to investigate. As she opened her door she smelled the river, out of sight but always sharp in the air. The silver can had rolled to a halt at the concrete curb, its guts emptying sideways on the road. Not much of a spill, just a couple of intact white kitchen-size trash bags peeking out. The woman stuffed them one-two back in and replaced the lid. Then, anchoring the bottom of the can against her sneaker, the woman pulled it back upright. Only then did she see the girl. Actually, just the hair at first, a real mop of it, pale blond and tangled like seaweed.

Now the woman leans in to investigate. The woman has not seen this particular girl before, and she knows all the children of the neighborhood. This one looks to be a grade-schooler – perhaps nine or ten. The girl is sobbing gently, indifferent to the rain as it soaks through her light cotton dress. Her thin fingers are pressed together as if she's praying while she rocks slowly back and forth. The pale woman sits down next to her and rests a hand lightly on the girl's back. The girl flinches but never looks up. Instead, she starts crying in earnest, putting her weight on the stranger's shoulder.

After a few moments the convulsions subside. The girl wipes her face with her fists as a toddler might, and looks up. The woman sees an ugly bruise covering the girl's cheekbone. She touches it gently with her thumb, pulling away the strands of tangled hair, and sees that the bruise isn't new. Whatever has the girl crying now hasn't surfaced yet. The girl starts speaking softly. It's not English but the woman understands some of what she's saying. The girl is speaking Russian with an unfamiliar accent, not the St. Petersburg lilt that is familiar to the woman. "He hits me," she makes out, "always he hits me." Then the girl haltingly begins to tell her story and the pale woman forgets the cold rain on her feet, the trashcan and everything else.

"Yelena, come here at once!" a voice barks in Russian, and the girl and the woman both jump. The girl trembles. A man is striding across the yard. The woman sees his eyes first. They are so dark that the pupil fades into the iris. The man meets the woman's startled stare with a basilisk's gaze. He is built as thick as the metal trashcan beside her, but he crosses the lawn in four paces without seeming to hurry. Tattoos swirl down the sides of his neck from the fringe of the blond hair on his closely shaven scalp and snake down his thick forearms. A smile is fixed on his face as he looks at the woman, but his eyes are dead flat.

The woman's instinct is to protect the girl, to shield her, but those reptilian eyes paralyze her and she does not move. As the thick man grabs hold of the girl's wrist, he says gruffly in stumbling English, "Thank you for watching my daughter. She is being very bad tonight." Then he pulls the girl onto her feet and drags her toward the house with the blue shutters. He speaks to the girl rapidly in Russian. The woman doesn't understand the man until she hears him say, "You stupid girl, now you will pay." Then the woman gasps involuntarily. The man stops immediately, standing stock still on the threshold of his doorway. "You speak Russian?" he asks slowly in Russian. The woman stares at him, still paralyzed by fear. Then, taking hold of herself she forces a smile, ignores the question and walks purposefully to her house. She steps through the front door, closes it and slams the deadbolt home. Without removing her raincoat she gradually slides down to the floor, her back against the door, sniffling at first and then descending into sobs. It takes her a few moments to regain her senses, to begin to think clearly.

She pulls herself up to the kitchen counter, grabs the phone and starts to dial 9-1-1, still shaking. She misdials twice and almost laughs at herself, at her inability to string three simple digits together. When she finally dials the number in sequence, the line rings twice and the 911 operator, says "9-1-1 – what is the nature of your emergency?" As the woman is about to respond, a hand clamps down on her mouth and the phone is suddenly not in her hands. She is pulled back off balance as she hears the words, "Hello? Hello?" in the accented voice that is burned into her memory. The man pauses for a moment, listening, then says contritely, "Very sorry I am trying to reach information for pizza delivery – Dominos." Then he chuckles, the sound coming out of his throat like lumps of coal clattering in a hollow stove, "Please excuse, I am very sorry." He hangs up the phone.

He releases his hand over the woman's mouth and nose and she gasps for air. Before she can scream he slaps her across the face with the back of his hand, stunning her. Waving a stubby finger in her face with disapproval, he speaks to her again in Russian: "Now, what are we going to do with you?"

Chapter One –

Friday

Angry voices spill from the darkness as I gently pull the door to the funeral home closed. From a distance, individual words are indecipherable, but the tone is unmistakable. A man and a woman stand twenty yards away on damp asphalt, centered in the pale circle of yellow light cast by a street lamp. The woman is barely over five feet tall, slender and pale with glossy, straight brown hair. She wears a black dress cut just below the knees and flat shoes. She is talking with her hands, jabbing her finger at the man's chest to punctuate her words. The man towers over her by at least a foot and a half. He has blond hair and the clean-scrubbed look of a commuter, an office-worker. His jaw is chiseled and he looks like the kind of guy whose photo a teenage girl would cut out of a magazine. Except for his eyes, which are clear blue but not kind. The man is leaning into the argument, trying to intimidate the women with his size, but the woman clearly has him off-balance. There's steam rising from his head as if he's been running. He tries to interrupt the woman and fails, and I see his eyes narrow to slits. Then something the woman says makes him swear and take a step toward her. She does not step back.

The look on the blond man's face freezes me in mid-step. My feet are carrying me in a different direction, toward my car. I want nothing more than to return to my motel room, put a hot towel over my head and let this awful day evaporate in the steam. But the conversation between these two strangers has crossed a line. I can feel it snap; the fragile filament of social contract between them is gone. I hesitate, and it saddens me. Time was I'd have stepped forward without a second thought. But as I look at the tall blond man looming over the short woman, I see him rocking on his heels, see his right hand clenching into a fist. I sigh and redirect my steps.

As I draw closer, the angry tones resolve into words. The man says, "*I'll be damned if I let some little bitch talk to me like that...*" Self-narration in the middle of an argument is not a good sign. A few yards closer and I can see that his face is the same shade as a cherry-flavored popsicle. He may not have thrown a punch yet, but his fists are clenching and unclenching rhythmically. He is large and fit, but he has lost emotional control and he's leaning forward onto his right foot, which puts him physically off-balance. His hands are callused at the knuckles, but not the way they get when you fight barehanded. His face is unmarked, and his nose has never been broken. He is right handed and not carrying a gun. If he has a knife, it's not someplace he can reach it quickly. I relax marginally. Whoever this man is, he's not a professional.

I consider how to defuse the argument as I approach the couple. When I get close enough for them to see me, I extend my hands in front of me with the palms up and fix an unnaturally broad smile on my face. As I open my mouth to speak, I hear the door to the funeral home open twenty yards behind me, followed by footfalls on the wooden porch. My mind transforms these sounds into shapes: a couple, the woman less than a hundred pounds in heels and the man about a hundred sixty, walking slowly with a cane. An elderly couple: I've seen them inside. I tune them out and step into the pale circle of light.

"Uh – pardon me – this is a little embarrassing but I think I'm turned around. I parked near Oak Street, do you know which way that is?" I speak a little louder than necessary and address the question to the small space between the man and the woman, causing them both to turn toward me. I see the man's angry blue eyes sweep over me once, quickly. He registers me as a half-foot shorter than him and thus not a threat. That's the lizard brain inside of him thinking. The woman's eyes dart toward me briefly. They are hazel and larger than I expect. But she will not be distracted and quickly shifts her attention back to the man. She holds herself like a little terrier barking after a Doberman: indignant and furious without any sense of her tiny stature or what happens if the big dog takes the bait.

The question hangs in the space between the two of them for a second before the man responds. "It's on the other side of the hill," he says, barely glancing at me. He doesn't make eye contact but jabs his finger in the direction I was heading, "that way."

"Thanks. I really should know better, but it's been a long time." I keep my voice even and friendly, pretending to be oblivious to the intense silence that follows. I let the moment stretch out for a spell before asking, "Were you at the memorial service?"

"Yes," the tall man responds. His voice lacks inflection. Hostility radiates off of him in waves. There's another moment of tense silence. I keep smiling and nodding, like an amiable idiot or perhaps an overbearing uncle who hasn't realized he's not welcome at the family reunion. Then something in the air shifts imperceptibly. The woman turns to me.

"How did you know Mel?" she asks, her eyes meeting mine for the first time. I can see her register that I'm throwing her a lifeline.

"We ... we dated in high school. I haven't seen her in ..." here I pause to count and then pause again as I realize the size of the number, "twelve years." My throat is suddenly dry as I try to swallow. *Twelve years.* Then the man turns toward me. His eyes lock on mine like the targeting radar on an F-22 Raptor. I instinctively widen my stance and balance forward onto the balls of my feet.

The woman's mouth drops open and a manicured hand quickly moves to cover it. "My God! Are you Mike Herne?" she asks.

I nod slowly, caught off-guard by the question. I take a closer look at this woman. She looks to be somewhere near my age, maybe just on the sunny side of thirty. She's pretty in a refined way. The little black dress accents the curves on her small frame. It hugs her well enough that I'd have trouble believing it's off the rack, though I'm no expert. A double-strand of pearls wraps her neck, large enough to flatter the dress but small enough to look elegant rather than vulgar. The jacket that hangs over it all, a sort of fitted black trench coat that she's left open, probably cost more than my last car. Her nails are manicured short and glossed with clear-coat. The flats she is wearing look expensive, the leather reflecting the glow of the street lamp from somewhere deep inside. She obviously comes from money and is just as obviously not from Conestoga.

"Well, my car is on the other side of the hill, too. Why don't you walk me there?" she says and steps forward, linking her arm through mine as if I'm escorting her to a cotillion. She pivots toward the tall blond man for a second as we step away. "We can finish this conversation later," she says firmly and turns her head, not waiting for a response. He stays rooted in place, glowering as we disappear into the gloom.

We walk in silence for a few moments, but once we've crested the hill and are safely out of earshot, she speaks.

"You weren't really lost, were you?" Then she shakes her head, answering her own question before I can. "I don't know what I was thinking, picking a fight with him. That was stupid. I could have gotten myself in trouble. Thank you for saving me from my own pig-headedness." She nods once sharply to accent her point.

I shrug. "Who was that guy?"

"George Jeffries. He was in Russia with us. Now he's telling everyone he was Mel's fiancé. Which is an outrageous fabrication. He's the reason she left the program. She came back home because of him!"

"Russia?"

"You don't know?"

"I don't know anything." It is true; I did not speak to Mel once in the last dozen years.

"I guess you don't," she says, and we continue on for another moment in silence. "But here's my car," she points to a silver Mercedes coupe, "and I need to call home soon, or my parents will worry. It's amazing that after college and grad school and four years abroad they still think I'm sixteen. Are you going to the funeral tomorrow?" She is speaking so rapidly that it takes me a second to identify the question. I nod slowly.

She opens a slim black purse and with two fingers extracts a silver case. Delicately she opens it and withdraws a card, which she hands to me. The paper is thick and textured in my rough hands.

"I'm Veronica," she says, extending her hand. I clasp it briefly. It is cool, the ambient temperature of the air around us. "Why don't we have coffee afterward? Mel talked a lot about you. I'd like to hear your story." She doesn't wait for me to answer, just smiles and slips into her car. A second later she's gone. I'm left standing in the middle of the damp road, holding her card. It has her name, Veronica Ryan, and a phone number printed on it in neat black letters. No company or title, not even an e-mail address. I shake my head. This is a nannies-ponies-and-private-school kind of girl. She doesn't belong here.

I sit in the bathroom of the small motel room with my head hanging forward over the tub. A threadbare white towel hangs over my head, dripping monotonously onto the faded white porcelain surface. I watch the beads of water gather into a tiny stream that twists slowly downhill to the drain, and wish they would spin counterclockwise as they do south of the equator. A light veil of steam rises from the towel, inhibited by the damp fall air. I breathe slowly and deeply as I count my pulse descending towards its resting rate of fifty beats per minute. With my fingers I trace the raised lines of the jagged scars on my neck, then the puckered one on my left shoulder.

My mind drifts back to my last days in Conestoga twelve years ago. I can still smell the overpoweringly sour fragrance of lilies at my dad's funeral. I remember the angry, strained look on my mother's face as we argue. Mostly I remember the lost look of my youngest sister Ginny as I close the door to my mother's house, leaving her on the wrong side, then walk away with a single duffle bag slung over my shoulder. The stink of my cowardice overpowers the cheap floral sent of motel soap. Eventually, I lie down on the narrow bed, close my eyes and wish to God that I smoked.

Chapter Two –

Saturday

Dawn comes late to Conestoga, as the sun must scale the bluffs on the east side of the Hudson before peering down on the town nestled against the river. My footfalls echo softly against the row of clapboard houses as I run through the sleeping town, now and then peering up at the gray sky. The houses on King's Road huddle together on their small plots like crows perched on a telephone wire. The colors on this street are muted, almost monochrome in their palate, with the exception of an azure blue house with yellow shutters sitting in the middle of the block like an orphan flower in a sea of weeds.

I reach River Road and turn left, heading north toward Main Street. Conestoga is still but for the occasional car that passes with headlights on or a stray head poking out from behind a door to snatch the newspaper from the front stoop. I'm conscious of retracing my childhood as I move through the deserted streets. I loop around Church Street onto High Bridge Road. Mel's parents live here. Their driveway is full and there are a number of cars with out-of-state plates parked on the road. The house is dark, excepting a single light in an upstairs bedroom. Three blocks further and I make the turn onto Green Farms Road. My childhood house looks the same, except that someone has painted the old swing chair on the front porch. Mom's battered Chevy pickup is parked in the driveway next to a spotless Cadillac Escalade that could only belong to my oldest sister Amelia and her husband Jeff. There is a beaten down Jeep Cherokee from the nineties sitting behind the Escalade and a Honda Civic parked on the street in front of the yard. *Everybody's home.*

I arrived at the funeral home late enough last night to miss my own family, though I did see Mel's. I'll see them this afternoon at the cemetery, though—no avoiding that. It can't be put off any more. The farther I get from Conestoga, the more it pulls at me. I shake off the thought as the house fades into the gloom and I turn onto Ridge Road, climbing in earnest. I keep up a brisk pace for three miles as the road twists and turns until I reach the old mill. I pull up just shy of the rusted chain link fence barring the entrance. This is where my father and grandfather spent every working day of their lives. This is the mill that closed two weeks before I graduated high school. The place has power for me, like a Native American burial ground.

Three towers thrust up from the site, looming over Conestoga like the witches from *Macbeth* over their cauldrons. In front of them are several buildings, the largest made of staged platforms with crazy pipes running through them. It looks like a competition diving platform constructed with a Lego kit. The platform structure is flanked by a schoolhouse-style administration building on one side and an enormous warehouse on the other. The buildings are crowded together—piled up against each other like old shoeboxes in a closet. The enormous yard in front of the mill has fallen into disuse, and grass has grown over the railroad tracks. A boxcar stands empty in the yard, waiting to be loaded. I see the first touch of red light hit the top of one of the towers in anticipation of the arriving dawn. Before I have a chance to think too much, I put my hand on the fence, testing the links. Then I back up a few yards and with three steps I am up and over. My real workout is just beginning.

The interment ceremony is brief. The cemetery behind Riverbend Church is the oldest in Conestoga, dating from the time of the town's first settlement as a royal charter to a wealthy merchant in 1745. Conestoga has been going downhill ever since. Mel—Melissa Jane Harris—was Catholic but because of the manner of her death, she can't be buried at Holy Oak Cemetery. Mel's parents managed to convince the parish priest to say a few words for her, which he does. Then some of Mel's friends and students say a few more words. I have certainly attended more funerals than any of the 300 Conestogans standing around me but this ceremony is especially raw. Nobody should have to bury a girl like Mel.

My mother is not around, which is just as well. She was never close to Mel. I haven't spoken a word to the woman for twelve years and a burial doesn't seem like the right place to break the silence. I'm standing between Amelia and Ginny, who is leaning on my shoulder and sobs through the whole wretched affair. My sister Jamie is on Ginny's right and Jeff is on the other side of Amelia. In the end, I put a shovelful of dirt onto the grave, hug my sisters, and shake hands with Jeff before walking silently from the gathering. I'm remembering my father's funeral. He's here somewhere, too.

Veronica stands waiting for me outside the cemetery. I didn't see her during the interment, but that's not surprising given the size of the crowd. It must have been intimidating for her. When a small town buries one of its children, it is a communal enterprise. Every family in Conestoga had some connection to Mel and would have even had she not been teaching half of their children. For days now, Ed and Beth Harris's home will have been overflowing with people stopping over to deliver pies and casseroles. They won't cook for months. For the next year, they'll get a call every few days from some fellow parishioner, asking them to play bridge or go to a movie. It will probably take them a few months to identify the pattern. For all of its flaws, Conestoga takes care of its own.

"Where should we go?" Veronica asks. She's wearing another simple but expensive-looking black dress under the same jacket with a different set of pearls. This strand is a bit longer, long enough for her to twist into a loop with her finger while she bites her lip, waiting for my reply.

I have to think for a moment. Conestoga has exactly one diner and three bars, but it will be difficult to talk privately at any of them. I suddenly realize that I'm already attracting stares from people leaving the cemetery. I can see a pair of middle-aged women looking at me as the one with a moon-shaped face points at me insistently with a jabbing gesture and whispers furiously into the other's ear. I think the thinner one is my mother's hairdresser. My return might rival the funeral itself for gossip value and I have a strong urge to disappear. Not Conestoga, then.

"Let's go to the coffee shop in Dill Springs," I suggest. "It's about twenty minutes' drive south."

I've walked to the cemetery from my motel, so Veronica drives. Her SLK-350 roadster with its 268 horsepower motor makes short work of route 9W as we head south. Dill Springs is the northernmost town in the Catskills within a two-hour drive of New York City and it wears an urbane air that marks it a world apart from Conestoga. The coffee shop is set in an old storefront with hardwood floors and a vast ceiling of worked tin. It's different from what I remember—it now looks more like a Starbucks without the generic Pottery Barn interior. Veronica orders a cappuccino while I puzzle over the menu for a moment, finally asking for the closest approximation to real black coffee that I can find. We sit down in leather armchairs set at an angle to one another and I have the transitory sensation that I'm in someone's living room. There are some impressively detailed portraits of kitchen appliances on the wall and I wonder for a second if they might be Ginny's but the name on them is Jennie Schaeffer.

"You said that you met Mel in Russia?" I ask after we've sat in silence for a few moments. The car ride was also quiet. I wonder if I've been rude.

Soil gets in your blood and the smells of my hometown—that mixture of red earth and river—have finally caught up with me. I realize that Veronica hasn't spoken not because she lacks curiosity, but because she's both intuitive enough to have figured this out for herself and patient enough to wait for me to start talking.

"Yes I did. We were roommates. We taught English on the Glasnost program. They pay your room and board, you get a small stipend and you get to learn Russian intensively while you teach English. Mel was there for two years—I lasted almost four."

"Four years is a long time to teach English abroad, isn't it? Where in Russia were you?"

"St. Petersburg. That's probably why I stayed so long. Most kids who join end up in some tiny village in the middle of nowhere and come back after a year or two. But St. Petersburg—it was just unbelievable. Even with the mosquitoes in the summer and the dreary winters it was just an amazing place. I still miss it."

"When did you get back?" I ask, because I realize I have no idea how Mel spent her life after I left home. I never asked.

"I came back about two years ago. Mel left a year before I did." Veronica starts telling me details about the time they spent in St. Petersburg. It's a lovely city. I went there a number of times for work. I listen to her describe her experiences and I can't help thinking how different the Mel she knew sounds from the seventeen-year-old girl I remember.

"What are you doing now?"

"Ah—now I'm writing silly feature stories for the *White Plains Gazette* while I dream about my future job as foreign correspondent for *The New York Times*. And living with my parents in Greenwich," she adds, waving her hand over her head in a southeasterly direction.

"You drove back there last night? How far is that?" In fact I know that it is over 90 miles and on the wrong side of the Hudson.

"No, I'm staying in a B&B in Rhinebeck for the weekend. It's amazing how nice everything is when you get just a little further south of Conestoga," she says off-handedly and then colors, adding, "I'm sorry," as she realizes she's insulted my hometown.

"Don't be. You're absolutely right. Fifty years ago, Conestoga was a solid working class town. Then the mill started losing business and laying people off every year and the town shrank with it. People who held on, like my family, were living on a tightrope. A lot of them drank or gambled," and here I think of my Dad, "and a lot of people got involved in bad things. After the mill closed," I swallow some of the hot black coffee, which is not bad in spite of its pretentious name and inflated price, "things got worse. A lot worse, I think." If what I've seen on my morning run is representative of the whole town, I'm downplaying the truth. The best sections of Conestoga now look like Newark, New Jersey, or the Compton section of Los Angeles. The houses are shabby and the yards unkempt, but there are expensive cars in some driveways. There is money in Conestoga, but it's the wrong kind.

"So, the guy you were," I pause, trying to find a polite phrase, "*talking to* last night—what's his story?"

Veronica smiles sourly. "George. Trouble. Big trouble, that's his story. I could see it in him from the beginning, but Mel didn't have that instinct. She trusted people, took them at their word. She was so naïve. And he was this big shot banker, very charming when he wanted to be, knew everyone in town and took her out places she couldn't afford to go. But he was a player, you know—there were probably ten other girls besides Mel at the same time, most of them Russian with no brains but legs up to here," she chops her hand at her Adam's apple, "who would do anything for a nice meal or a night out at a club. And he had a temper—almost as bad as mine." She smiles briefly, flashing perfectly straight white teeth. "One day, about a year after they started dating, Mel came home from a weekend with a bruise on her cheek and said that she tripped and hit a doorknob. Then a few weeks later it was a broken arm—this time she fell playing tennis. Then finally she showed up with a black eye and that's when I called her parents. She spent a whole weekend crying on and off the phone with them. I asked a friend of mine who had connections to do me a favor and the next week a messenger showed up at our door with an envelope. There were a whole bunch of pictures of George with other women. Mel left the country three days after that."

I think about that last part for a moment but don't say anything. I can tell that Veronica is aggrieved, really upset. George's appearance at the funeral home must have been a slap in the face. "How did they get back together here?" I ask.

"They didn't!" she hisses, almost spitting, "No way. He left St. Petersburg about six months after she did and moved to Manhattan. Then another six months later I get a call from her saying that George showed up at her school. It really scared her. I mean, that's like a five-hour drive round-trip, right? I actually flew back home to stay with her for a week. Then about a month later he appeared outside her place, pounding on her door in the middle of the night. She threatened to call the police and he finally left. When I got back she hadn't seen him for nearly a year. Then last year he started calling again and about two months ago he showed up at her place and tried to force her into his car. Her landlord started hitting George with a rake and someone called the police this time. Right afterward, Mel took out a restraining order on George and as far as I know he hasn't been around since then. Until last night."

"And last night he was saying that he was her fiancé?"

"Yes! Can you believe it? I'm standing there talking to Mrs. Harris and suddenly I hear his voice. He's chatting up some bimbo, telling her that he and Mel were engaged and giving her some sob story. He wouldn't dare say that to her parents, but can you imagine? Mel is lying there literally twenty feet away from him and he's hitting on some nineteen-year-old. So when he leaves I follow him out. I tell him exactly what I think of him. And that's just when you show up to rescue me," Veronica smiles charmingly, her soft pink lipstick glowing against those white teeth.

"George looked like he was about to take a swing at you," I observe.

Veronica nods vigorously. "How stupid am I? I'm standing there in the dark on a deserted street arguing with this crazy guy who beat up my best friend? I just got so angry and I thought, 'I'm not going to let him get away with that—not here.' And I don't stop to think that he might actually hurt *me.*" She puts a hand over her eyes, massaging her forehead, and leans back in her chair. Her feet slide out of her shoes and she props them up on the inlaid wood coffee table between us. Black wool stockings cover her legs. "That was very clever, by the way, how you handled George last night," she says, smiling at me.

I shrug again. I feel myself being pulled in an uncomfortable direction.

"No, seriously, it was. You just played dumb and whisked me away before he could even respond. No confrontation, no fight. Pretty smart. You're a man of twists and turns, aren't you?" she smiles. I raise an eyebrow because I get the reference, but I don't respond. "And here we've been sitting for nearly an hour and I keep talking and talking and you've hardly said two words about yourself."

I stop a moment to consider that. "It's been a long time since I was home and you're helping me catch up, which I appreciate."

"You know Melissa talked about you a lot. She really idolized you," Veronica says. Her voice quiets as her tone turns more serious.

She catches me off-guard again. I actually stutter when I respond.

"I-I would have thought that she hated me. I walked out on her—I abandoned her."

Veronica shakes her head with conviction. "She didn't think that. I mean … of course she missed you. I think she spent her first two weeks of college crying. But she didn't blame you. You left your mother, not Mel. And you still helped support your family, didn't you, even if you didn't stay in Conestoga? That's a lot to carry for an eighteen-year-old." I see a spark of compassion in Veronica's eyes and look away.

"It wasn't like that. I was a stupid kid."

I can feel my face burning. Veronica is so earnest that I can almost see things from her perspective. But what looks brave to her was just plain fear and immaturity. Yes, I was furious at my mother but even more mortified by my reaction to her ultimatum. "With your father gone, you have to help me support the family," she'd said to me exactly one day after my Dad's funeral. "Ned Vickers will give you a job at his machine shop." It wasn't a discussion, just a statement of fact. Like the solid sound of a prison door slamming shut. I ran upstairs and threw some clothes and a few personal items in a duffle and then I walked out of that house and never looked back. It was just a few weeks after my eighteenth birthday.

I couldn't go to Michigan and play football after my mother told me I'd be starving my sisters, but I was damn well not going to get stuck in Conestoga for the rest of my life. So I enlisted. I sent money back home every month: that was atonement. In all the time since, even after I left the Army, I've been too ashamed to come home and face my mother. At least once a month for the past few years, Ginny calls, pleading with me to make peace with mother. And Amelia tries to goad me by saying I'm too proud to make amends. The truth is worse. Thinking about my mother reminds me of the conceited self-image I had in high school and how quickly it fell apart when I was asked to make a real sacrifice. Running off and enlisting was a hasty, angry decision. I had no idea of the consequences, of the price I'd pay for that moment of rebellion. And I am only just beginning to understand how childish I was. My mother is not an easy person to like, but she has given her entire life to her family. I ran when I was asked to sacrifice a few years.

It was different with Mel, of course. We dated for three years in high school. She knew why I left Conestoga and abandoned my football scholarship and she understood my choice on some level. I stayed with her family while I was winding my way through the enlistment process. Maybe if I'd actually gone to Michigan when she headed to Syracuse, we would have ended up married. She wrote me nearly every day that summer before she went to school, but I was in basic training and it was hard for me to write back. Eventually our worlds became so different that the letters slowed down then stopped altogether. Despite everything Veronica has said, I don't know how Mel really felt about me.

But Veronica doesn't give up easily; I already know that about her. She shakes her head resolutely. "You were a soldier, weren't you? Mel talked about the medals you earned in Afghanistan."

Here it is, the conversation I've been trying to avoid. "That was a long time ago. I spent most of my time in the Army in a clerical division." Technically, this is almost true. Veronica looks skeptical, narrows her eyes, but lets it pass. I change the subject and ask her about her career. She chats animatedly about her editor and the difficulty of getting real estate developers to comment on zoning issues, the awful lack of good restaurants in Westchester County and her strong desire to land a job in the city and move out of her parent's place. When the conversation lulls again, we leave the coffee shop. She drops me at my motel, wrinkling her nose when she catches sight of it. She asks me for my cell number and I give it to her, thinking with a twinge of regret that I will probably never see her again.

I'm wrong, of course.

I stop ten feet from the door to my childhood house, realizing that I have no idea what I'm going to do when I see my mother. What can I possibly say to unravel a dozen years of silence? My pride is gone. Everything I've seen and experienced since I left home tells me that I've been a fool to not hold on tightly to my family. I just don't know how to take the first step. It doesn't occur to me that I already have.

The Herne house is a pre-war Victorian with a wraparound porch and a detached one-car garage. It is painted in a matte, off-white color that probably has some artsy sounding name like "eggshell" or "ochre". Still, the yard and the house itself have been cared for better than most of the other houses in the neighborhood, or the town for that matter. The grass in the yard is trimmed, a flowerbed of chrysanthemums is gamely holding on more than a month past Labor Day and a pile of autumnal leaves has been neatly raked to the side of the porch. It's a big house for Mom and Ginny, but Amelia and Jeff live just a town over and Jamie teaches in Albany, about an hour north.

Ginny answers the door and winks at me, then gives me a big hug. She's more excited than anyone and knows how hard this is for me. The smell of roast turkey hits me like a body blow, flooding me with memories. I walk stiffly into the living room and I get the sense that time has paused while I've been away. The TV is new, or at least newer than the 27-inch walnut console I remember, but the floral sofa and stuffed armchairs look not a day older. Amelia and Jeff are both in high spirits and Jamie pecks me on the cheek while she continues an animated conversation on her cell phone. I stand there in the living room, rooted in place until my mother emerges from the kitchen wearing a calico apron. I see immediately that she has passed through middle age. Her hair is steel gray and a network of lines maps the contours of her face. She's very near retirement age and has not lived an easy life. With a jolt, I realize that my mother has become old. I never saw my dad age and it's a shock to see how my mother has changed.

My mother stops a couple feet from me and regards me with those green-gray eyes. I am frozen. I can feel a collective inhale of breath from my sisters. After a second she simply nods at me and says, "Michael … you can peel potatoes in the sink." I numbly shuffle into the kitchen and taking up the peeler, use it to attack a stack of russet potatoes. *Hi Michael, do some chores,* I grumble to myself. I realize that I shouldn't have expected either a tearful greeting or an angry scolding. The woman who didn't shed a single tear through my father's depression and alcoholism, their constant fights, his layoff from the mill and his suicide, the woman who didn't cry at her husband's funeral or on the day when her eighteen-year-old son cursed her and left the house with a single bag slung over his shoulder—that woman is not going to get flustered by that boy's return. With the water running and the peeler moving smoothly, tears leak from my eyes. I can't remember the last time I cried, and I've seen some truly awful things since I left Conestoga. Only Ginny seems to notice. She puts a hand on my shoulder before grabbing another peeler to help me.

As I cut into a drumstick and pile peas and stuffing onto my fork, I realize that something inside me feels different. A familiar knot in my stomach is gone. I have no illusions: my mother will not become warm and affectionate and I doubt that my sister Amelia will ever stop reminding me of my drill Sergeant from basic training. But I've been accepted back into my family. In my life, I've been adopted twice: once by the Army and once by my classmates at Georgetown. But this is not the same. Blood matters.

"So how do you like civilian life? Is it weird to go a whole day without shooting someone?" Jamie teases.

"It's sad, very hard to pass the time," I reply with a straight face. Jamie looks shocked for a second before she laughs. Amelia rolls her eyes and asks for the mashed potatoes. She may be the only one who was angrier than Mom when I left home.

"How do you like your new job?" Jamie asks.

"It's great. Fascinating, but I'm only six months in." That's not entirely true. I'm not a hundred percent sure that I fit the sedentary life that I've worked so hard for. A suit doesn't feel comfortable on me. But it's the path I've chosen and if I learned anything in the Army, it's how to track a path to the end.

"And what is it that you do, exactly?" my mother asks in a tone that suggests she may not want too many details.

"I'm an intelligence analyst for the State Department."

"Oh my God! You're a spy!" Ginny says, savoring the last word.

I shake my head emphatically. "More like a reporter. It's a desk job. I look at things like satellite photos and intel reports, as well as publicly available stuff from the Internet, to put together stories. I have a little area of responsibility that I follow and I write articles for some classified journals that circulate in the intelligence community."

"What's your specialty area?" Jeff asks. I hesitate because I know he's obsessed with guns. I'm weighing an offer to join him tomorrow morning for a hunting trip before I head back to Washington.

"Generally speaking I work on arms transfers—when a country sells arms to another country through a defense contractor. I can't be more specific than that or I'll fail my next polygraph and lose my job."

"They make you take a lie detector test?" This from Ginny, who looks like she's smelled bad fish.

"It usually catches people who are nervous about the test…" I drift for a second, remembering the exact moment when I learned to flat-line a polygraph while telling the most outrageous lies.

Amelia turns away from me to mother and pointedly changes the topic. "So I snuck a peek at the blanket you're quilting for the baby. I love the pink trim!" And there it is. About six weeks ago she called and asked me to come home for the weekend. I said no. She said it was important. I apologized but held my ground. I found out later that she and Jeff announced that weekend that they are expecting a baby girl. Amelia never called to tell me. I realize that I have a lot of ground to make up with her and I think about that and being an uncle while the baby talk continues for the rest of the meal.

Later, as we're sipping cider and hot chocolate in the living room, the conversation turns to Mel.

"I know she was depressed and all when she came back from Russia, but I really can't believe she killed herself. She was always so cheerful and her kids just loved her. My friend Judy teaches in the same school and told me Mel was one of the best teachers there," Jamie says.

"It shocked me too, but I haven't seen her since I left," I reply. When Ginny called me in tears two days ago, I felt the blood drain from my head all at once. It was enough to get me to walk into my boss's office late on Thursday afternoon and ask for the next day off. Then it took me half the day on Friday to settle down enough to start driving, which is why I'd missed my family at the funeral home.

"Yeah, but didn't she detest guns? I can't believe she shot herself. That's so creepy," Ginny says, shivering. Mel had been the supportive older sister to Ginny that Amelia never was. I knew without asking that they'd stayed close after I left.

"No, you're right, she did hate guns," I said. I remember trying to get Mel excited about a deer hunt I was going on early in junior year. Hunting was a necessity in my family, an expedient way to cut the food bill in the colder months when demand for cement waned and my father found himself seasonally unemployed. Some of my few fond memories of the man were in the woods, where he taught me how to track, to move silently and to shoot quickly and accurately. Possibly the most valuable lesson was learning to stand perfectly still—no easy task for a teenager, but one that proved invaluable years later. I always thought of hunting as a basic skill, like carpentry or tuning a car, so Mel's visceral reaction to guns surprised me. "They're awful, evil things," she said, "and nothing good comes from them." I got angry and told her that just because her family could afford to eat without hunting didn't make them better than everyone else. That softened her and she apologized, but she never really changed her opinion.

"Yeah, a lot of people have been talking about it, saying that it seems wrong," Jamie adds. "It's totally not like her. I mean if I were going to go, it would be a handful of Vicodin," she continues and looks around puzzled when she realizes everyone is staring at her. "What? I'm just saying…"

My cell phone wakes me from a sound sleep. I'm sweating, which means that it caught me in the middle of a nightmare, but the details evaporate from my brain before I can catch them. I'm instantly awake like the lamp on the nightstand I flick on as I sit up. It's Veronica on the other end of the line.

"I'm so sorry to bother you, did I wake you?"

"No, I was reading," I lie instinctively and glance at my watch—it's just after midnight. I'm unaccountably relieved that years in the field have taken the sleep out of my voice.

"This is going to sound stupid, but I think George is stalking me. I'm with a friend who was also at the funeral. We met for dinner in New Paltz and as we were leaving the restaurant I could have sworn I saw George across the street. Now we're sitting in this bar down the block. We were heading home, but I looked out the window and he's there in a car right outside. I know I sound totally paranoid, but I'm a little freaked out. I'm so sorry to bother you, but you're the only—well, *guy* I know around here." I can barely hear her over the background noise. "And if I ask some stranger in the bar to help me I might just be trading one problem for another."

"Just stay put and tell me where you are," I reply, reaching for my pants.

A half hour later, I pull my black 2004 Pontiac GTO into a parking spot a block short of the bar. I looked in the rearview mirror as I pull a sage baseball cap with "Blackhawk" written on the front in modest letters low over my eyes. I step out of the GTO and amble forward, slouching deliberately with my hands thrust into jeans pockets and my eyes cast down. It's almost as good as invisibility for a man with a medium build.

I spot George immediately. New Paltz is not Conestoga—it attracts a good crop of wealthy city folk in the summertime and during ski season, but fewer at this time of year. Sitting behind the wheel of his new, cherry-red BMW coupe, George stands out like a strawberry on a pumpkin pie. I brush past the car on the sidewalk and confirm that he's not holding anything but the steering wheel. I walk two cars further down the block, then cross the street and turn back to Rascal's Lounge. A bouncer blocks the door—a wide Samoan who looks like an offensive tackle for an NFL team. The man eyes me and glances at my D.C. driver's license with a professional eye before waving me through.

Rascal's is a big place, considerably larger inside than it appears from the street. It has a Boston-pub-meets-Swiss-chalet feel to it. A long oak bar attended by three attractive women in buttoned vests exposing a healthy amount of cleavage runs the length of the main room. The twenty-something crowd is mostly standing in the space next to the bar, but a line of booths hunker against the wall under hunting trophies and old ski paraphernalia. The sour smell of beer competes with Old Spice and a pulsing song from the Cure for my attention. I take off my cap and run my fingers through my hair, which is approximately the color of squid ink and is starting to feel a little shaggy. This earns me a stare from a brunette in a halter-top with large breasts and thick makeup. I look away quickly, scanning the room. Veronica is sitting in a booth talking to another thin, pretty woman with thick dark eyebrows and curly brown hair. Veronica is wearing a black sweater that fits her snugly and a silver necklace with a small pendant in the center. She waves when she spots me and I thread my way through the crowd and slip into the booth next to her friend, who she introduces as Nicole.

"I think you've actually rescued us twice tonight," Veronica laughs, pointing to a short man with a bad hairpiece wandering back towards the bar with a tumbler of scotch. "That guy would not give up! Why is it that only short bald guys over fifty have any confidence?" she asks and Nicole laughs. Veronica's eyes crinkle a little at the corners as she smiles.

"I don't know," Nicole replies, "those guys who sent us drinks from the bar seemed pretty pleased with themselves."

Veronica frowns and pauses for effect before saying, "If it had been anything but chocolate martinis…" and the two of them burst into laughter that does not end until they are dabbing the tears out of their eyes.

"Sounds like a big night."

Nicole shakes her head. "You have no idea. Most of the time, hitting a bar is like being locked up in seventh-grade gym class. These places are full of guys who are big talkers around their friends and absolute cowards without them. Which wouldn't be so bad if they didn't have the charm of a torque wrench when you get them alone. And if you actually find one of them to date, you're lucky because the only other choices are married guys, the eternally uncommitted thirty-somethings and the real creeps like Jock Awesome outside. Did you get a look at him, by the way?" Nicole asks.

"Jock Awesome?"

"That's what we called George in Russia. You know, the kind of guy that always checks himself out in the mirror? Always has to be right, always in control? He was a freakin' nightmare." She shakes her head and rolls her eyes.

"He's sitting in a BMW right across the street."

Veronica nods. "I think he's been out there for a couple of hours because I noticed the car when we walked in. Then we were getting ready to go and I took a look out the window and saw him lurking..."

"It would make me nervous, too."

"What do we do?" Nicole asks. "I was thinking about having the bouncer walk us out, but Awesome could still follow Veronica."

"Does he know where you're staying?" I ask Veronica.

"I don't think so. It didn't come up last night. I don't see how he would know. There are a lot of B&Bs around here." Veronica bites her lip and twists the slender silver chain on her necklace as she thinks.

"How do you think he found you then?"

"That could be my fault," Nicole says. "I'm from Kingston and Awesome knows where I live. He saw me at the funeral today."

"Let's just walk out of here," I suggest. "I'll make sure he doesn't follow you home."

"Are you sure? George was an Olympic rower, and then he started taking karate or something... and I think he won a bunch of tournaments," Nicole says, looking anxious.

"Don't worry," I say.

A few moments later, Veronica and Nicole step through the door to the bar with me two paces behind. The door to the BMW coupe immediately swings open and George crosses the street in four rapid strides as the club bouncer moves aside to let the girls out. George has worked himself into a rage. His pupils are dilated and his face is flushed red. He's been drinking. He starts swearing before he reaches the curb, "Fucking bitches..."

Just as I'm about to move to intercept him, the Samoan bouncer puts his arm out and steps in front of me. He moves swiftly for a man of his size, interposing his bulk between George and the girls.

"Don't bother the ladies, pal," he says as he plants his feet. He is wider than the door to Rascal's, and looks strong as a horse. George tries to step around him and the Samoan sidesteps with him. George takes a half a step forward and the big man puts those two enormous paws on George's chest and shoves, backing George up three feet without breaking a sweat. George's red face brightens to the same shade of cherry as his BMW and he takes a step back toward the bouncer. The Samoan wags his finger "no" and for an instant it looks like it might end there. Then, without warning, George steps in on his right foot, planting it solidly. His left fist comes swinging towards the bouncer in a classic roundhouse. The Samoan puts up a beefy paw and blocks the telegraphed punch effortlessly. Then the big man steps in and grabs a handful of George's lapel in an effort to grapple him. George clamps his hand over the bouncer's big paw, simultaneously leaning in and to his left as he twists the man's wrist sharply. A cry of pain comes from the Samoan, who lurches to one side. Then George hits him in the solar plexus with his free right fist and the big man collapses forward. Without mercy, George's left knee sweeps up and connects solidly with the man's face, sending him sprawling to the pavement. A woman waiting outside the club screams, and someone else yells, "Call 9-1-1!"

George turns away from the man on the ground to face Veronica and Nicole, his fists still clenched. I step forward and put the back of my arm in front of them, gently moving them behind me. I look George squarely in the eye, meeting his gaze in a manner that I did not last night. "You should stop now," I say to him in a tone he's probably never heard before. This freezes him for an instant. He looks at me perplexedly, as if I'm a cockroach that's gotten between him and his meal. "He pushed you first," I say. "You should just walk away now."

"Get out of my way." George gives me the same look he'd give that cockroach just before grinding it under his heel.

I shake my head. George takes the opportunity to try to catch me off-guard, lashing out with his right foot. He kicks low, aiming for my left knee. It's not a Karate roundhouse but a *Muay Thai*-style shin kick. George is decently fast, but I've already raised my left foot up and catch the middle of his shin with the solid side edge of the lug sole of my shoe. They don't wear shoes in mixed-martial arts tournaments so George has probably never hit his shin quite so hard on a sharp edge. Trust me, it hurts. He swears loudly and jabs with his right fist but I've already stepped back. Then he jabs again with his left, using it as a decoy to set up a roundhouse with his right fist. He's good and angry and he steps into the punch, putting his weight behind it.

That's what I'm waiting for. I'm already spinning to my left as I catch his right wrist on the knife-edge of my right hand as it sweeps up and clamp onto it as I pivot past him. My left hand slides around the back of his elbow and I twist the wrist so that the joint bends back on itself, forcing him to turn with me to keep his wrist from breaking. It's a move he's undoubtedly seen before, but not executed as quickly. As he starts to recover, I release the wrist and jab three fingers into a spot below his armpit. His right arm spasms. Then with my other hand I immobilize his left arm. I pause to give him a chance to realize that he can't move either arm. George gasps as he tries to figure out how some guy he has fifty pounds on has just decommissioned him in three seconds, and it makes him even angrier.

We've reached the precise moment that I've been thinking about since Veronica called me an hour ago. I can easily put George on the ground right now, zip one of the plastic ties I've got in my jacket pocket around his wrists and wait for the police to show. He'll spend a night or possibly two in a holding cell and be arraigned and released by Monday. He will have a very good, very expensive lawyer who will keep him out of prison. Given what I know about George from Veronica and what I've seen of his temper, though, I don't think it will end there. It will take weeks or months for this guy to cool down. And that only really leaves me with one choice.

With some real regret, I bring my right leg up to the outside of his left knee. I'm standing behind George and just to his left, and as I shift my weight and his towards me, I exert a steady pressure with the sole of my shoe on the joint until I hear his anterior cruciate and medial collateral ligaments pop and feel the knee buckle. I ease George to the ground and whisper into his ear. "You just can't go around beating up girls. Let it go now. We won't have this discussion again." I know this guy beat up Mel, but I can't summon up any anger. I feel only the professional revulsion I have for people who can't overcome their base genetic programming. This guy has everything: brains, looks and money. Instead of doing something useful with all of that he pisses it away with anger and jealousy.

The look on George's face as I lay him on the ground does not fill me with hope that my message has gotten through to him. At least I've slowed him down. As I turn around, Veronica is staring at me with a strange expression—as if she hasn't really seen me before. Which may be true, but it still makes me uncomfortable. I lean over the bouncer, who looks at me with respect and introduces himself as Tana Tautolo. He assures me he will be fine even as he pulls a handkerchief from his pocket to staunch a steady flow of blood from his broken nose.

"Do you want to wait for the police?" I ask Veronica and Nicole. They both shake their heads vigorously. I look at the bouncer steadily and after a second he nods. We slip away from the gathering crowd. As we part company, I have a queasy feeling about the man I've left on the pavement.

I have good instincts.

Chapter Three -

Sunday

Joining the Army was never my dream. Enlisting was a hasty decision I made when confronted with the same bleak future that had doomed my father and grandfather to toil their lives away in Conestoga. Military service is a well-trodden path in my hometown. Teenagers have been running away to join armies since the time of Alexander, and small towns bear more than their fair share of the sacrifice. A group of kids I graduated high school with were headed to the military but I never paid them much notice. I had a clear image of my future fixed firmly in my mind: four years playing football at Michigan followed by a stint in the NFL. Then possibly back to college as a coach. So when I left Conestoga I had no idea what to expect.

For one thing, I had no idea how many jobs there are in the Army. All I knew was that I didn't want to spend four years confined to the sweaty interior of a tank – I was obsessed with that thought. So when the recruiter asked me to choose a military occupation specialty, I mumbled something about wanting to be outdoors. The man, a polite, clean-shaven poster boy for soldierhood wearing a Ranger tab, smiled like he'd just tasted the first peach of the season. "11x it is," he said, and in that moment I became an infantry-man. It seemed like a straightforward choice. I'd carry a rifle and do a lot of marching. I could handle that.

By the time I showed up at the induction center for the physical, I noticed that I was different from most of the other Army enlistees. That year I'd been named one of the top 100 high school football players in the country. I could clear 40 yards in 4.4 seconds and bench press twice my body weight. At Fort Benning, I ran the obstacle course faster than all the other recruits, faster than even the Drill Sergeant, who challenged me to a timed race. The man swore sideways when I beat him and broke the course record in the process.

My hunting experienced started to pay off almost immediately. I was so comfortable on the weapon ranges during Advanced Infantry Training that

I picked up a nickname, "X-ring," after the center ring on the bull's-eye of a paper target. The rifle instructor, a member of the U.S. Army Marksmanship Unit, arranged an informal competition with the M-24, the military version of the Remington 700—the same rifle I'd used all my life. I won the competition at 300 yards, beating several older men wearing Sergeant's stripes, with a shot grouping smaller than a silver dollar. The tracking skills I'd learned in the Catskills also proved invaluable during field exercises. Men leave more evidence of their passing than deer, even though most of the suburban kids I trained with couldn't see it.

In truth, the Army was a revelation to me. I wasn't great at everything in high school. I may have been a football star, but there were others who read faster and understood chemistry better than me. In the infantry, though, shooting straight and knowing how to track are huge advantages. The regular infantry doesn't much care how fast you run unless a sixty-pound pack is strapped to your back, but my speed helped later on.

Army life suited me. The physical regimen was no more strenuous than football workouts. Army discipline was a shade softer than the rule of law in my mother's house. My fellow enlistees respected me, even looked up to me, because the cockiness I'd had in high school was gone, doused by my father's suicide and snuffed out entirely when I'd abandoned my family and my future in one stroke. What I found in its place was a quiet determination to be good at something again.

Two weeks before I graduated from Advanced Infantry Training, I was called into the Office of the Commandant at Fort Benning. A tall man with sandy hair in civilian clothing sat behind the desk, reading from a file folder. He was not the school commandant. He motioned me to a chair by flicking two fingers downward without looking up. I'd had enough training at that point to know how to sit still and shut up, so I waited there for a full quarter hour before the man looked up from the file. He pulled a paper from it and slid it over to me. It was a copy of an article from the Albany Times Union covering the New York State High School Championship Football game from the previous winter. On the front page was a picture of me in mid-air at full extension, arms stretched out as I descended on the Buffalo quarterback. I knew the article word by word from memory and slid it back to him. The man looked at me for a moment, unblinking.

"Why did you give up the University of Michigan for this?" the man asked, spreading his hands outward and looking around the sparsely decorated office.

"My Father died. I have to help support my family now," I replied. I could hear the strain in my voice.

"You mean he killed himself. With a shotgun, correct?" The man's clear blue eyes suddenly fixed on me, challenging me to flinch.

I didn't bite. I recognized the tactic. It was like having an offensive tackle whisper nasty things at you, trying to get you angry and put you off balance so he could knock you on your ass.

"Yes, that's right, Sir," I said crisply. "It was a twelve-gauge, pump-action Ruger."

The man nodded, almost in approval. He continued to leaf through the file. "The Army," he said, "is more observant than it appears. We did not overlook the fact that you were a top college football prospect. We noticed that you've posted exemplary scores here in spite of a marked tendency to," and here he paused and raised those clear blue eyes from the folder for a second with a significant look, "challenge authority. Oh, and I don't know if you realized that you were competing with some of the Army's best snipers in that little sharp-shooting competition last week. One was an instructor at Sniper School here at Benning, another a member of the USAMU rifle team, and two of the other soldiers in question flew in from Fort Bragg." He paused to let that sink in. I was stunned. Sniper School was justly famous in the infantry, and everyone coveted the sniper certification even though no tab was awarded. The Army Marksmanship Unit supplied the Army participants for international shooting competitions, including the Olympic games. And I knew what the man's offhanded reference to Fort Bragg implied; Fort Bragg in North Carolina was headquarters for some of the Army's deadliest men—like those in the 82nd Airborne and the Special Forces. The corners of the sandy-haired man's lips twisted briefly into a shadow of a smile as he saw me processing this. "Their CO will not soon let them forget that they lost to a recruit."

There was another weighty pause. "I'd like to describe a career path for you and see if it might be of interest," the man continued. I nodded slowly.

"In two weeks you'll be sent to airborne school. Then you'll move directly on to Ranger School and if you make it through, you'll be posted to one of the battalions of the 75th Ranger Regiment. You'll stay there until your twentieth birthday, when you become eligible for the Special Forces. If your performance as a Ranger is exemplary, you'll be chosen for Special Forces selection and indoctrination on your first application. They'll spend about a year training you, then you'll spend at least two years with SF in the field. If you survive, you'll be assigned to my unit. To actually enter, though, you'll have to make it through Delta Force selection and operator training." The man put down the folder and leaned forward, staring intently into my eyes.

"Sir, you're with The Unit?" I asked with a new level of respect. The Delta Force, the Army's elite counterterrorist force had the reputation of being the toughest sons of bitches in the Army.

That ghostlike smile passed the man's lips again as he shook his head. "No, the Delta Force training just warms you up for what we'll put you through."

"Respectfully Sir, just who the hell are you?" His smile got a little broader at my challenge. In truth, I already knew part of the answer. The sandy-haired man had enough pull to commandeer the Commandant's office. He was obviously so well-connected that he could guide my career in and out of the Army's most elite units. And he was clearly unimaginably powerful if he felt perfectly comfortable making his pitch in jeans and a white button-down Oxford.

"You can call me Alpha. I run a clerical support company—one that doesn't do much clerical work. The name of the outfit doesn't matter; it changes all the time, as does its divisional designation. We were originally named the 'Intelligence Support Activity' and internally we still call our unit 'the Activity.' We were established after the failed hostage rescue of those students in Iran in 1980. Remember that, when those helos went down?"

I didn't remember because I hadn't been born yet, but I didn't interrupt.

"The accident was the result of poor field-level intelligence from non-military agencies. We exist to rectify that problem. We prepare the battle-field for special ops units by providing reliable reconnaissance and communications intelligence on the ground. Most of our work supports the Joint Special Operations Command units including DEVGRU— that's Seal Team Six—the Special Forces, Delta Force and a couple of outfits you've never heard of. This means we have to get in and out before they can do their work. We often cooperate with local governments or CIA officers on the ground, and we develop some of our own intelligence networks in key areas. You'll need to learn languages—at least two to a high degree of proficiency. That's why you'll spend time in Special Forces before you reach us. They'll start your language training and teach you how to understand foreign cultures.

"Most of our people are electronics and communications experts, but we need shooters for our direct action arm. They perform reconnaissance and infiltration assignments and provide security support for our field teams. If you join us, your life expectancy will be shorter than that of a North Sea Oil Driller. Most of your work will be alone. You will go into places that we haven't dared to send in a team so you can map it out for them. It's crazy work. But you will save lives. Every time you hear about a miraculous hostage rescue or a terrorist leader being killed, you will feel proud to have served in The Activity, even if your contributions are never publicly acknowledged. Do you understand?"

I nodded slowly. I knew this was a one-time offer. If I said no, I'd never see this man again. "What happens to my Army benefits if I join?" I asked. Part of the question was practical—I needed to know if the check I was sending home would shrink. The more significant question was unspoken: If I die, what happens to the benefits to my family if I'm not officially in combat?

"When you join the Activity, you'll be assigned to a clerical division in Virginia and promoted to the rank of Master Sergeant. The increase in base pay will help with the loss of combat pay. Your record after you leave Special Forces will not reflect your real duties and you will no longer receive medals or commendations. If you expire in our employ, your death will be listed as a training accident and your family will receive normal death benefits, plus a supplemental check from an anonymous Army veteran's support group every month for twenty years." Alpha paused. When he spoke next, it was with genuine compassion. "I'm very sorry, but I need your decision here and now, son."

There was nothing to decide. It was a dream job. "I'm in," I said, trying to sound stoic.

"I'll be in touch from time to time but you won't see me again for at least five years—and only then if you've done damned well every step of the way. Some of the places we'll be sending you have high attrition rates. Army Ranger School alone fails almost fifty percent of its students, half of them in RAP week, for example. So the odds are very good that you and I will never meet again. On the other hand, if I've assessed you correctly, you don't give a shit about the odds." Alpha stood up slowly and shook my hand, looking directly into my eyes for another moment. As I left the office, the short hairs on my neck stood on end. For the first time since I'd left Conestoga, I felt a sense of purpose.

"Son of a bitch, that's a solid eight-pointer," Buddy Peterson whispers, peering through a rugged-looking set of binoculars.

"It's also seven hundred yards away with a fifteen knot cross-wind," I counter, not bothering to keep my voice low. From this distance, I might as well be in another state as far as the deer is concerned. I track the antlered buck through the Leupold scope I've mounted on the bolt-action Winchester Model 70 rifle in my hands.

I wouldn't have chosen to use this particular rifle at all, but I never for a second dreamed that I would end up hunting deer on my first trip back home. It's not even deer season yet in Greene County. We've driven two hours north to Saratoga County in the Adirondacks, the chain of mountains north of the Catskills in upstate New York. My first instinct was to back out of the trip altogether and when the call came from Jeff at four-thirty this morning; I had my excuses down pat. I told him I'd be happy to join but unfortunately I didn't have a hunting permit, a rifle or suitable clothing with me. I hadn't imagined that all of those obstacles could be overcome before 5am on a Sunday.

"No problemo—way ahead of you," Jeff replied without hesitation. "I got you a permit at Stokeley's yesterday afternoon—they still had your information on file. Amelia found your father's old deer rifle in your mom's attic. It looks pretty clean to me and I've got an excellent new scope you can use with it. You'll be able to count the zits on a buck's ass, no kidding. Plus you can borrow a set of my camos. The pants might be a little short for you, but I'm sure the jacket will fit just fine." Which is a nice way of saying that Jeff is a couple of inches shorter than me but sports a beer gut. So now I'm wearing camouflaged gear that has my arms and legs sticking out awkwardly while my midsection swims in extra fabric. Swell.

I was even more surprised to see the Conestoga Sheriff's Ford Explorer pull up in front of my motel room a half hour after Jeff's call. Jeff popped out of the passenger's seat, explaining that Buddy Peterson had proposed the hunting trip when he heard I was coming back to town. Jeff is bidding for the auto glass contract for the township of Conestoga, which includes the vehicles of the Sheriff's office. Buddy is a fixture in town, having held the elected office for over twenty years, and no major decision is made in Conestoga without consulting him.

I stiffened when Buddy extended his hand. He is tall and lanky, with skin the texture of an old leather wallet. Buddy has hazel eyes and slick, straight brown hair cut short and parted on the right. His right cheek bulged slightly over a wad of Skoal. The last time I'd seen Buddy was at my father's funeral. He'd been one of the pallbearers carrying my father's casket to the grave.

In addition to being Sheriff, Buddy is the head of the booster's club for the Conestoga Cougars, my high school football team. In practical terms it means he hits up local businesses for donations to pay for gear and coaching salaries for the team. But during my time on the Cougars, Buddy expanded his role as our unbeaten streak lengthened. It was Buddy, not Coach Howard, who made the calls that got me written up in *Sports Illustrated* and later persuaded college scouts from USC, Florida, Ohio State and Michigan to attend the state championship game. Of course, if I hadn't played well that day, it wouldn't have mattered. But the ten tackles, two sacks and interception that day brought scholarship offers from USC and Michigan. Without

Buddy's help that dream would never have been possible, even though it was one I'd never realize.

When I grasped Buddy's outstretched hand, he surprised me by pulling me into an embrace and thumping me on the back. "It's good to see you, son," Buddy said. "I'm so glad you finally came back home. We're all really proud of you here."

That meant something to me.

The fourth man on the trip is a New Paltz businessman named Jack Millard. Jack owns a car dealership and several rental franchises around the Catskills and is one of Jeff's largest clients. Millard is also a hunting fanatic, although his experience is limited to four deer hunts—one more than Jeff. Much of the talk in the car centered on equipment; Jeff and Jack debated whether the Weatherby Mark V or the Sako 85 was the better rifle, then moved on to the comparative advantages of tree and ground blinds. I closed my eyes and their voices faded into a drone of white noise. I was asleep in seconds, waking only when the truck pulled into the small parking lot at the trailhead.

I expected to pair off with my brother-in-law, so I was surprised when Buddy insisted that Jeff and Jack set up a blind at the edge of a small meadow where Buddy had shot a buck the previous season. It was obvious that both men had been hoping to learn from either the Sheriff or the former soldier, but they quickly fell into an animated conversation as Buddy untangled their first hopeless attempt to set up the camouflaged deer blind. The blind was more or less just a tall tent without a bottom. I was relieved I wouldn't be confined in it with Jeff.

As we left, Buddy tossed the two men a walkie-talkie, telling them to call us if they had any luck. When we were safely out of earshot, Buddy chuckled and said, "Your brother-in-law's a good man but he's god-awful with a rifle."

I smiled. "He means well. But I can smell his deodorant from here."

"I think that boy's gonna need a lot of luck and one developmentally-impaired deer if he's gonna come home with anything today."

Buddy led me up a steep slope and along a narrow trail that skirted the ridgeline. We found a spot about a mile from where we'd left Jeff and Jack, on the opposite side of the ridge in a small stand of trees with a broad view of the valley below and the mountain peak above. Buddy didn't have a portable blind like Jeff, but he did have blankets and a couple of sandbags.

"I don't think we'll get anything from here," I said, looking around. "We won't see a lot of deer hanging out above the tree line and those clearings in the valley are a long ways away."

Buddy shrugged, "True, but there's a deer trail just up there where they cross the ridge," he pointed. "And besides, why spend all day staring at one dark patch of woods when you can get a great view like this?" He gestured to the east, where the sun was still low and red in the sky. Autumn in upstate New York is no less spectacular than in neighboring New England. The foliage was past the peak of color in the Adirondacks, but the hillside was still dappled with splashes of brilliant red, orange and yellow. We savored the last remnants of the season for a moment, as an unspoken companion to the hunt.

After a bit, I unzipped the soft padded rifle case that Jeff had handed me and withdrew the Winchester. Buddy whistled, "She's a beaut—does that have the pre-'64 feed?"

"The whole rifle is pre-'64," I answered as I examined the weapon closely.

"Was that your Daddy's gun?" Buddy asked, hesitating.

"Yes."

"Well son, you don't have to use that. You can shoot my rifle," Buddy said as he inserted a key into the brass lock on his hard-sided gun case. Buddy's rifle was secured in custom-molded compartments in two sections, the barrel separated from the stock. He removed the stock first and then inserted the barrel. A flat lever clicked down when he twisted it in place. I whistled.

"That's an H-S Precision Pro 2000, isn't it?" I asked. Buddy nodded, grinning broadly like a proud father.

"Are you planning to shoot deer or elephant?" I said as Buddy handed me the elegant rifle.

Buddy chuckled, "Well, maybe someday I'll head out West and take an elk."

I gingerly handed the gray rifle back to him. "I'll stick to something I can afford to touch." I turned back to the Winchester, which was my father's most prized possession. *I love this Winchester more than your Mother, don't forget that*, the old man said to me without irony the first time he let me fire it. I unzipped a compartment at the bottom of the bag and was relieved to find a small waterproof case. There were forty round-nosed shells inside and I examined each one closely for signs of rust or corrosion, but they were immaculate.

"Those aren't thirty-aught-six shells," Buddy observed, spitting a thin stream of liquid into a bush.

"No, this gun is chambered for the .375 Holland & Holland Magnum. I don't think Jeff knew that," I replied as I searched the deep pockets of Jeff's jacket for the box of ammunition he'd handed me in the car. They were 30-06 shells—useless in the Winchester.

I stripped down the rifle on the blanket and cleaned the grease my father had used to store the gun off carefully with mineral oil and a soft cloth. I partially reassembled it and mounted the new scope, but left out the bolt. Then I got up and paced out a hundred yards exactly. There was a tree at the hundred yard mark, and I pulled my Spyderco folding knife from a pocket and whittled an "X" at what I reckoned would be chest height for an average-sized buck. Returning to the rifle, I stabilized it on a sandbag and sighted my mark on the tree through the empty bore of the rifle. Then I slowly moved my eye up to the Leupold scope and adjusted it click by click until the same mark was centered in the crosshairs. Finally, I put the bolt back in, inserted the magazine and chambered a round. I gently squeezed the trigger, and saw that the shot was a few inches low and off to the right. Then I repeated the process, adjusting the sight a few clicks and fired again, this time dead on. I hit the cross dead center, sending a shower of chips blossoming from the tree.

"Now with all that racket we can be sure we won't see any deer this morning," I said. Buddy chuckled.

We lay there side by side for a few minutes before Buddy started talking. I wasn't surprised. When Buddy paired my brother-in-law and his client off together, I half guessed it was because he wanted to catch up with me. I even wondered if he might have engineered the whole trip for that purpose. He started off slowly, updating me on the town and the tough times the recession caused. Then when he ran out of gossip he paused for a moment and carefully said, "I told you how glad I was that you finally came home. Part of that reason was selfish. I never got a chance to talk to you after you decided to enlist. I've always wanted to tell you that I admired the courage you showed when you turned away from that Michigan scholarship to help your family."

That surprised me. Buddy had put himself out to get those scholarship offers for me. He risked more for me than anyone else in Conestoga. I would have thought he'd still be burning.

I shook my head vigorously. "I walked away from my family. Mother wanted me to give up college and take a job at a machine shop. I couldn't face," *being stuck in Conestoga* I was about to say but I bit my tongue, "... that life, so I enlisted. Nothing courageous about it."

The folds under Buddy's eyes deepened as his expression softened. "You did take care of your family, don't forget that. Maybe not the way your Mamma wanted, but good enough. I kept an eye on her and your sisters after you left. They did just fine with your help. And son, I can tell you as one former soldier to another that there isn't a coward born who gets to be Best Ranger at age 18. How on earth did you manage that?"

I wondered for a moment how Buddy knew that about me, but then I realized he was probably still reading *Stars & Stripes*, and even if he'd missed my name in the story, another local veteran would have told him. Stuff that wouldn't make a whiff of difference in a city is big news in a small town. I considered my answer carefully.

"I was too obstinate for the regular infantry and I like to run," I said. We shared a laugh.

The truth was more complex.

Two weeks after meeting Alpha, I received my field assignment. As Alpha had predicted, I was assigned to Airborne School. I loved the adrenaline rush of the jump, even the tame kind from a static line. Afterward, I was one of a handful of students to move directly to Ranger School without serving a stint in the 82nd or 101st Airborne divisions. To me, it felt like advanced hunting training with better weapons. Others found it grueling, but I thrived on the long hikes in the wood with heavy packs and even the nights we spent in the Florida swamps in the third phase. Shortly after Ranger School, I was approached by one of the instructors and persuaded to enter the Best Ranger competition in my first year as a Ranger, partnered with a veteran First Sergeant fifteen years my senior. We won the competition handily, and I became the youngest ranger to win the three-day athletic challenge in the seventeen years of the competition, and with it the title Best Ranger.

"I was pretty stubborn, too, but I wasn't any Ranger, just regular infantry," Buddy said, interrupting my thoughts, "And I didn't get the Silver Star, either."

"I was in the right place at the wrong time," I said. "And I was just trying to save my own sorry butt. I got hurt badly enough to spend the rest of my time in the Army in a clerical brigade."

I would have liked to tell Buddy the truth. In a way I felt he deserved to hear it. But it wasn't my truth to share.

After two years as a Ranger, I entered Special Forces selection. It was physically easier than Ranger School, but there was a new emphasis on individual problem solving. Move a jeep missing all four wheels 100 yards with four men and no tools—that kind of thing. It was fantastic. The thrill of picking apart a puzzle set to trip you up was another kind of adrenaline rush, one that lasted longer. I also started learning languages. Special Forces operators are often used as "force multipliers" in the modern army. They train local troops to fight alone or alongside U.S. military units. Learning local languages is vital for success in this type of mission. Selection and training took six months. Then suddenly, I found myself on a cargo plane with six other men, soaring through the mountains of Afghanistan on a clandestine mission. My first combat HALO jump felt like being ripped through a brick wall by a bear. Jumping in the Hindu-Kush Mountain Range is nothing like grazing the soft belly of a swampy rice paddy in North Carolina.

For nearly two years, I alternated between training and missions. That's the thing most people never hear about the Army. They invest more in training every soldier than any private business would ever dream of. On my first trip into the North West Frontier of Pakistan, I could barely spit out two phrases of Urdu. Two years later I could get by in four local languages and several dialects. For the first time since I'd left the Conestoga Cougars, I felt fully part of a team. The standard issue scraggly beard and weather-beaten tan I acquired for infiltration missions didn't separate me from the Army—it strengthened the bond.

Then one morning, I got a call from Alpha. It was the first I'd heard from the man since we'd met in person. If my career hadn't followed the exact path he'd outlined four years earlier, I would have long since forgotten him. "Are you watching the news?" Alpha asked. I wasn't. I'd just come off of a 72-hour field exercise. I still had a 60-pound ruck on my back.

"No sir," I replied, instantly alert.

"Bad things are happening. It's time for you to suit up. By February, you'll be heading to Fort Bragg to start Delta Selection. In the meantime you're going to have your hands full. Good luck," Alpha said and clicked off. I stood there dumbly for a moment, wondering how he'd got my cell number. It was September 11, 2001.

I dropped my ruck on my bunk and raced to the NCO's lounge. I was by then a newly minted Staff Sergeant with an E-6 pay grade. The room was packed but dead silent as the Rangers and Special Forces operators stared mutely at a television set. A building was burning on the flat screen. A Master Sergeant whispered, "Terrorists just hit the World Trade Center—both buildings." As I watched in disbelief, a plume of smoke rose and the tower collapsed in a cloud of dust.

The action Buddy Peterson asked me about took place in January of 2002, four months after the terrorist attacks. It was a raid on an Al Qaeda stronghold near Kandahar.

I was leading a squad of ten Special Forces operators from my A-Team from the front. Two squads had been designated to take down a target that looked like a single building from aerial surveillance photos. When we arrived there in the dead of night we found not one, but three separate buildings surrounding a courtyard full of gleaming new Toyota pickups filled with sleeping Taliban Mujahidin fighters wearing long dishdash cotton shirts. My squad was tasked with clearing the two structures to the right of the courtyard. The attack needed to be timed and coordinated with the first squad, so I divided my force. Half the squad took the smaller building while I led the other four men to the last building. On the signal from our team leader, a specialist breached the front door and we threw flash bang grenades in. Then I went in first, and all hell broke loose.

The moment I got through the front door, night-vision goggles peering right and left to re-create my peripheral vision, a hailstorm of coordinated fire came down on my guys from the second floor of the building. The man behind me never made it through the door. I moved through the building alone, trying to locate the source of the fire. I made it to the second floor and crept into a room where four men were lined up at blown-out windows, firing AK-47s at my guys. I was sighting in on them when a pipe hit my right shoulder, dislocating it. I pitched forward, hitting the floor hard, which popped my shoulder back into joint. But then the man who'd blindsided me with the pipe started beating me with it in earnest. I managed to bring the thin man down by scissoring his knees between my legs and rolling over, which flopped the terrorist directly onto his face.

Unfortunately, I trapped my right arm in the process. In desperation, I pulled my Beretta with my left hand from the mid-chest molded plastic Serpa holster secured to the molle system on my rig. It was a difficult draw with a dislocated shoulder. I brought the automatic up just in time to face the snout of an AK-47 as the men who had been targeting my guys heard the commotion and turned on me. I managed four kills left handed with my pupils still adjusting to the loss of illumination from the night vision goggles that had been knocked off my head when I'd fallen. Then the pipe wielder managed to twist around and knock the pistol from my hand. I could smell his sour breath as he stretched for my weapon. Before the Afghan could reach the pistol, I slipped a fixed-bladed SOG knife from its downward-facing sheath on my rig and buried it in the man's carotid. He was dead in seconds.

I remember thinking that I'd screwed up, letting myself get cut off from my men. I was sure I'd pay for the mistake with my life, and the lives of the men I was responsible for. Then suddenly I was a hero. One of my guys didn't make it. I was thinking about him when a general I'd never met handed me that medal.

It was my last official combat engagement. I was surprised to see an article saying that I had sustained "serious, debilitating injuries" during the action. I knew it would take some physical therapy to rehabilitate my shoulder after the dislocation, but I was otherwise unharmed. A few days later, Alpha called to congratulate me. He said that in light of my "serious injuries" I would be promoted to Master Sergeant and transferred to his clerical unit. Six weeks later I began Delta Force selection and training—the most difficult seven months of my life. Then Alpha finally welcomed me to the Activity, where I learned an entirely new set of skills.

Buddy eventually realized he would get no grand stories from me and lapsed into silence. Two hours passed, with neither of us stirring. Then Buddy placed a hand on my shoulder and pointed to a clearing in the distance. A buck stood on the edge of the meadow, unmoving. I grabbed binoculars, searching the direction Buddy had pointed.

"Son of a bitch, that's a solid eight-pointer," Buddy says, counting the number of tips on the end of the buck's antlers.

"It's also seven hundred yards with a fifteen knot cross-wind." I pause for a second to let that sink in before adding, "That's half a mile. You want to try that shot?"

"Nope—it's all yours. I haven't hit something that far away since Vietnam, and then it was a weather balloon," Buddy replies, chuckling.

I shake my head and look through the site at the buck. It's small even in the high magnification Leupold VX-7 scope. Without my brother-in-law's absurdly overpowered scope or the hot Holland & Holland load, the shot would be impossible. As it is, it's merely foolhardy. Missing the buck entirely is not the worst possibility. If I tag the buck without bringing him down, I'm going to spend hours tracking a wounded animal. But there's a challenge in Buddy's voice, one that my younger self responds to. So I still myself and start doing calculations in my head. Buddy has an expensive Leica rangefinder, which confirms my visual estimate within a few yards. I calculate how much the bullet will drop in that distance and adjust the scope. Then I make a correction for the wind after spotting some leaves moving in a tree above the buck. And I make a final correction for the humidity. I'm half hoping the buck will have wandered off by this time, but he's grazing away, unconcerned. I make myself absolutely still until I can hear my heartbeat in my ear. When I have the rhythm of my heart timed below fifty beats per minute I gently squeeze the trigger between beats. The recoil of the rifle pulls the telescopic site off the buck, but a second later Buddy hollers, "Sonofabitch! You dropped him right in his tracks!"

It is late afternoon before I reach the motel room in Conestoga. I should have checked out in the morning, but the extra $40 buys me a shower and a quick nap before hitting the road. The showerhead has two settings: a fine mist that doesn't feel like a shower at all or multiple thin jets that sting like needles. At least it's hot. I scrub myself with harsh soap extracted from a thin plastic package on the countertop and ponder my lack of joy at bringing down the buck. It was a remarkable shot—probably the farthest distance from which anyone has hit a deer in the Adirondacks in years. If I'd done it when I was seventeen, I wouldn't have slept for a week. Most of the hunting I did with my father was from a hundred yards or less—a fraction of the distance I managed this morning. I made much longer shots in the Army, only with better equipment. I don't doubt that Jeff and the hunting community in Conestoga will be buzzing about the kill for years.

But the elation I would have felt as a child is gone. What would have been a miraculous shot has been reduced to physics and mathematics by my training. When I took a deer with my father, we would always kneel down in front of the animal before dressing it and repeat a ritual phrase: *I respect the sacrifice of this animal because it gave its life to sustain mine.* There was something noble about consummating a kill. Today, the kill felt coldly practical. Taking the long shot at the buck got me away from the hunt and from Buddy's questions. It made my brother-in-law happy. I'd used the animal's life to solve a personal problem. It's something my younger self could never have done. Perhaps it's a slight offense, almost inconsiderable next to the multitude of sins I'll have to answer for one day, but it still eats at me as I attempt to scrub myself clean.

The vibration of my cell phone on the bathroom sink interrupts my thoughts. I slip from the shower and wrap a towel around my waist as I flip the phone open.

"It's Veronica."

"Hi."

"Can you come meet me? I'm still in Conestoga."

"I was about to head home to D.C."

"I think you're going to want to see this. I'm at Mel's place. I…I don't think she killed herself."

"Give me the address," I say, reaching for my clothing.

Mel's place is the downstairs rental unit of a converted two-story Victorian on an anonymous block of Orchard Road just off of Route 9W, close to the New York State Thruway. The owner, a widower, lives in the upstairs unit. Veronica has charmed him out of the key after calling Mel's parents, asking them if she can stop by to pick up a book she'd lent Mel and needed back. They'd offered to come over but Veronica had demurred, insisting she knew just where it was.

I pull the black GTO up to the curb in front of the place and listen for a second as the V-8 growls in protest when I shut it down. It's almost dark at 5pm and the street is not the best, even for Conestoga. The houses look decrepit, like old bones scrubbed bare by the wind. Some of the yards are tended while others have gone to seed. Even the trees lining the road, planted on the grass between the sidewalk and the asphalt, look skeletal and dyspeptic. The door to the unit is ajar and I step in. The interior of Mel's apartment is like an extension of her brain, one that I recognize even after all these years. There is a weird sort of order that would look like complete chaos to anyone who didn't know her. Stacks of papers dot the living room like ferns in a primeval forest. The picture window that looks out onto the driveway is covered with a hand-embroidered lace curtain. A green sofa that looks like it has spent the first fifty years of its life wrapped in plastic is nested under the large window. A rocking chair sits opposite, a silent companion.

Veronica is standing in the middle of the living room with a stack full of papers in her arms and a puzzled expression on her face. She looks down at the piles of papers around her feet. "This is like playing solitaire with five decks of cards…" then she looks up and smiles at me. She looks different in casual clothing—jeans and a pale blue sweater made from something that looks to be softer than wool. The sweater is snug and I snap my eyes upwards to her face before I am officially staring.

"This kind of mess I remember," I say, nodding. It was the source of endless fights between Mel and her mother as a teenager. "She always seemed to know where everything was."

Veronica nods slowly. "Exactly. It looks like a mess but she's got a system. That's why this is odd. There are twelve stacks of papers on the floor. Every one is a different assignment from one of her four classes. The papers are all in alphabetical order, except for this stack here. It's two different assignments from two different classes and the papers are all mixed together. Half of them are from the students with A-L last names from this stack over here. One of these papers is half graded—in fact, her pen trails off in the middle of this comment." Veronica hands me the paper, which is an essay on bird feeders. I remember Mel's distinctive handwriting, its loops and swirls.

"Okay. What's your point?" I ask cautiously. If I'm short with Veronica, it's because I'm not comfortable in Mel's place. Being here with Veronica somehow makes it feel worse.

"She wouldn't have left this paper half-graded. And if Mel was going to fling a bunch of papers down or something, why straighten them up and put them in some random order? Why wouldn't she just leave them where they landed if she was that distraught?"

"Her parents could have cleaned this up."

Veronica shakes her head. "They said they haven't been over here yet. It sounds like they're not looking forward to it. This place hasn't been cleaned. There are still bloodstains in the bathroom." Veronica stops herself from saying more and frowns, momentarily looking queasy. "The landlord, Harvey Kastriner, told me that nothing in here has been touched. The paramedics wouldn't have cleaned up and I doubt the police would be straightening up piles of paper either."

"There are a lot of possible explanations," I protest, although I do see how the living room looks like a puzzle put back together by someone who never saw the picture on the box.

"On its own perhaps, but then you have this," Veronica says as she takes three steps backwards into the kitchen area—really just a corner of the main living room with linoleum tiles instead of carpeting. She points to a portion of the countertop next to the fridge.

"What?" I ask. Aside from some clutter on the countertop, I don't see anything significant.

Veronica rolls her eyes. "It's sugar, flour, chocolate, butter, vanilla and eggs!"

"Meaning?" I ask, mystified.

"Men!" Veronica looks skyward. "She was obviously going to bake brownies. And she left the eggs out. I checked the fridge—other than milk that just expired yesterday, there's nothing out of date. She wouldn't have randomly pulled all this stuff out and left the eggs to rot right before she killed herself. That's not how women work. We don't decide to make brownies and finish grading papers and then get up and shoot ourselves in the head. We would think about what people would find here and we'd straighten up. Mel would have wanted her students to get their grades, for one thing." Veronica sounds indignant.

"You're assuming she was rational. People do weird things when they're depressed. I've seen it before," and here I'm thinking of some of the soldiers I knew afflicted by post-traumatic stress disorder after deployments. There were a string of suicides and homicide/suicides when I was posted at Fort Bragg in North Carolina.

"Maybe, maybe…" Veronica says, tapping a slim, manicured fingernail against her lower lip, "but there's more." She picks up the phone, a corded model that looks about a dozen years old and presses the redial button, turning the receiver up so we can both listen. Her hair glides across my neck as I lean in and I can smell the clean scent of her shampoo and a hint of something more complicated on her neck. It makes me uncomfortable.

"9-1-1, what is the nature of your emergency?" the female voice on the phone asks.

"I'm so sorry, my little boy dialed this number again by accident. I apologize, it won't happen again," Veronica says quickly, and the operator says its fine before disconnecting.

"Wait, don't they have to respond to that? Are we going to have the fire department on the doorstep here in five minutes?" I ask.

"Maybe in some places, but not here. This phone doesn't have a caller ID display, so I hit redial when I got here. I asked the woman who picked up the same question. She said no."

"Then obviously whoever found Mel called 9-1-1."

"That stands to reason, but it didn't happen that way. Harvey found her. I asked him what happened when he let me in tonight. He said he was upstairs when he heard the gunshot. He called 9-1-1 first before he came downstairs. He thought it was a break-in—there have been a bunch in this neighborhood."

"The EMT's could have called," I offer.

"Why would an ambulance driver call 9-1-1 on Mel's home phone?" Veronica asks and then wags her finger as I try to respond. "Okay, it's possible that someone else called but you have to admit it's suspicious. Now the final piece of the puzzle," Veronica says. She steps directly in front of me, forcing me to pivot outwards, which has the effect of preventing me from offering any more objections. She turns toward the back of the house and I follow her down the hallway that leads straight back, passing the door to Mel's bedroom on one side and the single bathroom on the other. There's a small laundry room at the back of the apartment, and a white door with louvered glass panes leading out to a fenced yard in back.

Veronica stops just shy of the door and pulls the knob towards her without turning the handle. The door swings open. She points to the doorframe, and I can see a piece missing where the door lock and deadbolt receivers ought to be. It wouldn't be too hard to jimmy a door like this—it's a wood door without a metal frame. The lock isn't the type you can open with a credit card, but a stout crowbar or even a Slim Jim handled by someone with a bit of experience would do the trick.

"Well, I can see why this might upset you," I say, examining the lock, "but there's no way to know when it happened. It could have been last week, last month or two years ago."

Veronica considers this for a few seconds before replying. "Maybe the old Mel wouldn't have worried about the lock on the back door, but after that incident with George last year, she wouldn't have let this go for more than a couple of days."

I shake my head, suddenly weary. "I'm not a cop, but I really doubt you'll change Sheriff Peterson's mind by showing him these things. There are small mysteries in everyone's house. It doesn't add up to murder."

As I say this, I realize there's one room we've avoided. Well, two actually, but I'm not going into the bedroom. As we walk back towards the living room I stop and put my hand on the tarnished brass knob on the bathroom door. I glance back at Veronica to see her tracking me with her eyes. She nods.

I hold my breath as I swing open the door to Mel's bathroom. It's not that I'm squeamish. I've seen things in war that I'd have trouble explaining to anyone who hasn't been there: the aftermath of a missile strike on an Afghan village that hit a school misidentified as a terrorist camp, a brown betty mine vaporizing a man two-dozen feet from me. A hundred other disturbing images flicker through my consciousness. In spite of all this, seeing the exact spot where my high school sweetheart shot herself is different.

The bathroom walls are the standard off-white rental color. White porcelain tiles looking at least fifty years old adorn both the floors and the walls. The sink is also an antique. It's constructed with real porcelain and has individual faucets for hot and cold water. It's obvious that Mel died in the bathtub. The bottom of the tub is mostly clean, but there is a smattering of dried blood in the far corner near the drain. The tiled wall above the faucet is splattered with a large, oval halo of dried blood and bits of crusted gore. There are flecks of crimson on the shower curtain as well. I kneel down on the bathroom floor and examine the grout between the floor tiles. I see no signs of blood and the grout is gray and moldy. It's obvious that the tiles have neither been cleaned nor replaced recently.

"I'm sorry to say it, but it really looks like Mel shot herself here," I say.

"How can you tell?" Veronica asks.

I pause and consider how to answer the question without revealing too much. "A bullet at close range makes a lot of … mess," I explain, searching for a delicate word. "But there's no blood outside the shower and the tub is mostly clean. That means that the shower was running and the curtain was closed when she shot herself. And if you're thinking that George killed Mel, it's hard to imagine that he'd have the presence of mind to think of these details when he was in a rage. Not unless he's done this before."

Veronica deflates a little as she lets my words sink in. I can see the question in her eyes— *How do you know this stuff?*—but she has the sense not to ask. She stands there for a moment, rooted in one spot, then turns and leaves the bathroom. When I catch up to her in the living room I can see tears leaking from her eyes. "I just can't believe Mel would have done this to herself," she whispers. I put a hand on her shoulder and she leans into me, her chest heaving silently. Then we step apart awkwardly as the moment fades. We walk out of the apartment.

"It's been really nice to meet you, Mike. I hope you'll call me the next time you're heading up this direction," Veronica says as we stand on the lawn near our cars.

"I might be back for Thanksgiving next month," I confess, "now that I'm speaking to my mother again."

Veronica smiles fleetingly. "It's a date then. Be well, Mike." She kisses me on the cheek, and the imprint of her lips lingers on my skin for a moment. As I slide into the GTO and pull the door shut, I realize that Mel is the only other person who called me Mike.

As I head toward the thruway, I start to have second thoughts. On their merits—even taken together—the minor inconsistencies that Veronica has pointed out don't really add up to much. But something in the bigger picture nags me. When I joined the Activity, I got to spend a lot of time with field intelligence folks—the kind of guys who spend weeks at a time in a white panel van listening to landline and mobile phone conversations and reading someone's e-mails and text messages. I remember something that one of the analysts told me early on that I'd always found to be true.

"When you've been listening in on some dirt bag for three, four weeks, you get a sense of his routine, the way he lives his life. Sometimes you'll see something that's just a little bit different and it's not a big deal but you get this feeling that something's not right. It might be this guy telling his wife that he's got to go out and meet someone or just an odd conversation on the phone, whatever. The point is, when you get this feeling, it's usually correct. You have to trust it and dig deeper. What we call a gut feeling is the subconscious mind putting together little pieces of data we could never organize consciously. Call it expert intuition. If you want to stay alive in this job, learn to trust it."

Even since leaving the Army, I'd found these words to be helpful. A few months ago I was looking at a satellite photo of a small container ship leaving port from Bandar Abbas, Iran, and I had a feeling just like that. Something just didn't look right. Only after two days of analysis did I figure out that the ship didn't fit any of the normal shipping patterns from that port and in fact didn't have a registered manifest or insurance. As green as I am at my analyst job, my intuition still guides me.

And now it's telling me that something is wrong with the story of Mel's death I'm supposed to believe. Veronica's theories are probably all nonsense. She's doing what people do when confronted with an unbearable truth—she is reconstructing reality. Her ideas are all flimsy and circumstantial, with no more weight to them than the yellow film of chewing tobacco residue on a 90-mph spitball. Still, I hesitate. Something feels out of place to me. With a start, I realize it's the most basic thing—the same thing that's bothered me since I heard that Mel killed itself and the same thing that bothered my sisters. I flat out don't believe that Mel would end her life with a gun.

I'm fast approaching the entrance ramp to the New York State Thruway. I replay the scene in Mel's apartment in my mind and I suddenly realize that there is at least one hole in the story that I can fill in. At the last moment, I pull off into a gas station and punch a number into my phone. A familiar voice answers immediately.

"Long time, Orion, how you been, dude?"

Orion was my call sign at the Activity.

"I've been well, Sammie, how about you?" I reply. Sammie Fernandes is a headquarters guy, not a field guy but he's probably worth more than a dozen of the rest of us. He is a data specialist whose abilities I'm only beginning to appreciate as I deal with other men and women who fill the same role for the Bureau of Intelligence and Research.

"I'm guessing this is not a social call?"

"I need a favor."

"Shoot."

"Are you at work or home?" I ask.

"I live, sleep, eat and breathe this man's Army."

"So you got killed in fantasy football this afternoon?" I can imagine Sammie at his data station in the Tactical Operations Center of The Activity, four expensive 50" flat screen monitors blossoming with player stats. Fortunately, Command Sergeant Majors are pretty forgiving of that kind of stuff.

"I don't know what you're talking about, Master Sergeant," Sammie says carefully, with exaggerated innocence.

"Can you check on a call to 9-1-1 in New York State last week?"

"Sure, if you've got the originating phone number," Sammie replies. I give him Mel's number, which I saw on the phone in her apartment.

"Okay, Sergeant, just hang on here a second while I get into the right network."

I listen to the clicking of keys for a few moments.

"Ah, here we go. I actually see three calls into 9-1-1 from that number in the last week. Two were today..."

"Yeah, don't worry about those."

"The other was last Wednesday at 6:11pm."

"Can I hear the recording of that call?"

"Sure, but I'll have to get that tomorrow. This gets into a grey area with *Posse Comitatus*. We have an understanding with the FBI counterintelligence folks that allow us to exchange little tidbits like this with no questions asked, but I'd need to contact them during working hours unless you want some alarm bells to start ringing."

"No, tomorrow is just fine. I really appreciate it."

"No problem, boss. Just let me know if there's anything else I can do you for." These little requests are the currency in our profession and both of us know that as an intelligence analyst at State, I'm in a pretty good position to return the favor.

I thank him and hang up. Then I dial Veronica, catching her in her car on the way back to Greenwich. It sounds as if she has some sort of hands free device, maybe a Bluetooth system in her car. I tell her that I've confirmed a 9-1-1 call was placed on the day of Mel's death and I ask her if she knows the exact time that Mel purportedly killed herself. She does not. I tell her that I'll be able to hear the recording tomorrow and that I'll call her when I do. She's silent for a moment then thanks me for believing her.

I stand outside the GTO, pumping gas with my collar turned up against a stiff cold breeze blowing off the river. I know I can get on the Interstate, go to work tomorrow and put everything out of my mind until I get the call from Sammie. I know that odds are that the call will be perfectly legitimate and that it will give both Veronica and me some closure. The problem is, whatever the odds are, I don't believe them anymore. I'm not ready to leave town. So I have one more call to make.

"Pol-Mil, this is Susan," the voice on the phone is professional but distracted. The most important calls to my workplace in the State Department do not come through the public phone lines.

"Hey Suz, this is Michael."

"Hey, Michael, how are you? I'm so sorry to hear about your ex," Susan says. Her concern is genuine. It's a small office.

"I'm okay. It's obviously a bad situation but it's been nice seeing my family. Eileen is on with you this weekend, right?" I already know the answer. The twelve analysts in the Arms and Technology Transfer Division of the Office of Politico-Military Affairs in the Bureau of Intelligence and Research at the U.S. Department of State are responsible for covering the weekends a pair at a time between them. Susan works on the technology part of arms and tech transfer while Eileen, who holds a master's degree from the Fletcher School of Law & Diplomacy at Tufts University, is one of my co-workers on the arms side. I glance at my watch. It is after six. I'm lucky to have reached the day shift.

"She's wrapping up in the Vault—do you want her to call you when she's out?"

The Vault is the secure office where all material classified "Top Secret" and compartmentalized by codeword is viewed. Each analyst at INR/PMA/AT has two desks. The first resides in a minimally secured location and it comes with a green phone that dials outside numbers and a grey phone that links to a closed system within the U.S. government. We also have a computer with access to the Internet and outside e-mail addresses from this desk. Our second workspace is in the Vault, which does not resemble a bank vault. It is actually a much more modern workspace, and a highly secured one. Only in the Vault can we review satellite photos from the National Photographic Interpretation Center, intercepted communications from the National Security Agency and human intelligence reports from the CIA. The phone system in the vault only reaches other secure locations within the intelligence community—the CIA, Defense Intelligence, the NSA as well as counterintelligence agencies like the FBI and Homeland Security. Cell phones don't operate in the Vault and there is no access to the Internet.

"Sure, have her give me a call," I reply and leave my cell number with Susan before I disconnect.

While I wait for a call back, I dial Ginny. She is surprised to hear from me, thinking that I've already left town, and offers to meet me for pizza. I turn the GTO around and drive back into Conestoga. I am halfway to Main Street when Eileen calls back.

"How was the weekend?" I ask. Weekend duty is usually drudgery unless something unusual happens. On one of my first weekends on the job, while I was an intern still finishing my degree at Georgetown, Russian tanks rolled into Georgia. I was suddenly swamped with queries from the political desks in State about the capabilities of the Georgian military. Subsequent weekends have not been as interesting.

"Quiet. How about you? How did it go with your family?" Eileen is my best friend at State, the only one who knows the whole story about my family issues. She is older than me, a tall, willowy blonde in her mid-thirties who walks fast, eats at her desk and can read and write six languages. She has mentored me almost from my first day as an intern. I like the fact that she has no higher career aspirations and no interest in politics.

"Better than I expected. It's been a long time," I pause for a moment. "Listen, I'm still in Conestoga and I'm going to have dinner with my sister. I can drive back to D.C. late and be back in the office tomorrow, but I'd like to hang around here for another day or two. Can you talk to the Admiral for me?" I use our nickname for bureau chief Jim Larimore. He is a straight arrow, a former Coast Guard captain who completed his doctoral degree at the School of Advanced International Studies of Johns Hopkins University.

"I told him when you left on Thursday evening there was a good chance you'd need to be gone a few more days, so you're okay. I'll e-mail him and make sure we get you officially signed out by extending your personal leave request form tomorrow morning. I'll set it up for a full week and if you get back sooner you can just change the req, okay?"

"Thanks, you're a life saver," I say, relieved.

"That's the job" Eileen replies smartly before she disconnects.

I have the key in the door to my motel room when the intense beam of light hits me. I spotted the Sheriff's cruiser from a block away as I walked back from DeLoria's Pizza on Main Street. There are two deputies in the car, and I don't recognize either of them. They seem tense, but the shotgun is still locked upright between the seats. In a town the size of Conestoga, the odds that they're on a random stakeout of my motel are pretty low. I don't believe in coincidences, anyway, especially not a couple of hours after I've been poking my nose into police business. So I continue on my way until the moment the light from the cruiser hits the back of my head and I hear the command voice they teach police rookies projected from a loudspeaker.

"Put your hands up against the door," the voice booms. After ten at night on a Sunday in Conestoga, a whisper would be sufficient to get my attention from ten feet away. I see curtains part from a nearby motel room as curious eyes peek out. I comply without hesitation. "Spread your legs." I do.

The two deputies move in. Once pats me down professionally but indifferently, removing a small folding knife from my pocket. Then he clicks handcuffs on me and turns me around, keeping one hand on my shoulder and one on the back of my head. The second deputy holsters his weapon and opens the rear door on the driver's side of the cruiser. The deputy who cuffed me pushes me forward gently and guides my head down as I step into the vehicle.

I don't bother to ask questions; I know I won't get anything useful from these two. They are silent for the short drive to town hall, which houses the mayor's office, the town registrar and sheriff's department for Conestoga. The building is quiet, and only a few vehicles are parked outside. There are several other cruisers, but I do not see the Sheriff's SUV. Inside the office, the deputies empty my pockets and fill out an inventory list. They seal the envelope containing my wallet, cell phone, keys and the 3" folding Spyderco knife they've confiscated, then both sign it in the presence of a desk clerk and hand it over to her. She opens a safe and stashes the envelope inside. Then the two deputies lead me toward the back of the office. The magnetic lock for a solid-looking steel door clicks as we approach and the larger man opens it. Inside are a half dozen holding cells in a row, each with two steel cots. A few of the cells are occupied. The lights in the cellblock are already out and the men are sleeping—or at least lying down. The deputies escort me to an empty cell and after locking it instruct me to turn around. They remove the handcuffs through the bars and leave me standing in the cell. Neither deputy has spoken a word to me since cuffing me outside the motel.

I stand there for a moment as questions and implications race through my mind. I realize that I haven't been Mirandized, fingerprinted or photographed. So I haven't actually been arrested, just detained. I lie down on the bed, on top of the rough wool blanket, and close my eyes. Speculation is useless: answers will come soon enough. I am asleep before the lights wink out.

Chapter Four –

Monday

I sit uncomfortably -on the hard gymnasium floor with my legs tucked under my knees. My ankles ache after the first few moments, but I will not allow myself to move. I have flown a military transport for sixteen hours from Virginia to reach the northern island of Hokkaido in Japan, accompanied by Dasher, my training supervisor at The Activity.

I've survived Delta Force selection and training and have been whisked away by the Activity, not without some regrets. The Intelligence Support Activity, codenamed "Gray Fox" at the time I join, is headquartered in a non-descript building in Arlington, Virginia. The purpose of the unit, as Alpha told me several years earlier, is to provide field level intelligence for the covert units of the Joint Special Operations Command. When the ISA was founded, there was a great deal of distrust between military commando units and the CIA. The ISA was set up to give units like DEVGRU – Seal Team Six – and the Delta Force the information they needed to mount counterterrorism operations. The ISA was essentially a special-purpose integrated field surveillance unit. As the Internet evolved, the ISA evolved with it until it employed as many computer experts – hackers – as communications experts.

On my first day in the ISA, Alpha introduced me to Dasher, the Command Master Sergeant for the direct action arm of the ISA. "We're shooters," Dasher explained to me. "Except that when we shoot, nobody can know about it. We infiltrate enemy locations to map them out and identify targets. Sometimes we're also tasked with completing special assignments that are best carried out by an individual rather than a team, because we're the only unit in the special ops community that trains and deploys shooters as individuals. That's why you go through Delta selection and training before you can even step foot inside this building. We do everything they do except we do it alone, without maps and without the Army Rangers to bail our asses out if we screw up. Before you go on your first field deployment, you're going to break into the network operations room of a Fortune

500 company and the main vault of a bank right here in Arlington without leaving so much as a drop of sweat to show you were there. You'll learn to tell an SAS officer from a U.S. Marine Force Recon Sergeant or a Navy Seal Master Chief just by how they walk in civvies. You'll get so you know if someone is telling you the truth without a machine, and you'll learn to fool any polygraph or voice-stress analysis. And of course there will be no medals. Nobody outside this unit will ever know what you've done here."

Dasher is like a personal trainer, rotating me through an ever-changing series of exercises. My days alternate between learning the basics of electronic communications from NSA specialists, maintaining my pistol and rifle skills at the FBI range in Quantico and learning field surveillance from the CIA at a place in Virginia called "the Farm." I have been put into an advanced program of daily Ju-Jitsu instruction with a Brazilian master based in the D.C. area, and I've reached the point where I can reliably take down any man or woman in my class except for the instructor. I also continue my language training, concentrating on the dialects I will need for my regional specialization – the Caspian Sea/Hindu Kush area including Iran, Russia, Afghanistan and Pakistan.

About twenty-four hours ago, Dasher calls me at six a.m., just as I'm getting home to the small basement apartment in Arlington I rent but rarely see, and tells me to grab my "go bag" and meet him on the helo pad at ISA headquarters. We make the brief ride to Langley Air Force Base by helicopter then board a military passenger jet. Sixteen hours later we land in Sapporo, Japan. A car takes us directly from the runway to a non-descript public high school in the middle of the city, where a bespectacled young man escorts us into the gymnasium. It's dark outside. The young man invites us to kneel at the edge of a gym mat and observe the class. There are no other onlookers.

The class starts off with a prolonged period of silent meditation. The instructor is an old man with gray hair who can't be an inch above five feet tall standing on his hat. His face is worn like the hide of an elephant and he's wire thin. The only unusual thing about him I spot are his wrists, which seem unnaturally thick.

The instructor is wearing a white Gi – the two-piece standard martial arts uniform made of sturdy white cotton – and a hakama, a black skirt worn only by Japanese fencing masters and Aikido black belts. I don't see any bamboo swords, so I guess that this is an Aikido class. Aikido is distinguished by joint locks and throws, which use the strength and motion of an opponent to power them. The rap against Aikido is that it's "soft." As a martial art, Aikido is strictly defensive. Injuring an attacker with Aikido is considered a grave offense. And unlike Ju-Jitsu, there are no Aikido tournaments.

The class progresses more or less as I expect: a period of stretching follows the meditation, then students break into pairs to practice throwing techniques. I notice that even the least experienced students seem to have a good awareness of the other pairs around them. The class of twenty male students is crowded onto a few small gym mats. Practitioners are constantly throwing their partners, who roll through the paths of other students, yet there are no collisions. Still, by the time an hour has passed, I am wondering what imaginable reason Dasher has for dragging me all the way to Japan to observe a glorified aerobics demonstration.

As the class winds to a close, the instructor motions the students to kneel. He points to his three most senior students – all black belts wearing the hakama skirts – and commands them with a few terse words in Japanese. They rise to their feet and surround him. On command they attack simultaneously, using standard karate punches and kicks. They do not pull their punches, but none of them manages to lay a finger on the instructor. He appears to move slowly, dancing through them in circular motions, using the momentum of one student to block the attack of another. It is impressive. The instructor seems to have eyes in the back of his head, always sensing an attack and whirling out of the way or intercepting and redirecting it in midstream before it reaches him. The students roll gracefully each time and return immediately to the attack. This goes on for about five minutes, after which the master claps twice and the students bow and return to their kneeling positions, panting. I admit I'm impressed, although I hardly think that wearing out my opponents aerobically is something I'd care to try in CQB.

"This traditional Aikido," the master says in halting English, addressing me directly and bowing slightly. I return the bow, and remembering the in-flight pamphlet on Japanese customs that Dasher handed me when we departed Virginia, bow much deeper than the master, who smiles. He waits a minute and claps again. The same three students rise. Again they attack their instructor. This time, however, the master's reaction is different. As each attack arrives, he again moves off-axis to redirect the force. This time, however, he adds a small jerk of his shoulder or a tap of his hand into the element. The arm or leg he targets begins to tremble. Then he puts the students on the ground, one by one, twisting them into knots where they appear unable to move until he leans down to release them. He repeats this demonstration several times in different combinations before having the students grapple him directly. One starts with a half-nelson lock around his neck while the other two each control an arm. In a few seconds he has reversed the position, again leaving the students trembling on the ground. As hard as I look, I can't see exactly how he's doing this. I've heard my

Ju-Jitsu instructor talk about nerve strikes, but nothing like this. The master continues to repeat the technique from different starting holds, with similar results. Then he bows to us again and motions to me. I look at Dasher questioningly. "You're not actually going to believe this is for real unless you feel it yourself, are you?" Dasher asks. I nod and rise stiffly to my feet.

"Please attack," the instructor says. I hesitate. I've just seen this guy take down three young black belts in a variety of situations. But I am still irrationally reluctant to strike a man older than my mother and considerably smaller than my youngest sister. The dull ache of jetlag is still in my bones,though, and I want to see if this man is for real, so I take a step forward and throw a jab. The instructor retreats a half step and the blow hits air. I jab again and the master takes another step back, patiently waiting as if nothing has happened. I get the point. Without warning, I crouch and dive in low to execute an under-arm hook takedown – a simple Ju-Jitsu move that I am particularly fond of because the initial approach mirrors a football tackle. The basic technique involves grappling the opponent around the chest under both arms, stepping a foot around one of his legs and then using your lower center of gravity to pull the opponent down over your leg. I explode into the tackle, using my years of experience as a linebacker tempered by my more recent daily martial arts workouts.

The result is not at all what I expect. Instead of tackling the instructor, my arms grasp empty air. Then before I know what is happening, the gym mat hits my chest at ninety miles an hour. My six-foot-three, 250-pound Ju-Jitsu instructor has never put me down with equal force. As I try to get up, I realize I can't move. My right arm is inexplicably sticking out straight behind my back, up into the air, and it is quivering. My left arm won't move, either. I am intensely aware of the chuckles from the seated students.

Five times, I try to take the instructor down with different approaches, scientifically ferreting out a weakness. Five times I fail. I only touch the man once, as I make a sideways approach for a leg tackle and a sudden instinct tells me to adjust at the last moment. My open hand grazes the small man's bony thigh. But that is all, the opportunity is gone as soon as it appears and I am pitched forward in a manner that will break my neck if I don't roll. Then the instructor again brings me to the mat before I can recover my feet. Finally, the tiny man bows to me with another smile and I bow back with genuine respect. I hobble over to Dasher, my muscles more sore than they had been at the end of the final 40-mile march during Delta Force selection. "Tough little son-of-a-bitch, ain't he?" Dasher says, smiling broadly and slapping me unnecessarily hard on the back.

A moment later, the instructor turns to Dasher and pointing to me he says, "Student. O-Kay," prolonging the "O" with some ceremony. Dasher's mouth falls open. He turns to me with a look of consternation, and explains. "Alpha found this guy ten years ago. We heard rumors about him for years before that. We bring him shooters three years in a row and he tests them out and says no. Doesn't make any fuckin' sense. This guy is a janitor. I'm serious, that's his full time job; he's the janitor for this school. We offer him two year's salary to take on someone for a few months. He says no. Then we double the offer. Still no. After three years of asking, we gave up. Last week Alpha calls me in and tells me to bring you to Master Shioda – Hikaru Shioda, that's his name. I tell him he's nuts but he just gives me that look, you know the one. And fuck me if it didn't work. What the hell did you do? Looked to me like you got your ass kicked just as well as the rest of them." Dasher actually looks bitter, something I have not seen from him before.

Master Shioda, whose English I will soon learn is flawless, keeps his gaze locked on Dasher as the big man speaks to me. Then, he says gently to the big man, "When you come first time, you use this," he pats Dasher's impressive bicep. "This one," he says, gesturing to me, "also use this," and here Master Shioda taps my forehead. Dasher rolls his eyes and makes a face at me, plainly disgusted. "Enjoy your stay with Mr. Miagi. I'll see you in three months, Soldier. And if you ever try any of this shit on me, I'll kill you."

"George Jeffries was brought into the emergency room at St. Luke's Cornwall Hospital by ambulance just after 1am on Sunday morning. His left knee had multiple torn ligaments as well as damage to the meniscus. An orthopedic surgeon performed arthroscopic surgery yesterday to repair the meniscus and assess the damage to the ligaments. George was released from St. Luke's yesterday afternoon at 6pm. He took a taxi from there to his car, which was parked in New Paltz, then drove it – against medical advice – to the Days Inn in Kingston, where he had been staying for the weekend. It appears that Mr. Jeffries was surprised there by an assailant who shot him and took the cash and credit cards from his wallet, as well as his watch." Sheriff Buddy Peterson pauses to slide a photo to me across his desk.

George is lying facedown on the floor of a motel room. He's been shot in the back of the head, at close range. From the position of the body, he was kneeling when he was shot, which must have been excruciatingly painful after what I'd done to him. I can see a dozen little details that tell me the killer is a pro, but I keep my mouth shut. I rub my neck. It's stiff from sleeping on the little cot in the holding cell. My back has grown used to better mattresses since I left the service. My watch has not been returned to me, but I can see from the clock on the paneled wall beside the Sheriff's desk that it is nine-thirty in the morning. At least I've caught up on my sleep.

"Not two hours after this homicide occurred yesterday, I answered a call from a White Plains reporter asking to meet me today to speak about the death of Mel Harris. This reporter suggested to me in the strongest terms that her death was not self-inflicted and that she believed Mr. Jeffries to be the cause. I made some enquiries and learned that Mr. Jeffries had just been released from a local hospital, so I sent my deputies to his motel room to bring him in for questioning. I also discovered that Mr. Jeffries had been in a bar fight in New Paltz, leading to his injuries. I was able to talk to the bar manager, who explained that Mr. Jeffries had assaulted their bouncer and broke his nose, and that a young man approximately six feet tall with black hair and an athletic build intervened and disabled Mr. Jeffries, causing the injuries that sent him to the hospital. I was told this man left the scene before the police arrived ..." Buddy pauses here and looks up, making eye contact with me. "It was obvious to me that this was you. Then no sooner do I start wondering what the hell is going on between you and this George Jeffries than my deputies call back in a panic saying they've found him murdered in his motel room."

"What time did they find George?" I ask.

"Just after eight last night."

"I was having dinner with my sister Ginny – you can ask her. There's a credit card receipt in my wallet." Buddy stops to ponder this for a moment.

"I'm sure you have an alibi, son," he says slowly in that patient, matter-of-fact tone you use to explain things to someone who's a little slow. "In fact, I'm absolutely convinced of that. But let me lay this out for you straight, okay? Forget about the assault at the bar. You're in a world of trouble here.

"Do you know how the justice system works in Ulster County? It's not very sophisticated. There are rural magistrates. In some towns, they're not even full time and they actually move from place to place. They aren't like big city judges in New York or Washington. The magistrate that hears arraignments in Kingston doesn't even have a law degree – he's a second cousin of the State Assemblyman from that district. So if the police in Kingston tie you to this murder, they're going to arraign you. And I can almost guarantee that he'll hold you over for trial.

"Now you may be able to get a fancy lawyer to prove that you didn't kill George. But then again you might not. George was threatening your ex-girlfriend – I have the restraining order right here. You're a decorated war veteran. You put George in the hospital on Saturday night and then this reporter tells you that he killed your ex. I don't think anyone around here would hesitate to believe your sister would lie about an alibi to protect you.

Either way, even if you win, you're going to lose your security clearance and your job in the process. Your career will be over. That's a sad fact, but that's just the way things go." Buddy lets this sink in for a moment. I realize he's not bluffing – it's a conceivable scenario.

"Son, I'm your friend. I don't want to see this happen. But I'm in a tight situation here. This reporter friend of yours is threatening to write a story about Mel's death. That would be very embarrassing to me and my department. More importantly, it would force me to reopen the investigation, and you would certainly get caught up in that.

"I bear some of the responsibility. I was pretty distraught over Mel's death just like everyone else here. We didn't investigate the way we probably should have. And for what it's worth, Ms. Ryan's story about Mr. Jeffries is plausible. I was over at the house this morning and it does appear that it was broken into. And now that I know about the restraining order, I can put two and two together. I should have figured this out last week, but I didn't. But Mel's been buried and the man who killed her is dead, so if we want to start proving what actually happened, it'll get pretty messy.

"Frankly, son, I'm not a big city cop, I'm just a small town peace officer. From my perspective, whether or not you killed Mr. Jeffries, justice was done. He paid the price for something terrible that he did. And I don't think you're any danger to society. You're a hero to the people of this town and I'm not interested in tarnishing your name." I see where this is heading as Buddy speaks and I wait patiently for him to pull the hook he's baited.

"The Kingston police haven't tied you to Mr. Jeffries' death. They don't know you were the one who attacked George on Saturday night," Buddy says as he spits a stream of yellow tobacco juice into an old-fashioned spittoon next to his wastebasket. I refrain from pointing out that George attacked me, not the other way around. "And like us, they have enough crime in their town that they might think this was a random break-in. So I'm willing to let this rest and keep my mouth shut. But it won't work if your reporter friend starts stirring things up by writing a story. That can only lead folks to you. It probably wouldn't hurt either if you got the hell out of town to let things die down for a while. Do you catch my drift?"

I nod. "I read you five by five."

I have the midnight black GTO spooled up to 80 miles an hour on the New York State Thruway heading south when my cell phone rings. I've ignored the five increasingly urgent text and voice messages from Veronica that started coming through last night because I need time to think. But this call is not from her. It's Sammie.

"Dude, I think you gave me the wrong phone number for that 9-1-1 call," he says.

"Come again?"

"I don't know what I was expecting to hear, but it sure wasn't this," he says and plays the recording to me.

"9-1-1 – what is the nature of your emergency?" a female voice asks.

"Hello? Hello?" a male voice with a Slavic accent: Russian or possibly Ukrainian. "Very sorry I am trying to reach information for pizza delivery – Dominos." The voice pauses and the 9-1-1 operator interjects, "Sir, this is 9-1-1 – the number for emergencies. Please hang up and dial 4-1-1 for information." The Russian voice laughs and replies, "Please excuse, I am very sorry." The 9-1-1 operator says, "That's alright, sir, have a good day." Then the phone disconnects.

"That's not the voice I was expecting to hear either. Can you read back the number you checked?" I ask and Sammie does. It is the same number I'd given him. "Can you check to see who the phone is listed under?"

"I did – the number is registered to Melissa Harris on Orchard Road in Conestoga, New York," he replies.

"That's the right one. Can they have mixed up the call logs?"

"Yeah, that was my first thought, too, but there's no mistake. The systems are routinely audited and double-checked. They have to be able to send the police or fire department to the address of anyone who calls in, even if the caller doesn't know their own address, so accuracy is a big deal for them. I think you can be 99.9% certain that the call came from that house," Sammy concludes briskly. "Anyway, is this at all helpful?"

"In a way," I reply and ponder for a second. "Is there any way of finding out if anyone else has pulled this recording?"

"Hold on the line and let me check," Sammy says. I wait a few minutes before he returns. "It looks like a Sheriff Peterson from Conestoga requested it on Thursday, the day after the call," Sammy confirms.

I exhale a whistle. "That's very helpful. I'll be in touch, Sammie."

I run through the sequence of events again in my mind before dialing information in New York City, asking for the business number for the bank where George worked. When the receptionist answers I ask for George Jeffries. A moment later another woman picks up the phone.

"George Jeffries' line, this is Nancy," the woman says smoothly.

"I'm trying to reach George Jeffries," I reply.

"I'm sorry, he's not in at the moment, would you like to leave a message?"

"When can I reach him?" I press.

"Are you a friend of Mr. Jeffries?" the woman asks.

"We've met," I reply truthfully.

"Well, I'm sorry to say that Mr. Jeffries is…deceased," the woman says after a few seconds of consideration. Then I hear her falter over the phone. "I'm very sorry but we just found out about this and everyone here is in shock."

"No, I apologize," I offer. "I'm very sorry to hear that. Perhaps you can help me, though. I sent a package by courier over to your group last week and it was received at 6:30pm on Wednesday night. I'm trying to track it and couldn't read the signature. Could it have been George who signed for it?"

"Let me check his calendar…" the woman says, and I hear computer keys clicking. "Ah yes, I remember. We were finalizing a deal that evening and Mr. Jeffries was in the office all night. He actually didn't leave until late the next afternoon. I'd be surprised if he signed for a courier delivery, though. I stayed late that night as well and that's what he has – I mean, had me for."

"Thanks, I appreciate it," I say and hang up before she can ask me any questions. Then I call Veronica.

She's clearly angry with me until I explain that I didn't return her calls because I've spent a night in jail. Then she apologizes, sounding both horrified and remorseful. She tells me that she left a message for the Sheriff before we met, but she was too embarrassed to tell me when I dismissed her concerns. She wanted to find out what time Mel killed herself to see if the 9-1-1 call came before or after. Sheriff Peterson called her back just after I had called her from my car last night, and dragged the entire story out of her. In no uncertain terms he ordered her to meet him at 7am this morning, then had her take him through all the things she showed me. Then he promised to investigate and asked her to hold off speaking to her editors for a couple of days. He didn't tell her anything about George's death, which she is shocked to hear about from me. I relay the Sheriff's ultimatum.

"Well thank God you know Sheriff Peterson personally," she says, "because he's right about the magistrate system in this state. It's a mess – it's been written up in the *New York Times*. Who knows what would have happened to you if you got caught up in all that?"

"I'm still in it. I can't ask you not to write a story about this. That's your job, isn't it?"

"My job is writing feature stories for a suburban newspaper, not speculating about murders! Even if I wanted to, do you have any idea what it would take to get a story like this printed? You don't want to know. Don't worry, you're safe."

"I don't think so. We've still got two problems," I say, sighing.

"Which are?"

"I was able to listen to the recording of the 9-1-1 call last Wednesday night from Mel's apartment. It wasn't George's voice. The speaker was Russian or maybe Ukrainian. After I heard the recording, I called George's bank. I talked to his assistant. It turns out that George was at work all night on Wednesday. He was there finalizing some deal until mid-day on Thursday, in fact. He couldn't have killed Mel."

I slow the GTO, checking for traffic in the rearview mirror. Then I pull quickly across two lanes, exiting the Thruway at the last minute. "That's the first problem," I say to Veronica as I bring the GTO to a halt in front of the traffic light at the end of the exit ramp.

"What's the second problem?" she asks.

"When he was interrogating me this morning, Buddy Peterson was hiding something. He was lying to me."

"How do you know that?" Veronica asks.

"He listened to the recording of that 9-1-1 call last week. That should have been enough to investigate the cause of Mel's death," I tell her. It's true enough. But I didn't need to know about the recording to know Buddy Peterson wasn't telling the truth.

So the obvious question is this: if I know Buddy is lying to me and covering something up, why am I leaving Conestoga as fast as my ride will carry me? It's not because I'm afraid of getting locked up. I'm not worried about losing my job. I know that if I dig into this my own way, I'll figure out what's really going on. I'm good at that, world class. No, that's not what has me running. The real reason is this: I know that if I put myself in the middle of this mess, people are going to get hurt, and not just the ones who deserve it. It's already happened to George, although I don't entirely put him in the innocent bystander category. This is the burden I promised myself I wasn't going to carry around any more.

But it's too late now; I've crossed the Rubicon. I've asked too many questions and I know too much. Someone I've respected since I was a child just lied to my face, and now I've confirmed it. I make two quick turns and then I'm on the Thruway again, heading back north towards Conestoga.

"What is Buddy Peterson hiding?" I muse aloud as I sip coffee and push a lone French fry around the rim of my plate with a fork. I look over Veronica's shoulder at a couple passing outside the diner, fingers casually entwined. I stare for a moment then look away.

"Are you sure he's hiding something? He seems like a pretty good guy."

"I thought so too. But it's all too convenient. George gets killed almost immediately after you finger him to the Sheriff. And Buddy is suddenly convinced that he made a mistake about Mel's suicide after hearing some sketchy circumstantial evidence?"

"Sketchy?" Veronica sounds indignant but looks amused.

"How about 'inconclusive'?" I amend, and she shrugs her agreement. "My point is that Buddy Peterson is not an idiot. I spent most of the day with him yesterday. He's cautious and thorough. He thinks things through. So hearing him flip-flop from calling Mel's death a suicide to a murder in a nanosecond, then pinning it on George – conveniently dead…I just don't buy it."

"He's obviously trying to protect someone," Veronica taps a lacquered nail against her coffee cup as she says what I'm thinking.

"Yes, but who?"

"Himself. People almost always lie to protect themselves or someone very close to them. Unless his wife or kids are responsible, I'd say he's involved somehow," Veronica observes. It's the first time she's sounded like a reporter to me. "Are you absolutely sure that the 9-1-1 call you heard was real?" she asks.

"Pretty close. This is a system tested and verified a bunch of different ways. They use those addresses to direct emergency responders, so they have to be accurate. Apparently they can keep the line open even if you hang it up," I explain, repeating what Sammie has told me. "The more interesting question is, what does it mean if it's really the call from Mel's place?"

Veronica pauses to consider this. "I don't know," she says finally.

"Let's assume that the person who killed Mel did break in through the rear door. That means the murder wasn't just about some argument that got out of hand, like a parent angry about his kid's grades. Someone like that would have pushed his way in through the front door. George might have broken down the rear door if he'd been thinking clearly enough to want to avoid being seen knocking down Mel's front door. But the voice on the 9-1-1 recording wasn't George's, because George was in New York City at the time. So the other possibility is that someone decided he had to kill Mel and had to do it quickly. If you assume that, the killer did a pretty good job."

"What do you mean?"

"Whoever killed her must have done it spontaneously, but he obviously didn't want to get caught. So he thinks, how can I make this look like a suicide? Because if he tries to make it look like an accident, like Mel slipped in the bathtub and broke her neck or electrocuted herself accidentally, there's going to be more of a forensic investigation, and those kinds of setups fall apart quickly unless they're well planned. I mean, this guy has already broken the lock on the back door, right? So he needs something that will keep the cops from looking too closely. Suicide does that. Unless there's a reason to suspect foul play, there isn't much of an investigation."

"But that's ridiculous. Mel had a restraining order out against George and everyone knew it. Even if he didn't kill Mel, wouldn't that at least get the cops wondering and asking questions about her supposed suicide?"

"Yes, that's the other problem. Buddy Peterson personally requested a copy of the 9-1-1 recording the day after the shooting. So that means he had his own reasons for going along with the scene staged in that apartment."

"Which were?" Veronica taps her lips slowly.

I shake my head sharply. "No idea. And there's no way to ask Buddy now. In fact, I'd say it's pretty important that he doesn't think we're poking around this at all."

"So what do we do?"

"Didn't you say Mel's landlord lived upstairs from her?"

"Yes, what's his name?" Veronica asks herself as she flips through a slender notepad encased in antiqued green leather. "Harvey. Harvey Kastriner."

"Is he retired?"

"Maybe. He said he was a widower." Veronica squints and I can almost see her replaying her brief meeting with Kastriner in her mind.

"Let's go talk to Harvey," I suggest, rising. "Maybe he can tell us what time he heard the gunshot." I drop a twenty-dollar bill on the check before Veronica can protest.

Mel's neighborhood does not come alive in the daylight. Hundred-year oaks planted too close together loom over Orchard Road, their branches extended like bony fingers over the worn pavement. The sidewalk is uneven and disused. An abandoned Radio Flyer lies on its side at the edge of the yard. The house is painted a dull blue, faded almost to gray with white trim around the windows. A narrow walkway with cement stones leads from the sidewalk to the house. Three steps bring us up to a small landing. The landlord's door faces us and the entrance to Mel's ground-floor apartment is to the right. Veronica rings the bell to the upstairs apartment.

I can hear Harvey Kastriner making his way down the staircase slowly, his cane preceding his feet on each stair. The creak of the old wood follows each of Harvey's heavy footfalls and we both hear Kastriner's puffs of exertion and exchange a glance. When the door opens, I see a weather-beaten man in his seventies. Kastriner wears a plaid bathrobe tied over boxer shorts and a dingy undershirt that peeks through as he balances two hands on his cane. His steel gray hair is combed neatly to one side, and his face is clean behind enormous steel-framed glasses, lending the impression that it is the only part of himself that he regularly observes in a mirror. The blue paint on the staircase Harvey has descended is peeling, a sign of neglect mirrored in the rickety railing and chipped mirror by the banister. Kastriner's face seems to soften a little as he recognizes Veronica.

"You're Melissa's friend from the other day, right?" he asks. Veronica nods and I wonder if she has also noticed that he didn't say "yesterday."

"I'm very sorry to bother you again, but we wanted to ask you a couple of questions."

Harvey looks around, checking the space behind us nervously before asking, "What about?"

"The day of Melissa's death."

Harvey shakes his head, "I don't know, I already talked to the police. Why do you ask? You must know that your friend killed herself."

I take a closer look at Harvey. His fingernails are neatly trimmed, cut to the quick. The man has thick knuckles afflicted by arthritis and beefy hands covered in calluses. His eyes dart around, exploring the perimeter of his vision. I guess the man's age and calculate backwards. "You served in Korea, didn't you?" I ask.

Harvey's head snaps back in surprise. Then he inhales and seems to swell a bit, "Why, yes I did. Twenty-seventh Infantry Regiment, '50 to '54," he says proudly. "How did you know?"

"Infantrymen can spot one another," I reply. "So you're a Wolfhound? You must have seen a lot of action. Did you cross the Han River?" Veronica looks from me to the older man, not following the conversation.

"Yessir. Toughest day of my life. But we won the Presidential unit citation for that one. What unit did you serve in, son?"

"I was in combat with the Fifth Special Forces Group," I reply evenly.

"Then you must be the Herne boy. Thought I recognized you. I heard you won the Silver Star in Afghanistan," Harvey adds enthusiastically. I can see that Veronica is surprised by the transformation in Kastriner, who seems to have shed a decade. I've seen it before.

"Yes sir, but I'm sure it was nothing compared to what you guys saw in Pusan."

We fall into conversation for a few minutes. When Harvey asks me a question, I divert the conversation back to him. He's a tough old sonofabitch, I can tell that much. I would have liked to serve with him.

"You were Melissa's boyfriend in school, weren't you?" Harvey asks gently. I nod.

"I'm so sorry, son. Sorry about your father, too. He was a good man. I worked with him for twenty years at the Godfrey Mill." He places a large hand on top of mine. I'm surprised. I haven't heard many men speak fondly of my Dad.

"Look, we're not trying to stir up any trouble," I say, "but I'm sure you understand that I have some questions about Mel's death."

"It was senseless," Harvey shakes his head, "such a bright, beautiful young girl."

"Did anything happen around here the evening she died?"

"Nope, it was quiet as a church," Kastriner said, "until the gunshot, of course."

"Do you remember what time that was?" I ask, hoping.

"Yes, it was right at the end of the evening news …6:30."

Veronica and I exchange a glance. Now we know that a man called 9-1-1 from Mel's apartment nearly twenty minutes before Mel died.

"What did you do after you heard the gun go off?"

"Well, I could tell it was a pistol and that the noise came from downstairs, so I called 9-1-1 from my place. I know the trouble Melissa had with that old boyfriend of hers and I don't move too quickly these days," Harvey shakes his head ruefully. "I was afraid I might tumble down the stairs and then nobody would have called the authorities. I looked out front for a moment and I didn't see anything. Then I grabbed the keys and went downstairs. I was knocking on Melissa's front door when the Sheriff arrived, and I let him in."

"He beat the ambulance to the house?" I ask, only half-surprised. Harvey ponders this for a moment.

"By a minute or so, yes."

"And you don't remember hearing anything at all before that?"

"No, not at all. I was watching Katie Couric."

On instinct, I take another tact. "What can you tell me about the rest of the neighbors on the block?" I gesture to the right and left of the house.

"Well, the Simons are retired, they're pretty quiet," he says, pointing directly across the street to a blue colonial, "and the Martins are upstate for a couple of weeks," he continues, gesturing to a somewhat larger brick house next door to the Simons'. "Over to the left, that's a young couple, Jen and Brad Kyle – they have a two- and a four-year-old. Kyle works at Simmon's garage. And the house on the right – that was a foreign family, but they moved out over the weekend." The last house, the closest to Harvey's door, is a Colonial painted a faded yellow and only in marginally better shape than Kastriner's.

"Foreign?" I ask. The little hairs on the back of my neck are tingling.

"European or something," Harvey says uncertainly, "but not very friendly. I went over to say hello after they moved in and the father just said 'not speaking English' and closed the door on me. Good-sized family, but you never saw any of them outside. And lots of visitors, at all times of day and night. I didn't like them. They didn't understand what we mean by neighbors around here."

"And they moved out this weekend?" I ask, studying the yellow house.

"Come to think, it must have been Thursday. A big white panel truck came and took the stuff away. They were gone in a couple of hours. Not that it mattered. They were only here for a coupla' months. Not even long enough to take the 'For Sale' sign down," Harvey gestures towards the road with a large callused hand.

I thank Harvey and watch the big man retreat slowly back into the house, the cane preceding him step by step. That's what it comes to.

"Do you think it's the guy from the 9-1-1 call?" Veronica asks as we walk onto the lawn of the yellow colonial.

"I don't know, maybe. Maybe he was in his back yard when he heard the shot. He went in and found Mel, called 9-1-1 then changed his mind and decided he didn't want to get involved."

"But the 9-1-1 call came before the shot," Veronica points out.

"If Harvey's right about the time, but I wouldn't bet the farm on his memory. What if the neighbor was an illegal?" I speculate, unconvinced by my own scenario. "Still, I'd like to get a look inside the house," I say, reaching into the front pocket of my jeans.

"Do you think it's open?" Veronica asks.

"No, but if you're willing to be my wife for an hour I think we can get a guided tour," I tell her as I dial the number for the realty agency on the sale sign out front. I observe the look on Veronica's face as she considers the possibilities.

"This is such a lovely neighborhood, I can see why you two want to live here. Are you expecting, honey?" Mary Edwards asks, as she vigorously shakes Veronica's hand. I have to stifle the urge to laugh. Edwards is an attractive woman in her late thirties or early forties with straight brown hair spun up above her head in some complicated hairdo that involves a healthy volume of hairspray. Her slightly dark, rust-colored lip gloss complements brown eyes covered by a pair of small rectangular glasses with horn rims. She pulls a stray hair behind her ear as she speaks, emphasizing her talking points with a pen. Her navy pantsuit gives her an air of managerial authority, only slightly undercut by the elaborate brooch on her lapel.

Veronica is about to make an angry retort but I squeeze her hand and she bites her lip. It's a fair enough reaction, because Veronica's stomach – or at least her sweater – is washboard-flat. I interject, "We're not quite ready to talk about that if you know what I mean," I wink at Edwards, "but we'd like to be in a nice neighborhood. How's the school system?" I ask, instantly regretting the question. I do want to get inside the house, after all.

"Well, there aren't many top-rated schools in this area, but Conestoga High School has its advantages," Edwards says brightly. An emergency room within two miles is all I can come up with.

"So we heard this house just opened up," Veronica comments, eager to move the conversation away from her reproductive health.

"Let's see," Edwards says as she consults her clipboard, "No, you must be wrong, this house has been listed for seven months. I can't tell you much more because I didn't rep this property personally. Let's see who did … hmm, that's odd. The listing agent is Charles Vanderhook, but I didn't think he handled any properties personally any more – he's the founder of our firm." Edwards looks momentarily puzzled but then shakes it off like a Labrador after a bath and moves purposefully towards the house. She uses a small key to open the lockbox on the door and withdraws the house key. It clicks neatly into the front door lock, which I notice is a new deadbolt in better condition than the rest of the place. Edwards strides purposefully into the house and Veronica and I step in behind her.

The air in the house has a peculiar smell, and Edwards immediately pulls out an embroidered handkerchief and starts waving it around. "I'm so sorry - they really should have aired this place out," she says as she struggles to open a window. "It's a bank-owned property," she adds by way of explanation or apology.

"It's okay. Why don't you just give us a moment to take a look around on our own? If we have questions, we'll ask you," Veronica says smiling, and pecks me on the cheek. Edwards hesitates for a second, conflicted because she knows she's not supposed to let us wander unsupervised. Then she sneezes, which makes the decision for her, and she shrugs and steps onto the front stoop as we walk up the half-flight of stairs separating the sunken living room from the bedrooms on the upper level.

I whistle before we even reach the first bedroom. "They really cleaned the place out," I remark. Veronica looks at me questioningly.

"Look at the door," I say. I pull the open door towards us until it closes. There is a hole just below eye-level. Then I examine the hole closely. "There was a deadbolt here," I explain. I move through the room, the bare pine floors creaking. I see holes drilled in the window frame. As we move from bedroom to bedroom, we see identical holes on each door, and the windows in each of the four bedrooms have all been drilled. The rooms are otherwise immaculate, devoid of any sign that a family has lived here just days before. There is a strong smell of disinfectant, as if the house has been scrubbed clean. It isn't any more pleasant than the sour smell in the living room.

I lean against the door of the black GTO, my arms crossed in front of me. I flick Mary Edwards's business card between my fingers like a poker chip, giving the illusion that it is tumbling downhill.

"So what do you think?" Veronica asks me.

"There's definitely something odd about that house. It wasn't just deadbolts on the bedroom doors – there were bars on the windows. Whoever lived there was trying to keep someone in, not out."

"It smelled really odd in there, too. I feel like I know that odor, but I just can't put my finger on what exactly it was," Veronica adds, gathering her thoughts for a moment. "Did it sound to you like the owner of that real estate firm was illegally subletting a foreclosed house to that family?"

"Yes, that's exactly what I was thinking. It sounds like a pretty good sideline for a realtor these days," I reply, wondering how any real estate agent in this area managed to survive the recession.

"So if these people got scared off and left, doesn't it make sense that they'd go somewhere else – maybe another house that's been empty for awhile?" I nod. "So how do we find them? It seems like half this town is vacant."

"Oh, I don't think that will be very difficult at all," I answer, and the ghost of a smile passes my lips.

"That'll be $96.35," the man behind the register tells me, and I wince as I hand over five twenties. I take possession of a handful of helium balloons from the florist along with a hefty vase of flowers. I pause before leaving the shop.

"Listen, I'm going to surprise my girlfriend at work. Is there any chance I could borrow a hat and apron from your shop?"

The florist, an angular man with thinning white hair and a pair of reading glasses perched near the tip of his nose considers the question for a moment. "Can I trust you with the responsibility that goes along with wearing the Phil's Florist hat?" he asks seriously. I stare at him blankly for a second. Then he smiles. "I've got an extra set from my assistant who just quit, but you'll need to promise to bring them back or give me an extra $20 so I can replace them. I nod and hand the man another twenty.

Vanderhook Realty is based in a converted row house just off Main Street in Conestoga. Main Street itself shows few signs of life on a cloudy Tuesday afternoon, and the block Vanderhook sits on is positively moribund. The row house at least has a fresh coat of paint in that jaunty yellow that only a real estate agency or an ice cream shop can pull off. As I approach the building, I pull the Phil's florist cap down low over my eyes.

Any good performer knows that magic is about directing the audience's eyes to where you want them to be. As I push through the door to Vanderhook Realty, a brace of mylar helium balloons and a dozen yellow roses almost ensures that nobody is looking at my face. There are six desks on the main floor, but only a couple of agents are here as it's nearing the end of the day. Veronica has called ahead to ensure that Mary Edwards is not about. I walk over to the receptionist. A plaque tells me that her name is Dolores Ledbetter. She is a middle-aged redhead with long, fake, elaborately lacquered nails and a pen stuck behind her ear that she's forgotten about. As I approach her I can see that she's on the real-diets.com website, calculating points for her meals. She looks hopeful as she catches sight of the roses.

"I have a delivery for Mr. Vanderhook," I say politely but not too warmly. Dolores looks skeptical.

"This is Vanderhook Realty, are you sure those aren't someone for else here?"

"Uh, it says Charles Vanderhook. Is there someone by that name here?"

"Well, he won't be here until Thursday," Dolores looks both cross and uninterested, as the flowers clearly aren't for her. I can see her reappraising the value of the yellow roses downwards. "Could'ja come back then?"

"Uh, I'm sorry, I kind of have to delivery them now. Umm, I can put them on Mr. Vanderhook's desk if you want. They'll keep for a few days if you water them. But they're pretty heavy so I'd appreciate it if you could point his desk out to me." Dolores gets up from her station, leaning forward to grab a set of keys. She tries to catch me taking a peek down her sweater but I'm not looking at anything in that vicinity. She sighs and steps around in front of me.

"Okay, I hope you don't mind a set of stairs," she says and leads me up to the upper level. Vanderhook's office is the large one at the end of the hallway. Dolores uses her key to open a deadbolt lock. It's a large room with a traditional walnut desk with a wingback leather chair between the desk and a matching credenza. A lateral steel filing cabinet sits just inside the door to the right and a small round conference table with two chairs is to my left. I put the vase down on the table, taking a good look out the rear window to the office as I do. There isn't much of a view through the old paned window. The townhouse shares walls with a hairdresser and a veterinary clinic. Vanderhook's office looks out back to the small employee parking area shared with the other businesses. There are a few trees between it and the residential buildings behind.

"Should I leave the balloons here or do you want me to put them over there?" I ask, pointing to the credenza on the interior wall. As Dolores looks to where I am pointing to consider, I reach my hand back without looking and thumb open the lock to the window next to Vanderhook's conference table. My eyes quickly confirm that there's no jamb or key lock on the frame.

"I wonder who these are from?" Dolores muses, almost to herself.

"You'd be surprised by some of the people who send flowers," I say and before she can thank me, I'm gone.

"So this is your idea of a first date? Breaking and entering?" Veronica asks, leaning over me to peer up at the Vanderhook building. It is just after eight and there is still enough traffic around to provide some background noise. A miasma of clouds hovering over the town covers the moon, which should be nearly full tonight. Good luck.

"Do you have addresses for me?" I ask, ignoring the joke. I've slipped on a pair of black Chuck Taylors to complement dark jeans and a black fleece over a grey t-shirt.

"I found five residential houses in Conestoga that were listed on the cached version of the Vanderhook website from last week that weren't listed this week, but two of them were also in the "new sales" column and had the sale price listed. So here are the addresses of the other three – the one's that just disappeared this week, as well as Mel's address if you don't remember it," Veronica hands me a Post-It. I glance at the yellow square, memorizing the addresses, and hand it back.

"Okay, got it. Dial me if anyone pulls into the lot and just drive away. My phone is on vibrate," I say as I slip from the passenger's side of the Mercedes. I don't like using her car. It's too flashy for Conestoga and too easy to remember, but we can't use the GTO because Veronica doesn't drive stick. I'm not thrilled to be breaking into the realtor's office even after my reconnaissance. This would have been a ridiculously easy job in my old life, but things can always go wrong, and the stakes are very high. If someone calls the cops, I'm going to be sitting in Buddy Peterson's lockup for a long time to come.

I take a careful look around. The veterinarian and hairdresser are closed for the evening and the lot is vacant except for Veronica's Mercedes. The parking area is sunken a few feet below the level of the street and shielded by trees, only visible to a single window of an end unit in the neighboring condo complex, which is dark. I don't see or even feel anyone else within sight. I turn back to Vanderhook's office and the row house resolves itself into a series of geometric shapes and vectors. It only takes me a couple of seconds to pick my route. There are two windows on the lower floor, spaced about five feet apart. Each window has a side sill protruding from the building by a good three inches.

I step a few paces to the left of the office and give myself a ten-foot runway. I take a deep breath before sprinting towards the structure, angling my approach so that I am nearly parallel to the wall before I jump. I take two steps on the side of the brick building between the two windows, moving myself laterally but also nearly six feet up the side of the building in the process. I hit the side sill of the window on the right with the ball of my left foot and then spring backwards towards the left window, pushing myself up at the same time. In parkour, which has become part of my exercise routine since I started school at Georgetown, the move is called a tic-tac. Pushing back the opposite direction, I hit the side sill of the left window with the ball of my right foot, then use the momentum I generate to spring back to the right window frame, executing another tic-tac that hits just below the top of the frame. One final spring off of my left foot lands me on the top sill of the left frame. I scramble with both feet to find purchase, then flatten my body and hands against the white siding of the house until my momentum diminishes. Finally, I raise my hands and jump three feet up, grabbing the ledge of the upper windowsill, and hoist myself up as quietly as possible. I slip a small can of lubricant from my pocket and squirt the track of the window frame to help the old window move without squealing. Then I raise it slowly. It moves without hesitation. I slide through the open window. It has taken me less than thirty seconds to break into Charles Vanderhook's office.

Inside the dark room, I stand stock-still, listening attentively. When I hear nothing, I slide the old pane window closed behind me, then lower the blinds and twist them shut. I pull a small headlamp from my jacket pocket and turn it onto the lowest setting as I move to the filing cabinet. It is locked. I briefly considered tipping the entire cabinet up to slip the locking rod by using a hole in the bottom of the metal casing, but the unit is four feet long and looks heavy. I don't know what kind of noise it might make if I lift it. Instead I carefully slide the improvised lock-pick set I've brought along from an inner pocket in my fleece. I've cut up a soda can and folded a section over several times to create a shim that I slide into the lock, almost immediately feeling the five pins that are preventing the lock from turning. Then I insert a flattened metal dental pick I've picked up for two dollars at Walgreens into the lock below the shim to create tension. With two rakes of the shim, the pins click into place and I am able to twist the lock open.

Breaking into a filing cabinet is never as difficult as making sense of what you find inside, and Vanderhook's private files are no different. There are tax files, a folder of ancient student loan documents, instructions for every appliance that the man has ever bought and the lease agreement for his Lincoln Navigator in the bottom lateral drawer. The top two drawers all contain real estate files. They seem to be deals that Vanderhook has closed himself, all of them more than half a decade old. None of the folders correspond to the addresses I've memorized. After a half hour, I decide I'm not going to have any luck with the files inside the cabinet and I move on. The credenza has more of the same old jumble, as do the filing drawers in the desk. I find an appointment book in the main sliding drawer of Vanderhook's desk, but it is untouched. I've almost given up hope when I noticed the conspicuous absence of dust on the lower right corner of the framed picture of what looks to be the first house Vanderhook ever sold, circa 1960. Sliding my fingers beneath the frame, I feel a latch. Pulling it allows the picture frame to swing out, revealing a wall safe.

The safe is a SecureLogic model with a biometric scanner, making it the newest piece of equipment in the entire office. The lock is keyed to the fingerprints of the owner, and placing a finger into the scanner will open it. Only Vanderhook can open the safe because fingerprints are unique.

That's the theory, anyway.

I take a careful look at the safe and the fingerprint scanner and then, flicking off my headlamp, leave the office. I descend the darkened staircase and make my way to the receptionist's desk, careful not to let my silhouette fall into the pool of light from a streetlamp shining through the front door of the office. I pull two pencils and a manual sharpener from a jar on Dolores' desk and remove the spool of tape from her tape dispenser. Then

I slide open her desk drawer and locate the last item I need – an emery board. Moving back to the staircase, I pull a clean sheet of paper from the copier at the bottom of the stairs. Then I return to the office, seat myself at Vanderhook's desk and begin methodically scrubbing graphite from the tip of each pencil, sharpening repeatedly to get rid of the wood. When I have a fine pile of graphite dust on the center of the clean piece of paper, I look around. Vanderhook has a Dell computer in the corner of his desk, a small concession to modernity. I carefully pick up the ends of the copier paper so the sheet forms a tunnel. Then I tap graphite dust over the left mouse button. When enough has accumulated, I blow lightly on the graphite. A fingerprint appears. Grabbing the cellophane tape, I carefully put a piece over the print and peel it off. The print transfers. It's not ideal, but it's clean enough for the scanner on the SecureLogic. I seal the print with another piece of tape. I walk the tape over to the biometric safe, activate the scanner and slip in my finger with the tape where my fingerprint would go. The lock slides open.

I take a step back when the beam of my Tikka headlamp hits the interior of the safe. It is divided horizontally into two compartments. The bottom area is stacked with cash; at least a hundred thousand dollars. A pile of documents teeters precariously in the top compartment. Vanderhook's personal records include his passport, savings account, house titles and birth certificate. Then I spot a black leather-bound notebook tucked in to the side of the stack, looking as if it's been used frequently.

It is a book of green-ruled accountant's paper. I sit down at Vanderhook's desk to examine it. Two thirds of the pages are full of inked entries. Each page has dates at the top and a set of addresses down the left side. I assume the entries are dollar figures. The numbers make me catch my breath. There are at least twenty properties on each page. The total monthly take for each property is many times more than any house in Conestoga could command in rent. This volume has two years of records. On the second-to-last used page of the book I find the address of the yellow colonial that stands next to Mel's apartment as well as two of the three addresses that Veronica has given me from the website. The last inscribed page is filled with addresses but has no payments recorded and it includes a line for another of the addresses Veronica showed me.

I consider my options for a moment and decide to risk making a copy of the book. I don't want Vanderhook to know that anyone has been in his office, but I need some proof of what I've seen. Using my fleece to block the light escaping from the Xerox machine, I photocopy the entire volume. Then I replace it carefully in the safe before re-locking it. I methodically clean up the traces of my visit, returning the emery board, tape and sharpener to Dolores' desk drawer. I lock Vanderhook's office from the inside and carefully wipe down everything I've touched. Then I scan the parking lot through a slit in the blinds, only opening the window after I see that Veronica is still in her car and still alone in the lot. She is idling her Mercedes nose outwards with the lights off. I step onto the windowsill and carefully close the window behind me. Then I turn and drop, catching the second story window frame before I drop the remaining eight feet.

We sit in my car, underneath the grasping branches of a hundred-year oak on Sycamore Street, some forty yards away from one of the Vanderhook houses. It's raining the fat cold drops of autumn and the air is heavy with moisture. I slowly work my way through the copied pages of the ledger book by penlight, committing them to memory. Veronica is reading them at the same time, leaning across the padded armrest covering the driveshaft of the GTO. Just as a forced smile releases real endorphins that can trigger authentic joy, our proximity as we lean together over the small document kindles a sense of intimacy. As we talk in muted tones, Veronica's hand brushes mine on the armrest. She doesn't withdraw it.

We've spent nearly five hours taking a tour of four of the addresses from the Vanderhook ledger. As we observe these dilapidated houses from a distance, a pattern soon emerges. All of the houses have Vanderhook "For Sale" signs up, but they're all occupied. Despite being past the hour of the evening when most Conestoga families have long since settled in, the Vanderhook properties seem busier than Chuck's Diner after church on Sunday. Cars arrive at regular intervals. The routine is identical at each property. A car pulls into the driveway, rolling to a stop a few feet short of the garage door. The car hovers there for a moment, then the garage door opens. The delay is longer than you'd expect for someone fumbling for a remote, and the garage doors glide open without the usual clatter. There is invariably a second car in the garage with a cover thrown over it. The pattern proceeds with military precision. Twenty minutes later, the garage door opens again; this time the other car leaves. Exactly twenty minutes after that, another car arrives to fill the open slot, and so on. We've only seen two departures from this pattern. On Van Buren Street at a rose-colored ranch house, a black Lincoln MKZ pulls up to the dark house late, having missed the expected interval by ten minutes. The garage door never opens and the car drives away after a moment. On the street we're observing, a shiny black Mercedes slides into the garage just after we start observing. It's a new S550, easily a hundred-grand car. In Conestoga, not even the meth dealers can afford a ride like that. We've been sitting for more than an hour, and the car hasn't emerged yet, nor has anyone else entered.

"This isn't just some unauthorized subletting to illegal immigrants," I murmur as I flip back through the copied pages of the Vanderhook ledger.

Veronica arches an eyebrow in an expressive way that says "no shit."

"Yeah, yeah – obviously," I mutter.

"Prostitution?"

"Probably," I reply and stop for a second, replaying our tour of the yellow colonial next to Mel's apartment in my head. "But more than that, I think. I think we're looking at a sex trafficking operation."

"You mean white slavery? That kind of thing?"

"It's the only reason you'd put deadbolts on the bedroom doors and bars on the windows. You're trying to keep someone in, not out. Gangs out of Eastern Europe run most of the sex trafficking trade. They lure girls in with advertising for good paying jobs like modeling, then addict them to drugs and force them into prostitution."

"Why go to all that trouble? Aren't there plenty of prostitutes in the U.S. already?"

"They make more money because they don't pay the girls. Plus they get a steady supply of new blood."

"It's disgusting," Veronica says acidly and I nod. "And this real estate agent is part of this?"

"It's actually a pretty clever scheme. I bet all of these houses are foreclosures. That means they're vacant and banks don't keep tabs on them as well as homeowners would. If the neighbors get suspicious, these people can just disappear and pop up in another house in another neighborhood the next day. That could be what happened with the house next to Mel."

"And you think the Sheriff's part of this?"

"It makes sense. If the neighbors notice something unusual, they'd call the police. All the Sheriff has to do is make sure the operation moves immediately and everyone stays happy."

"Unless someone gets a glimpse of what's really going on," Veronica says, catching the disturbing implication of this line of thinking.

"Right. If someone actually figured this out, they'd threaten the entire operation. That's a lot of cash. So there would be a big incentive to get rid of anyone who got too nosy."

"What could Mel have seen?"

"I don't know. But she speaks Russian, right? What if she somehow talked to one of the girls? Or just saw enough of what we saw to figure things out? If Russians or Ukrainians are running this ring, they don't fool around." As I say this, I remember a particular trip to Sevastpol, the transshipment point for many bad things on the Black Sea.

"So what do we do? Confront the Sheriff?"

"No, definitely not. I have a friend at the FBI. I think if I tell him what we saw and give him a copy of this ledger, it'll be enough for him to wind this up pretty quickly."

"What about Mel? How will we find out who killed her?"

I think about this for a moment. The hardest thing for me to know is my own feelings. What we've seen convinces me that the killer will be sent to jail with all of the other felons running this racket. Is that enough? Then I realize that we have another possible approach. "Buddy Peterson must have been tipped off by whoever killed Mel, or he wouldn't have beat EMS to her place. I bet he'd cut a deal to save himself and give up the murderer. We can talk to the FBI about that."

It doesn't feel satisfying to either of us. But I'm not planning to try to twist Buddy Peterson's arm to figure out what he knows. Those days are over.

I'm laying on a bed in my motel room in Conestoga when I hear the door to the bathroom squeak open. By the time we finished our surveillance it was nearly two a.m. and Veronica asked if she could crash in my motel room. I didn't know exactly how to interpret the request, but I said yes. My room comes equipped with two beds and I feel a combination of relief and disappointment when she drops a small overnight bag on the second bed, the one that my duffel is not sitting on. She offers me the bathroom first and I take it, cleaning up and changing into sweats. Then she disappears into the bathroom for a half-hour. As the door finally opens, I catch sight of her framed by the light of the forty-watt bulb that hangs naked over the sink mirror. She is wearing a blue college sweatshirt over gray sweatpants.

I put my book, a Civil War history by James McPherson, down as she slides under the covers of the twin bed next to mine. She starts talking randomly, which seems to be her habit when she's nervous. But after a few moments we both relax and the talk drifts off. I've just turned off the light when another idea comes into my head. It's not a good thought.

"Something has been bothering me about that yellow house, the one next to Mel's place," I say, flicking the light back on. Veronica lifts herself up on her elbows and squints at me. "This whole business could be something worse than we were thinking."

She looks at me with those green eyes. I don't think I've quite noticed the color before.

"White slavery rings usually control the girls with drugs and with money – piling big bills up on them and making them earn it back. But the window bars and deadbolts we saw in that yellow house don't exactly fit with that scenario. A twenty-year-old Czech or Romanian girl in a small town in upstate New York would already be pretty well isolated. She'd be here illegally and wouldn't speak the language. So I doubt they'd need the bars to control the girls, unless…unless possibly we're talking about under-age girls. Young girls. That would also make the numbers in the Vanderhook ledger make more sense. Given what he's making for just supplying the houses, these Russians are sitting on a goldmine. One that they would kill to protect."

When I look at her again, there are tears in Veronica's eyes. "And Mel, if she thought a child was being hurt…she would have done anything to stop it."

I nod and see that Veronica has suddenly gone pale. For a second I wonder if she's going to faint.

"Mike, there's something. I … I may know something more about this," she says.

She must see me stiffen, feel the coldness that flows through me suddenly, because she shakes her head emphatically. "It's not like that. But there was something – something that happened in Russia when Mel and I were there. I need to think about it. If I tell you and I'm wrong I could ruin someone's life. Let me sleep on it, okay?" I look at her closely. She's not lying, at least.

In a few minutes her eyes close and she's out cold from sheer exhaustion. I don't sleep much at all.

Chapter Five –

Tuesday

A confetti spray of waxy green bits of foliage erupts inches from my head as I tumble sideways over the four-foot hedge. It takes a second for my brain to catch up with my body and understand why instinct has hurtled me into somebody's front yard. As my hip clears the prickly shrubs by an inch and puffs of erupting dirt in the yard tell me that 9mm rounds have just missed me, I replay the last five seconds of my life. I was jogging, enjoying the pre-dawn chill in the air. It was quiet. I may be the last person in America who runs without an iPod, but the training gets ingrained: it's impossible to be aware of your environment when you're listening to hip-hop. The trigger that awoke my dormant survival reflex was the combination of three sounds: the V-8 engine of a last-generation Ford Crown Victoria slowing to a bare murmur as it pulled up ten yards behind me, followed by the slight whine of an electric window being lowered and the barest clink of metal tapping glass. Before my conscious mind could process these things, I was flying sideways over the hedge. As the ground rises to meet me, my body twists in the air like a cat so that I land flat on my stomach, facing the two-story Victorian whose yard I've violated.

As my head snaps up toward the house, I'm suddenly nose-to-nose with a 120-pound Rottweiler, dripping saliva from bared yellow fangs. I can see the rippling muscles in the big dog's hindquarters coiling to spring at me and I start to raise my forearm protectively when puffs of brittle, un-raked leaves erupt in a straight line heading towards me from my right side. As one lands neatly between the dogs paws, the Rott yips and springs to my right. I roll to the left. The string of bullets follows me. The rounds come from a silenced Heckler & Koch MP5, one of the deadliest little machine pistols around. The silenced gunfire sounds like an air rifle, louder and more metallic than the "pluff" noise-suppressed weapons invariably make in the movies. The last round of the burst almost stitches me, which is impressive marksmanship considering that I'm concealed by the hedge. I make a mental note that the shooter anticipated my move even though he couldn't see it. As I roll past the end of the house, the bullets abruptly stop flying and I get my feet under me and run at a crouch through the side yard to the back of the Victorian. I hear a door on the big Ford open and slam shut as just as I reach the back yard and duck behind the protective cover of the house.

I scan the yard and assess my options, knowing I have only seconds before I'm face to face with my assailant. The V-8 engine of the Crown Vic roars and I hear a loud squeal as the driver lays down some rubber. The footfalls on the sidewalk tell me that a single person has exited the vehicle. I hear him vault the hedge and sprint towards the rear of the house. I can make it over the six-foot slatted wooden fence separating the Victorian from the house behind it, but only just barely. There's a decent chance I'll give my pursuer a clean shot if I do. Even if I make it, the Crown Victoria will have time to get around the block to Birch Street before I can cross over, hemming me in between the car and my pursuer on foot. If I start threading my way from backyard to backyard on Birch, I'll be caught between the runner and the car and they'll flush me out just like dogs beating the bushes for a fox.

I see another option: it's riskier but it gives me two ways to get clear. I take three strides forward and launch myself onto the top of a sturdy-looking doghouse. It's the route I would take to vault the fence, but instead I turn to the right. With two light steps on the roof of the doghouse, I jump to the top bar of a child's swing set, which sits at a ninety-degree angle to both the doghouse and the Victorian. I pivot again and take three long strides along the top bar of the swing set like a high wire artist, then jump, hitting the lower roof of the Victorian over the garage with my hands, and haul myself quickly up. I barely have time to spin around and flatten myself on the roof before my pursuer comes around the corner of the house. It may be a fool's move, but most things we chase keep fleeing until they escape or are caught. The hunter's instinct is always to assume the prey is moving away from him unless it is directly in his sights. I'm wearing a waterproof nylon shell over an insulated base layer, which are both as black as my coal-dark hair, so I have a chance of blending into the asphalt tiles of the roof.

The man stops and I get a look at him. He's about my height – six feet plus or minus an inch – and slender. I can see a fringe of fine brown hair peeking from beneath a knit black seaman's cap. He's sporting a navy pea coat and black boots with a Vibram lug sole under dark, wide wale corduroy trousers. He's carrying a Fabrique National p90, a vicious little bullpup-style machine pistol that holds 50 rounds in the magazine and can penetrate level II body armor. It has a GemTech silencer, making it a military-spec weapon. This is not the gun that sent me over the hedge, which tells me I'm being hunted by at least three men – the driver of the Crown Vic, the original shooter and this man. He scans the yard, looking speculatively at the tall wooden fence to the rear and as he turns his head I catch a glimpse of a tattoo on his neck. The sinuous bodies of two intertwined snakes creep us his nape. The tat is inked in black and shades of gray but comes alive as the tendons in the man's neck make the snakes ripple. I've seen tattoos like it before, and it's not good news.

The man peers narrowly at the lawn, trying to read my movements. My footprints are there, leading towards the doghouse and then disappearing. I can read his thoughts – did I vault the fence from the doghouse or do something unexpected? It's what I'd be weighing in the same spot. After a moment of consideration, he scans the yard, pivoting slowly towards the Victorian. In a second his gaze is going to reach the roof and he's going to spot me.

I swear inwardly and tense myself, getting ready to jump, knowing full well that I'm dead if he sees me before I move. I'm probably dead either way. It's okay. It serves me right for sticking my nose where it never should have been, for shedding the hard-won anonymity I've protected so greedily. And anyway, these fatalistic thoughts comfort me just like the warm embrace of an old lover – one I haven't known for the three and a half years since I left The Activity.

In the instant before the man spots me, I hear a bark and a vicious growl as the Rottweiler explodes from the narrow alleyway on the other side of the house. The man raises the P90 casually and I hear the stutter of the silenced bullets tearing into the dog. As the Rottweiler flies through the air, the man steps aside like a matador, and the dog hurls past him, landing dead on the sodden soil with a heavy thud. Without a second glance at the animal, the man pulls a small Motorola walkie-talkie from his pocket and speaks urgently into it. I strain to pick out the words. He's talking too quickly and faintly to understand, but the language is unmistakably Russian. After his walkie-talkie squawks in reply, he stows the unit back in his jacket and takes off at a canter, vaulting the back fence to the yard without breaking stride.

As soon as he's gone, I turn around and creep up the roof, peering over the crest into the front yard. As I expect, the Crown Victoria is long gone. I leap down off the roof and sprint across the front yard, hurdling the hedge back onto Ridge Road. I glance briefly downhill, but dismiss the idea. I won't make it back to town before the Russians catch up with me. There aren't many roads up here on the side of the hill and I don't want any more bullets flying around in a residential area, anyway. I decide to continue up the hill on my original route. As I run, skirting fences while I listen carefully for the big Ford, I visualize the Russian who shot the Rottweiler. Those tattoos are gang symbols for the Russian mafia. I haven't seen the exact pattern, but the style is distinctive. The snakes look like a more menacing version of the medical symbol called the Caduceus.

There's another thought running through my mind as I ascend the ridge. The men who are trying to kill me are no run-of-the-mill gangsters. The Russian with the p90 handled the Rottweiler too smoothly for a street thug. And the gunman firing from the car was far too accurate to be a petty crook. These guys have serious military training, special operations kind of training. If I let them keep the initiative, they'll put me down just like that dog. I increase my pace as the hill plateaus.

The gate to the Godfrey Mill is still locked as I reach it. I don't pause to fuss with the lock but instead use it as a foothold to vault the eight-foot fence. A hundred yards of open ground crisscrossed with train tracks separate the fence from the administration building for the mill. The four-story building is flanked to the right by an enormous warehouse and to the left by a structure built on four platform levels that looks like leftover parts from an outsized Erector set. Pipelines and oddly shaped supports shoot through the four platform levels, which are rigged with scaffolding. Conveyors and chutes link the platforms to the three cylindrical towers looming behind them. The towers can be seen from almost anywhere in Conestoga, a constant reminder of the town's dismal past. Railroad cars idle in the yard like forgotten toys in a teenager's closet. There are piled along the multiple tracks leading to a second warehouse at the extreme left of the complex. I pass within a few yards of one of the rusted hulks as I move through the yard toward the administration building.

The railway no longer functions. It's a dead spur on a defunct line. The railway gates to the mill are long since rusted shut and the tracks outside the property have grown over in prickly-edged grass and weeds. The mill itself doesn't support any growing thing. A toxic mixture of calcium silicates, calcium sulfate, gypsum, clay, shale, sand, iron ore, bauxite and slag keeps all but the most tenacious weeds at bay. The grounds of the mill are strewn with clinker, the primary raw material of Portland Cement. It looks like large, irregular gravel. It requires intense concentration to navigate the yard at high speed.

As I move, I replay my visit to the mill on Saturday, when I used the abandoned structure for a parkour workout. The schematic comes to life in my mind as I visualize the jump distances, the various protrusions and structural weaknesses. A plan begins to form in my head. This complex is big enough that I can lose the Russians right now, but that's not what I want. If I let them go without learning more they'll still have the initiative. Veronica woke just as I was leaving the motel room for my run. I still don't know what she knows, or how she's connected to these Russians. I've spent some time pondering the improbability of my Russian-speaking high school girlfriend randomly living next to a houseful of Russian thugs and prostitutes in Conestoga. I don't for one second believe Mel would have been part of anything sordid, but it's just too much of a coincidence. I need to talk to Veronica, but first I need to know more about these Russians who look like gangsters and act like soldiers. I need to identify at least one of them. I've left tracks in the dust on the road up to the mill, so I know they'll find me soon enough.

A sturdy steel door built to withstand the hammering fists of union protestors bars entry to the administration building, but I know from my last visit that it is unlocked. On the inside, I push the door shut and slide a rusty deadbolt home. It's not secure, but I'm counting on it to slow the Russians down for a few seconds. A thin fracture runs through the smooth cement floor of the large, open room. Only one desk, a Steelcase relic from the 1950s, remains in what was once the payroll area. An enormous, ancient IBM Selectric typewriter sits on the desk, patiently waiting for a typist. There are stacks of dusty office supplies and half-packed boxes, as if the job of closing down the mill was abandoned in midstream.

I take a quick look out the window to confirm that the Russians haven't found the mill yet, and then search the desk and the assorted boxes. I find a dozen staplers and a full set of desk accessories reproduced in cement. A two-level cement in-box with louvered sides sits delicately next to a blotter of thin cement. The cement blotter has a paper pad festooned with coffee rings still resting on it alongside a cement pencil cup and a cement letter opener that can't have seen much use. The cement ashtray is a gem – it is so heavy that it is impossible to imagine anyone tipping it into a wastebasket. That gives me an idea. A plan takes shape in my mind. I rifle through the boxes and find a big ball of sturdy twine.

By the time the Russians pull up in the Crown Victoria, I'm on the third deck of the platform structure next to the administration building, concealed behind a metal conveyor and pressing myself flat against the cold concrete. I've survived the fifteen-foot leap from a window on the side of the top floor of the administration building without losing the end of the twine, which is now completely unrolled. I made a similar jump on my last trip to the Mill. That time was easier, though, because it didn't involve diving through a window at flank speed with a loop of twine tied to my belt. Fortunately, the mill platform is six feet below the window I exited and has a loading dock for a crane on the third deck that left me a comfortable space to roll and absorb the impact of the fall.

As the Crown Victoria pulls up to the mill gate I feel the lack of a good pair of binoculars. At a distance, I can still pick out some details. The driver is skinny and exits the vehicle awkwardly – I can tell from his movements that he's not in the same league with the Russian who killed the Rottweiler. That man exits the rear passenger side seat and checks his weapon professionally. A barrel-chested, blond-headed Russian in a warm-up suit gets out from behind the driver. He's carrying an MP5 with his index finger extended, laying flat across the trigger guard and in spite of his size, he moves like a big cat. Another professional – he's probably the one in charge. The fourth man looks like a turnip in a hotdog bun. He's fat, awkward and his white down jacket looks like it's been picked off the discount rack of a ski shop in July. Like the skinny driver, this man carries an AK-47 and doesn't look like he knows one end from the other. So there are two professionals with two amateurs: better odds than I expected.

As I watch, the dog-killer examines the lock on the front gate and, stepping to one side, puts a bullet from the P90 through it, then pulls it open and tosses it away. He unravels the chain and swings the gate open. The four men advance into the mill yard, the skinny Russian obviously having trouble with the clinker. As they draw to within a dozen feet of the administration building, they're finally within earshot. I keep myself dead still. The human eye is not particularly a fine instrument compared to those of most predators, but we're good at spotting movement, even more so as we age. That blond Russian looks to be in his forties and I'd bet a paycheck that he'd spot a flea buzzing at a hundred yards.

"Don't let him slip out, Misha," the blond leader says to Dog-killer in Russian. Misha nods and drops back twenty yards, already scanning the perimeter. It's a smart move. The P90 is not very accurate at a distance, but the blond man has clearly put his best man where he can try to keep me from escaping.

The leader now turns to the fat man, pulling roughly on the lapels of his wool coat. "Get behind that mill on the other side and radio me if you see anything. Don't just watch the fucking building in front of you; remember to look left and right. Call me if you see anything move, even a fucking jackrabbit, right?" I can't place the accent, although he's certainly not a Muscovite. The fat man nods dumbly. "If that fucker gets by you, I'll eat your lard ass on a sandwich," the blond man says, tapping the fat Russian between the eyes with his index finger for emphasis. "Is your fucking radio on?" the leader rasps, exasperated as the thick man pulls a Motorola walkie-talkie from a pocket and fumbles with the dials. The blond man grabs it from him, quickly finding the right knob and twisting it. The Motorola gives a chirp and its red display lights up. Then I see the blond man flashing the channel by hand sign to Misha who adjusts his radio quickly and without taking his eyes off the complex. *Spetznaz, that's who you guys are*, I think, although it's not saying much. The word translates to something like "commando" and there are different Spetnaz units attached to all of the services in the armed forces as well as to the secret police in Russia.

"And take your goddamn finger off the trigger unless you're going to fire – I don't want to be pulling lead out of my ass today." The fat man hustles around the building, looking furtively up at the looming structures to his left and right, nearly making eye contact with me in the process. Misha moves slowly backwards, trying to get the entire site into his field of vision. The leader turns to the skinny Russian in the wool coat. "You're with me," he growls.

"Yes, Yuri," the man replies. *Yuri, that's your name.* Yuri and the rail-thin Russian start walking towards the schoolhouse-like administration building.

The four-story building has a porch of sorts, really just three concrete stairs leading to a small landing in front of the main door to the building, which I've bolted shut. I see Yuri consider it for a moment. The skinny Russian moves onto the platform, just to Yuri's right, crowding him a little. Perfect. I pull the twine in my hand, a little at first to get it taut and then a swift yank, hoping it doesn't break before the job is done. There's the slight sound of a clatter on the fourth floor of the administration building as a chair pitches forward. Yuri hears it and vaults off the stoop, over the railing and down to the ground. The skinny man doesn't move, he just stares at Yuri with a puzzled expression right up to the moment when that old IBM Selectric typewriter lands on his head. I know from the sound it makes that it's killed the unfortunate man, even though I'm already on the move and can't see it. I hear the stutter of the P90 as Misha empties a full clip through the window from which the typewriter dropped. Fortunately, I'm not there anymore.

Moving silently through the old mill complex is about as difficult as anything I've attempted. Steel rivets that were secure a dozen years ago have corroded, clinker is everywhere and the main yard is wide open except for the protective cover of half a dozen derelict freight cars. I manage to get off the platform building during the moment of distraction after the typewriter hits the skinny Russian. Then I loop around the warehouse at the extreme left of the complex, keeping a close eye on the fat man with the AK-47. He's standing in between the administration building and the three furnace towers and he already looks bored. He hasn't even heard the typewriter drop or the suppressed gunfire from Misha's P90. His walkie-talkie crackles as I'm just about to round the corner of the warehouse building. He doesn't so much as cast a glance my way.

Once I've made it around the warehouse, I use the abandoned boxcars to screen my movement as I work my way around Misha. He is still watching the entire complex from the front. I could possibly slip by him and out the front gate, but I respect his skill with that P90 too much to try. Yuri is not in sight and I assume he's still working his way upward through the administration building. That means I have precious little time until he discovers my little ruse and warns his comrades. As I slip around the last boxcar, I am twenty feet behind Misha. I move carefully, deliberately and silently and thank god this is a skill I haven't yet lost. When I'm three feet behind him, Misha senses me and whips around, but it's too late. I've disabled his gun hand and have him face-forward on the ground before he can make his move. Then my little folding Spyderco knife slips between the vertebras in his neck, severing his spinal cord. Death comes silently and quickly. I turn him over and check his pockets. I slip his wallet into my pocket and take the little Motorola radio. In his coat, I find a replacement magazine for the P90. I hesitate for a moment and then close the man's eyes before I hurry away to the front gate. I've just hot-wired the Crown Victoria when I hear Yuri's voice squawk through the Motorola. "It's a trick!" he yells in Russian, "He's not in this building, watch out for him!" Then I hit the throttle, sending the Crown Victoria into reverse as fast as it will go. After a hundred yards I hit the brake as I pull the wheel around and the car pirouettes smoothly on its axis. In a few seconds, I'm driving away from the mill, back toward town.

Light leaks from the door to Room 103 of the Motor Mountain Lodge, piercing the gloom of the early morning in Conestoga. It is a cold morning, more like the first day of winter than an average day in the middle of the autumn. The door is slightly ajar. It is the room Veronica and I shared last night, and I've approached it obliquely. The Crown Victoria is two blocks away. I tried calling Veronica on her cell from the car as I sped towards the motel, but she didn't pick up. She could be in the shower, but I don't have that kind of luck. Before I left the Crown Victoria, I took a closer look at the items I pulled off of Misha at the Godfrey Mill. The Russian's wallet held just a single credit card, two hundred dollars in cash and a driver's license in the name of Michail Grigor Alekseev. The license looked authentic, although I can't say I can tell a real NY driver's license from a good quality forgery at a glance. Sitting in the front seat of the Ford, I grasped the P90 and pushing back on the magazine catch at the top of the weapon, lifted the magazine upward. The clear polycarbonate magazine holds 50 rounds of 5.7x28mm ammunition, double-stacked at a ninety-degree angle to the main system receiver. I lifted the magazine out, then pulled the cocking handle back and released it, which ejected a single chambered round downward from the pistol grip of the weapon.

Only then did I unscrew the silencer. Putting it down next to the magazine, I depressed the receiver lock and pulled the barrel support assembly forward out of the stock. I pushed the breech through the magazine opening and pulled the butt plate of the weapon upward and off. Finally, I raised the locking latch on the hammer group and pulled backward on the rear wall, withdrawing it. Field stripping the P90 took me less than 20 seconds, and after examining each part for dirt or corrosion; it took me half that time to reassemble it. The weapon was immaculate, as I had expected it would be. Unfortunately, the spare magazine was empty.

I left the P90 in the Crown Victoria and advanced toward the motel from the side. As I reached the structure, I peered down the cement walkway fronting a row of six identical units. The only light I observed came from my room, whose door was slightly ajar.

Now I crouch down and slowly move past the units, keeping my head below the level of the picture windows fronting the parking lot. It is still early, just after 6am, and there is no activity from the rooms or the road. My black GTO is parked two doors down from my room. Force of habit kept me from pulling it right up to the door last night, though Veronica gave me an odd look. I'm thankful for that now.

I slide around the GTO and open the trunk slowly. The trunk light does not illuminate; I've long ago disabled it. With the lid halfway up, I snake my left hand along the front edge of the carpeted cargo floor, finding the seam in the floor panel concealing the spare tire. I lift the panel up, exposing the top of the spare, which has a huge gash in it. I lean in and reach behind the tire, releasing a hidden latch. The visible two inches of tire swing upward – the defective spare is a decoy. A false bottom epoxied to a metal liner creates a hidden compartment in the trunk. There is a square black metal case about the size of a thick briefcase in the compartment. Dialing a combination on the locking plate on the front, I pop the lock and flip the case open. It has molded openings for a pistol, magazines, a silencer and set of Gen IV military night vision goggles. I gently lift the pistol out. It is a .45 ACP Kimber Custom ICQB, a modern update of the century-old Colt 1911. The 1911 Colt is a favorite in the U.S. special operations community because of its reliability and stopping power, which is far superior to 9mm weapons. I've owned this gun for nearly a decade and I fire it weekly, although I haven't hit anything more sinister than a silhouette target in almost four years. I screw on the silencer and insert a magazine, pulling the slide gently back to chamber a round. I close the case and the trunk, keeping the pistol low and against my body.

I check to my left and right as I approach the door to my motel room. There are a couple of lights on, but all of the curtains are closed in the adjacent rooms. I raise the Kimber in front of me in a two-handed hold. I push the door open with my toe and wait a moment before crouching and peering cautiously into the room over the barrel of the Kimber. A thin man with a pockmarked face, wearing a tailored gray flannel suit with a Glock automatic in his right hand resting casually on his knees is sitting in an armchair he's pulled around to face the door. A burly goon in a tight-fitting blue muscle shirt stands behind the man, holding a revolver – a Smith & Wesson .375 Magnum. The big revolver is pointed at me. Unfortunately, this is more or less what I'm expecting.

"Come in, Mr. Herne," the pockmarked man says. His accent places him from St. Petersburg. At least I feel like I'm getting somewhere. I step inside the door, keeping my gun trained on the man. The suited man is calm as he continues to rest the Glock casually on his lap and leans back in the cheap faux-leather chair. "We have your girlfriend, Mr. Herne," he warns, glancing pointedly at my weapon. The burly thug makes a move towards me and I swing the Kimber towards him. Things get tense. Then the pockmarked Russian raises a hand and the larger man freezes.

"You can speak to her if you wish," the seated man intones, slowly reaching into an outer pocket in his suit jacket and pulling out a clamshell cell phone, which he flips open with his left hand. He presses the redial button and brings the phone to his ear. "Put the girl on," he says in Russian after a few seconds. Then he activates his speakerphone and turns the phone toward me. The line crackles.

"Mike, I'm so sorry," Veronica sobs.

"Are you okay?" I ask. My voice betrays no emotion.

"Yes, I'm in…" Veronica begins. The pockmarked man flips the phone shut before she can say more.

"You have already caused us a great deal of inconvenience, Mr. Herne," the man continues. I meet his dark blue eyes briefly, then focus on the Smith & Wesson in the larger Russian's hands. I'm watching the goon's knuckles, looking for any sign of whitening that signals increased pressure on the trigger. In double action mode, the Smith & Wesson has a hefty trigger pull, and the hammer is not cocked. I keep my Kimber trained on the larger man even as I listen to the pockmarked Russian.

"We now know that you work for the U.S. government, Mr. Herne. We have no desire to draw any more attention to our activities. I apologize for the unfortunate incident this morning. My colleagues exceeded their orders," the pockmarked man shrugs wordlessly as if to say *you know how these types are.* He's lying, of course. I listen to the man's voice closely, imprinting the pattern of his speech in my memory.

"I assure you that if you surrender your weapon and come with us now, you will not be harmed. We will lock you and Ms. Ryan in a safe place for a few hours until we can disappear completely." More lies. He motions to the bed with a bony finger, showing me where to drop the Kimber.

I look at him for a second. It is hard to believe that this guy works for the same group that hired two stone-cold professionals like Michail Alekseev and Yuri. I can't say that I wasn't expecting some kind of ultimatum, but I'm still surprised by this clumsy bluff.

The man clears his throat impatiently. "On the other hand, if you don't put your weapon down immediately and come with us, I regret to say that we'll be forced to kill Ms. Ryan." The Russian smiles like a chess master who has just announced checkmate in five moves.

"I doubt that," I reply as I squeeze the trigger of the Kimber twice, double-tapping the burly Russian through the forehead with powerful .45ACP rounds before the big man can react. The pockmarked man's eyes widen in surprise and his smile turns to a frown as he struggles to raise the automatic he has been handling so casually. He's too slow. I put a round through his throat and another through his forehead before he can reach the blue steel trigger of the Glock.

I pull the motel door shut behind me and close the curtains completely before evaluating the scene. I see that the big Russian has the same snake tattoos as Yuri and Alekseev, but the pockmarked man has none. I consider taking the Glock and the Smith & Wesson, but I don't need them. Besides, this is my motel room. When the day of reckoning comes, the weapons will at least give me a shot at claiming self-defense. Or would if the police weren't in on the game, I realize, frowning. I pat down the pockmarked Russian. The breast pocket of his suit jacket holds a slim card case containing a black card made of a light metal – possibly titanium – with the American Express Centurion symbol on it. He has a New York State driver's license in the name of Victor Sherbatsky. A money clip in his pocket has a folded stack of hundred dollar bills, over two grand in all. I take the cash and leave the credit card and license after memorizing the numbers. Then I flip open my cell phone and call Sammie on his cell. He answers groggily after three rings.

"Jesus, God, what time is it?"

"Six-thirty. Sorry to wake you." I wait for a second to let Sammie get his bearings before I continue. "I need to find the physical location of a phone. It may be a cell phone and if so it won't be active for very long."

"I can do that from here," Sammie says after a moment. "Give me the number." I flip open Victor's phone and navigate the menu to find the last number dialed, then read it out to him.

"Anything else?"

"Not as urgent, but I need information on two New York residents, Michail Grigor Alekseev and Victor Sherbatsky," I wait as Sammie copies down the names and then give him the two driver's license numbers and the credit card information.

"What kind of guys are we talking about? I'm asking because it will help me know where to look," Sammie asks.

"Russian mafia, I think. Alekseev probably has a military record, as well."

Sammie whistles. "What kind of trouble are you getting yourself into, Orion? No – strike that – I really don't want to know."

"How long will the phone number take you?" I ask.

"Give me about ten minutes. Less if it's a landline." Sammie replies. I consider this for a moment.

"I'll call you back. Don't call my cell," I say and hang up.

I quickly change, then gather my possessions and Veronica's and leave the room, locking it from the outside. I hang the "do not disturb" sign on the doorknob. I put the Kimber back into the metal case and take it out of the trunk before depositing my duffel and Veronica's overnight bag. Then I stop in the motel office and pay for three more nights with Victor's cash. I pull the GTO out of the parking lot and drive around to a side street, parallel-parking it behind an old Chevy Trailblazer. As I am walking back to the Crown Victoria, I pass a pickup truck with a sign for "Roberts' Landscaping" on the side. It is loaded with supplies. I pull my cell phone out, silence the ringer and casually drop it into the back of the truck between two bags of mulch, without breaking stride.

As I reach the Blue Crown Victoria, Victor's phone rings. "Victor, where are you? Do you have Herne?" a voice asks in Russian.

"He's dead, I'm heading back," I respond in Russian, trying to mimic Victor's accent as closely as I can. I snap the clamshell phone shut before the man on the other end can ask any more questions and pull out the battery, dropping both pieces of the phone in front of the rear wheel of the Crown Vic. I pull onto Lark's Lane and thread my way to Route 9W. I drive south for a half-hour before pulling into the parking lot of the Wal-Mart in Kingston. It's one of their 24-hour supercenters and I'm just as happy to be here when the crowd is light.

I walk into the enormous store, thinking about Veronica and wondering if she will be alive when I reach her – if I reach her. I know that I made the only rational play. Giving myself up to Victor would have gotten us both killed. That was the plan; if I hadn't already guessed it I would have confirmed it when Victor lied to me. With Victor dead, the Russians will probably keep Veronica alive at least until they figure out what's going on. They won't kill her as long as they think she might still serve as a bargaining chip or a human shield. Unless they figure out who I really am, that is.

Now the pages from Vanderhook's ledger won't be enough to break the ring. By the time the FBI can make it to Conestoga, every last trace of the Russians' activities in the houses we've identified will be obliterated. But if the Russians are stockpiling girls they'll be putting them in the same place they've got Veronica, so finding her is my number one priority. I pull out the wad of cash I took from Yuri's pocket and count it again, being careful to turn away from the surveillance camera covering my aisle as I do. Even after paying for the motel room I have $2200 in hundreds. I stuff it back into my Blackhawk shell. Time to go shopping.

I call Sammie from the parking lot next to the far end of the platform at the Rhinecliff train station, just across the Hudson River from Kingston. The lot is nearly full as those unfortunate souls enduring the 100-minute daily commute to New York City on the Amtrak train have mostly departed for the morning. I scan the platform, finding it empty except for a stray couple standing at the far end and arguing as they wait for a train. I hold the burner – a pre-paid cellular phone – between my shoulder and my ear as I rummage through one of the Wal-Mart bags and pull out a Black & Decker power screwdriver and a package of four AA batteries. After struggling to open the hard plastic packaging without lacerating myself, I insert the four batteries into the handle of the screwdriver and select the smallest Philips head.

I step out of the Ford and amble around to the front of the car, glancing right and left for traffic. Then I casually stretch and bend down as if to tie my shoelace. Instead I screw off the front plate of the Chevy Malibu parked next to the Crown Vic and swap it with the same plate on the front of the Ford. Then I walk over to the Chrysler LeBaron parked on the other side of the Crown Victoria and swap its front plate for my rear plate. Sammie answers his work phone as I'm changing the second plate. He gives me map coordinates and an address on the far northern fringe of Conestoga, and asks me to call him back in an hour for information on the Russians. I pull out a topographic Catskills map that covers most of Conestoga and mark it up, then key the coordinates in to a shiny new handheld GPS.

I sit in the car and after considering the still-early hour for a moment, call Dan Menetti at the FBI. I know a few different people at the FBI, although I don't work with them as closely as the folks at Homeland Security or ATF at Treasury. Those two agencies are more keenly attuned to the risks of arms entering the United States illegally and I sometimes see the foreign side of those transactions in my role at State. The FBI is a tricky organization to do business with, both because it's intensely political and its technology is ridiculously outdated. FBI Field agents only started using e-mail a few years ago – a good decade and a half after the rest of the world. Still, for the problem I'm facing right now, these are the right people. Menetti is a Section Chief at the FBI and I know he served a stint at the Human Smuggling Trafficking Center, which is jointly run with Homeland Security and the State Department.

"Menetti," he answers his own phone crisply.

"Dan, this is Michael Herne from INR," I say.

"Michael, how are you? Vicky and I have been meaning to invite you over for dinner. She's got a co-worker she wants you to meet."

I grimace. "I'd be happy to. Listen, I need to run a hypothetical by you. Can you do that?"

"Sure," Menetti says and he's all business. I have his full attention.

"Let's say that I've managed to trip across a human smuggling ring run by a group of Russian gang members. Let's say I have some good intel on their activities: dollars, addresses, that kind of thing. But they figured I was onto them and kidnapped a friend of mine. Let's say they're holding her hostage in the same place as their human smuggling victims. And let's say the local authorities are very chummy with the Russians and not so friendly to me."

"Jesus," Menetti says. I sense excitement at the fringes of his shock and concern. He can see both the danger and the opportunity.

"Exactly," I agree. "So the question is, if I could hypothetically get you an address where my friend is being held, could you crash the party?"

"Can you give us anything definitive that would prove there's a hostage? Or clear evidence of a human smuggling operation?"

"Not directly. I can give you secondary locations where you could gather enough forensic evidence and paperwork to make your case, but it will probably be too late for my friend by then."

"That's difficult. I doubt we would get a warrant without something a little more solid." I nod to myself. This is what I've been thinking.

"Hypothetically, what if I were to call you from inside the facility after I get hold of my friend?"

"If you see direct evidence of a crime, that would be enough. I can register you as a CI and get a warrant based on that, but I can't cover your back on what goes down before we get there." And there's the dilemma, neatly stated. I can go in and try to pull Veronica out, but if I report it to the FBI, I'll end up behind bars if I've done something illegal in the process, which is unavoidable. If I don't report it, the FBI can't roll up the white slavery operation.

"How long would it take for you to get boots on the ground?"

"Where?"

"An hour south of Albany, New York." There is a long pause. I imagine him calculating flight times for the Hostage Rescue Team out of Virginia.

"Two and a half hours, if you're willing to stake both of our careers on it."

"I'll let you know."

"Listen, I know something about your background, so I'm not going to tell you not to do this. Hypothetically speaking, anyway. But be careful. I'd hate to lose my best contact at State."

There should be a choice, a decision to make, but there really isn't. This is the path I've been heading down since I heard the 9-1-1 recording, since I looked into Buddy Peterson's eyes and saw that he was lying to me. I'm not going to get any help from a corrupt sheriff, and the best-case scenario with the FBI will probably land me in federal prison. If there are more men like Yuri and Misha holding Veronica, I'll more than likely be dead before this day ends, anyway. So I might as well do things my way.

My way isn't very subtle.

An hour after leaving Rhinebeck, I pull into the parking lot behind Stokeley's in Conestoga. The business is housed in what looks like an old red barn. It has a green roof and awnings that make it look like an old-fashioned general store. It's the only sporting good store in Conestoga, and the largest in the region. The same man has run it for over twenty years, and he's survived both the mill closing and the arrival of Wal-Mart in the area. The shop won't open for an hour yet but I knock on the back door after spotting an ancient Ford Bronco in the small lot behind the building. An eye peeks from behind the drawn shade and after a second I hear the clicking as deadbolt locks open. Donald Miller, a shambling, enormous man in his late fifties with a grizzled beard and a mop of gray hear, steps out and pulls me into a fierce bear hug.

"Damn, son, if you ain't a sight for tired old eyes! Why'd you wait so long to come back and visit?" Miller asks. He was a close friend of my father. He doesn't wait for me to answer. "I saw that buck you took on Sunday. Your brother-in-law said you made the kill from 700 yards, is that true?"

I shrug, "Lucky shot."

"Hogwash, boy. You always could shoot the dick off a bullfrog. That's what a real Conestoga boy does. Not like the little shits running around here these days," Miller shakes his head.

We talk for a few minutes and I answer more questions about my life than I want to. When I sense Miller is waiting for me to state my business, I lock eyes with him and slowly and clearly say, "Don, I need to buy some things from you. Including some items from your back room. Now."

Miller stares at me blankly for a second, then asks, "Boy are you in some kind of trouble?" I nod. "Not trouble I looked for, but trouble I found. I'll end it, I promise you."

Miller takes a moment to ponder this. "You've been gone from this town for a long time, son. Conestoga isn't the place you remember. People will do just about anything to survive. Those of us who hung on here, we've let this town…we've let it become something our parents would be ashamed of. All of us. Son, you might just want to get into that car and start driving. Nobody in this town is fit to lick your boots."

I shake my head sadly. There's nothing I want more. "I can't do that. Some people – people who aren't from around here – have taken a friend of mine. They're going to hurt her. I can't walk away."

"Well, why don't you call Buddy…" Miller's voice trails off as he starts to suggest calling the sherriff.

"I think you know he's involved, don't you Don?" I say evenly, with a flash of insight. The big man swallows.

"I think I do. Son, I can't help you. These people you're talking about, they just about own me. They own the mortgage to my shop, they own my inventory and they're almost half of my business these days. So I have to say no. Just no. As a matter of fact, I can't even talk to you about this any more. I could get into a pot of hot water just for doing that. Right now, I think I need to walk over to the Cumberland Farms and get myself a nice cup of black coffee and a bear claw. That could take a good forty minutes. When I come back I don't expect that I'll see you here. Tonight after I close the shop I'm going to do a store inventory. If anything's missing I'm going to call Buddy Peterson tomorrow and tell him that some things went missing since the last check. I'm sorry, son, but I've got to be goin' now." With a look of infinite sadness, the big man turns away and ambles around the side of the building. He leaves the back door to the store ajar.

I stand outside the building for a moment, slightly dazed at the enormity of the risk Don Miller is taking for me. Then I wipe my hands on my jacket and enter the shop. Stokeley's is organized into sections for hunting, camping and fishing, but there is also a small tactical section. I pull a TAG tactical vest off of a rack, checking it for size. It is a plain black vest with seven horizontal rings of nylon webbing running around it, designed to fit over body armor. The nylon straps are anchored every few inches, forming a matrix off of which different accessories can be attached – a so-called "molle" system. I grab a pair of Nomex Blackhawk gloves with hardened knuckles. Finally, I carefully select a SOG Seal Pup knife from a display case and confirm that its sheath will mount on the molle system of the vest. Then I grab two large load-out bags, framed duffels with multiple sections, and begin to fill them with more gear. I'm aware of the size of the bill I must be running up, but I rationalize that after today Don Miller is either going to have a big insurance claim or no co-owners. I pull the remainder of the cash I took off the dead Russian from my pocket and leave it next to the register.

When I've assembled the kit I need from the tactical room, I step behind the counter and put my hand under the cash register. I slide it along the underside of the counter until I find a button. It's not a silent alarm but the release for the hidden door to the back room. I have never been inside, but I saw my father disappear into the room with Miller on more than one occasion as a child.

The room is bigger inside than I anticipate and I catch my breath as I enter. There are rows of newly legal assault weapons in vertical gun racks as well as items restricted for police use. I grab a black Kevlar helmet with a mounting rail for fourth-gen night vision goggles and try it on. Then I pull a level II body armor vest off of a hanging rack. It is sturdy enough to stop the bullets from most handguns but still lightweight and flexible. It has pouches for ceramic plates, but I have no intention of wearing them. Mobility is more important. The store's cache of ammunition is stored in this room and I collect rounds for my Kimber and the P90. Finally, I take a peek inside the stout cast-iron gun safe, which is cracked open at the end of the room. My eyebrows rise involuntarily as I see what's inside. *Dear Lord*, I think, *Christmas comes early.*

I finally break down and call Dan Menetti at the FBI right at 5pm. All day I've been watching the warehouse at the address Sammie gave me from the roof of a vacant commercial building a half-block away. Sammie called me just before noon to let me know that the signal had vanished, but by then

I was already pretty sure I had the right building. I didn't see Veronica, but there was a steady influx of white panel vans pulling up to the three loading bays in the rear parking lot of the building. After switching vantage points twice, I finally got a look behind one of the vans while they were unloading. The cargo is human. They are very young girls, most of them looking under ten years old. My stomach churns when I see them. Not much gets me angry anymore, but this does. Unfortunately the compact autofocus camera I picked up at Wal-Mart doesn't have the optical zoom I'd need for the kind of picture that would convince the FBI to raid the building. I know I can't make any kind of move on the building before dark, so I spend the day preparing, all the while hoping they'll try to move Veronica. The cold, practical side of me wishes I had insisted she tell me what she knows about the gangsters, what she alluded to last night. But if she had, I couldn't pretend now that I need to rescue her for unsentimental reasons. On the other hand, if Veronica is involved somehow, these Russians could still be playing me for a fool. I spit a bad taste out of my mouth with dust from the roof. It doesn't matter. Once I saw little girls being treated like cattle, I was never going to walk away. It ends today, one way or another.

When Sammie called he also gave me information on the two Russians. Michael Alekseev was the son of a minor communist party official who attended military school before joining the FSB, the post-soviet successor to the KGB. Alekseev was assigned to a unit called the Special Operations Service, a Spetznaz unit. He quit just over two years ago, more than a year after I parted ways with the Army. Alekseev had no known associations after leaving the FSB until he was sponsored for an H1-B visa by a New York corporation called the Hudson Valley Service Group, which owns the building I'm looking at. The pockmarked Russian, Victor Sherbatsky, on the other hand, has been linked to the Tambov Gang. This is a St. Petersburgh-based gang that originated in the Tambov Oblast. The gang specializes in the drug trade, prostitution and protection. They also own a huge number of legitimate front businesses. They're the most powerful criminal enterprise in St. Petersburg. Sammie was able to verify for me that the tattoo I've seen on Yuri's neck as well as Alekseev's is an identifying symbol of the Tambov gang.

I asked Sammie to get me blueprints for the building I'm watching, which he obtained from the commercial realtor. The brick warehouse is shaped like an "L." The main section is two stories high but the smaller section that houses three administrative offices is just one story tall, built onto the side of a hill so that it shares a single roof with the main warehouse floor. The entire building is small by commercial standards: the main section is just 10,000 square feet. There are half a dozen cars in the parking lot and three panel vans. Three loading bays jut from the main warehouse and one of the vans is backed up to the middle one. The aluminum roof is slightly canted, looking more modern than the rest of the brick structure. There are skylights bored into the rooftop at regular intervals, undoubtedly installed to cut electricity consumption in the warehouse. The offices on the administrative level are accessible directly from a blue metal staircase in the back parking lot. Three windows look over the parking lot from the offices and a high-positioned narrow slit window stands above the parking area on the warehouse section, allowing additional indirect light onto the warehouse floor. The warehouse doesn't have any windows at all facing the road or other buildings. It is an ideal location for storing and distributing things you don't want anyone else to see.

By 5pm, I've given up on the hope that the Russians will try to move Veronica quickly. It looks like they are pulling girls from all of their houses. My best guess is that there are at least 50 children in that warehouse. That makes my task infinitely more complex. I also have to assume that the men inside the building will be expecting me. My Army file – my real file – is deeply classified; it is hard to imagine that these men could have gotten hold of it. But even if the Russians Google me they'll learn I was a decorated Special Forces soldier who served in Afghanistan. So they'll be expecting trouble. Adding fifty human shields to the equation – plus Veronica – makes it a logistic nightmare. I have to assume they have a picture of me, too, so I can't do any reconnaissance in disguise. They'd most likely see through me. So I spend the day planning and preparing.

It's a difficult conversation I have with Menetti. I tell him the full story, from the moment I arrived in Conestoga. I tell him the locations of the houses that the Tambov Gang has been using as well as Vanderhook's role, and where to find his little black book. That goes well enough. But then I have to ask him to use all of his political juice to send the most elite unit in the FBI halfway up the eastern seaboard without informing the local authorities and assure him that I will give them ample probable cause to enter the warehouse building when they arrive, followed by lots of glory and a first rate photo-op for the media. I have to get a very firm time commitment from him down to the second, even if it means that UH 60 helicopters will be hovering a town away for ten or fifteen minutes. And Menetti knows full well that I'm going to have to commit some capital crimes to give his guys the right pretext to enter the building. He warns me again that he can't shield me from the consequences. There's only one way I know to buy myself immunity and it involves a step down a path I swore I would never tread again. Even for that to work, I'll need more information than I have at the moment. So the taste in my mouth is bitter as I hang up the phone. If I believed that Veronica would survive the night, I'd make a different call and just walk away. I keep telling myself that, anyway.

But it's too late now. As darkness descends, I slip off the roof and quietly, carefully make preparations for what is to come. There's real work to do because the clock is now ticking and I have motion sensors, an alarm system and video feeds to defeat, and some nasty tricks to rig up.

When the white Ford panel van explodes, the blast wave slaps me like a pro bowl center even though I'm 100 feet away, lying flat on the rooftop of the warehouse. I'm momentarily worried that I've overdone it – it's hard to be very precise with the ingredients you can buy at Wal-Mart. Fortunately, the primary force of the explosion is upward, as I've intended it to be, although it blows out all the windows in the warehouse and incinerates a seven-series BMW parked next to the van. On this far edge of Conestoga, I figure I have at least seven minutes until the volunteer fire department responds.

I count to three before I hit the detonator that blows in the two skylights to the largest office in the administrative wing of the warehouse, as well as the power to the building. Everything now depends on timing, and a countdown is running on my watch and in my head. The skylights don't make the kind of mess the van did because I found Primacord at Stokely's along with some other illegal treats seemingly destined for the very men I'm about to drop in on.

As soon as the skylight is clear, I drop a CTS model 7290 flash bang grenade through the hole, directly onto the conference table that sits beneath it, then pull away from the opening before it detonates. It's a police model, not mil-spec, and without it and the Primacord I probably wouldn't be attempting this foolishness at all, so my feelings are mixed about finding the unexpected jackpot. The flash bangs weren't all that surprising – there are plenty of meth labs in Greene and Columbia counties and Conestoga has a SWAT unit within the sheriff's department. The detcord is strictly regulated, though, and highly illegal.

As soon as the flash goes off, I'm through the skylight headfirst, anchored by a carabiner to the rooftop. Three of the men in the room are kneeling or crouching with their hands over their ears and their eyes shut. But there are still five good men with automatic weapons, waiting for something to come through one of the skylights. I hit them one by one with the P90 on its burst mode while hanging upside down halfway through the skylight. Only one Russian, a bear of a man holding an AK-47, manages to raise his weapon toward me before I put a third round through his right eye. All of the men are dead by the time I swing my legs over my head and flip, simultaneously pulling myself up on the rope a bit, creating enough slack to unhook the carabineer anchoring my Blackhawk CQB belt to the mountaineering rope secured to the roof.

I drop silently onto the conference table, securing the P90 to my back and drawing the Kimber. I screw on the silencer as I drop to the floor. I survey the bodies to ensure I'm not going to be shot in the back as I move through the room by a man I failed to disable. Eight men are dead. I have some sympathy for them. I've been on the other side of this scene. During Delta training, it's one of the first things you experience, in a hanger specially set-up to practice nothing but these types of entries. Even if you've been in combat, there is nothing as disorienting as a quick detcord explosion followed by stun grenades and precision shooting. The Delta exercises are conducted with live ammo, so when the mannequin standing in for a live terrorist two feet from you takes two rounds through the forehead, it's hard not to check your own body for holes. After you make the entries yourself four or five hundred times, some of the magic goes out of it, but it's just as effective. Explosive entry is practiced in teams of four by Delta, so I count myself lucky to have my feet on solid ground without having been shot.

Twenty seconds.

The door to the large office is open, revealing a hallway flanked by two smaller offices. The hall ends at a steel door that connects the administrative area to the main warehouse floor. As I move into the hallway, a thick Russian with a scar running from his right eye to the edge of his dark mustache steps from the door to the office on the left holding an assault rifle. I put two rounds into the man's neck, not breaking stride as I reach into a pouch attached to the checkerboard molle system on my TAG vest and pull out another flash bang.

I roll the grenade into the first office, the windowless room to my right whose doorway is nearest to the bigger office. I hear a shout as I duck behind the wall, then the flash bang detonates. I flip my night vision goggles down from the tactical helmet and enter the room low, shooting two men. One is swinging a SCAR-H assault rifle wildly like a club, the other is waving a Beretta, a hand over his eyes.

I step back out into the hallway, which is still illuminated by the fire from the van, and flip the night vision goggles back up. I proceed down the hallway toward the steel fire door. As I reach the second office, a burly Russian comes flying through the door, nearly colliding with me as he passes. I stick a foot out in time to trip the man and start to turn toward him and away from the open doorway. The hairs on the back of my neck stand up and I stop cold, deciding in an instant to draw the flat-bladed SOG seal pup left-handed from its downward-facing sheath on the Blackhawk vest. I swing the knife backward without looking and bury it cleanly in the side of the man's neck, severing the carotid artery. At the same time, I raise the Kimber in my right hand and fire two rounds point blank into the chest of a second man who has just appeared in the doorway. This Russian is older and is carrying a sawed-off 12-gauge Mossberg shotgun. The weapon discharges as the man drops, nearly tagging me even though I've thrown myself instinctively to the side. I blink once then pick myself up, moving at a crouch into the last office. A lone man remains, huddled over a keyboard. He is unarmed and trembling.

Forty Seconds.

I pull the man roughly backward, toppling him off of his swivel chair. He is bespectacled and thin, completely unlike the other Russians I have encountered in this place. I roll the thin Russian onto his stomach and put a boot on his neck while I fish through a pouch on my vest until I find a string of plastic whip-ties I've liberated from a box of heavy-duty trash bags, and a roll of duct tape. I bind the man's wrists behind his back and lash his feet together. Then I hog-tie the man's feet to his wrists with duct tape and roll him over.

"I'm letting you live so you can pass on a message. Don't cross the *Solntsevskaya bratva,*" I say to him in fluent Russian, picking the name of the only other Russian mafia cartel I can think of. The thin man's eyes widen and a damp patch blossoms on the front of his polyester trousers.

Ninety Seconds.

I don't have much time. I was hoping to find Veronica in the administrative section of the warehouse, but she's not here. I step out of the room and examine the door to the warehouse. There is a deadbolt, which I slide closed. Then I pull two doorjambs from a pouch attached to my vest and kick them into place under the door. I leave the building the same way I came in, and soon I am back on the roof, running swiftly toward the main section of the warehouse.

I see a car pulling out of the parking lot just as I breach the skylight at the far end of the main warehouse. A lone man drives the Taurus, but I can't identify him or read the plates as he peels away. I can't waste any more time, though. I drop two flash-bangs down the hole and run a dozen feet to drop two more through another skylight. Returning to the first, I hook myself into a line and rappel down ten feet, where I drop onto a massive steel beam that runs the length of the warehouse floor. The room is shrouded in darkness, only faintly illuminated by the dying flames from the smoldering van that leak in through the high slit window above the loading bay doors, which are shut. The lights that were illuminating the parking lot have been extinguished as well.

I drop prone on the beam, unstrapping a rifle from my back as soon as I'm stable. It is my best find at Stokeley's: a VSS sniper rifle. I appreciate the irony as I adjust the scope: this piece was undoubtedly smuggled in for the men I'm aiming it at. The Vintorez, as it's commonly known, was developed in the Tula Arsenal south of Moscow for Spetznaz commandos of the MVD in the late 1980s. It isn't the most elegant or even accurate weapon, but it has two huge advantages over most other sniper rifles for the kind of close-quarter nighttime work I'm about to engage in. First, it is very compact, with a folding rear stock. Second, it has an integrated silencer and a large twenty-round magazine. With any luck, it will help keep me concealed for long enough to finish the job I've started.

Two minutes.

I peer through the PKN-03 night scope on the Vintorez. The scene below me is mayhem. The warehouse has an enormous open floor with six large cages set in the middle, about six feet from each other, organized like the dots that form the number six on dice. In the green illumination of the sniper scope, I can see clusters of figures in the cages, some huddled together and some crouched alone. Among the Tambov men, the smartest are huddling between the cages, crouched down while they wait for their eyes and ears to recover from the flash bangs. Others are not so wise, running about wildly in the dark. One man has collapsed near the stairs to the upper extension of the warehouse, and he's screaming loudly, adding the perceptible feel of panic to the confusion.

I count eighteen men in total. As I watch, three of them break cover at once and make a beeline for the door adjacent to the loading bay that leads to the parking lot. I see that they are armed and I caress the trigger of the Vintorez, smoothly dropping them one, two, three. I sweep the scope across the warehouse floor and catch the motion of two more men with SCAR-H assault rifles; one with his right hand on the other's shoulders run at a crouch towards the upper landing. I take down the leader first and then the man behind him. They didn't make it fifteen feet. I am scanning for more targets when I feel the ricochet of bullets against the steel beam below me and hear the characteristic crack of an AK assault rifle. I twist sharply towards the muzzle flash I've caught from the corner of my eye and I spot the shooter. As light blossoms from the rifle again; I put two rounds into the man. I feel a searing pain in my shoulder and, pulling off my glove, explore it with two fingers. A bullet has grazed the fleshy part of my upper arm. I am bleeding, but not badly. The body armor can't stop a rifle projectile, but has neverthe-less diverted the off-angle shot enough to spare me serious injury. It can wait. I shake my head. It is an unbelievable shot with an assault rifle in the dark at a prone target 100 yards away. Either the shooter was lucky or I was.

Three Minutes.

The warehouse floor has dissolved to chaos as I survey it again. I take down three more Russians brandishing weapons. Then a single man stands and puts his rifle down carefully on the ground, raising his hands above his head. Four more men follow his lead, surrendering. I pause for a moment to consider this. Then I pull a handful of glow sticks from another pouch on my vest. Wrapping them in a chamois cloth, I crack them and toss them in a bunch towards the warehouse floor. They separate from the chammy halfway to the floor and rain down like the arc of a rainbow in four different colors.

"Drop your weapons and move to the light markers with your hands above your head," my voice booms in Russian. I shout upward, towards the aluminum warehouse ceiling, hoping to mask my location. There is a moment of utter and complete silence when I wonder if I've just identified myself as a target. Then the clatter of another assault rifle shatters the silence as another Tambov thug drops it to the ground. Through the scope I see other stragglers follow suit. Eight men in total shuffle to the vacant area on the floor ten feet from the cages and drop first to their knees and then flat on their stomachs, hands stretched forward and legs crossed behind them. That's all of them, or at least all that I counted.

I secure a line around the steel girder with a carabineer, drop it and fast-rope down to the warehouse floor, with both the Vintorez and the P90 strapped to my back. As I hit the ground, one of the Russians on the end of the line of prone men rolls and half-stands, pulling a small automatic from his pants. I drop to one knee and smoothly draw the Kimber, which roars as I squeeze the trigger. The man is blown back off his feet, and the top half of his head dissolves in a spray of blood. Nobody else moves after that.

I single out the smallest Russian on the ground and kick him in the leg. When the longhaired Russian looks up, I drop a set of quick zip trash bag fasteners at his feet before stepping back and ordering him to bind his compatriots at the wrists and ankles. When the other men are secure, I holster the Kimber then secure my assistant before pulling out a thick roll of duct tape to ensure that the Russians will take some time to escape their bindings. I look at my watch. The entire action has taken less than six minutes, but the FBI helicopters will be overhead in two more. Worse still, I can hear sirens in the distance. It is most likely the Conestoga volunteer fire department, but Sheriff Peterson won't be far behind them. I have no time to waste.

I pull a sturdy metal flashlight from my chest rig and trot over to the cages, shining the narrow beam inside. What I see stops me cold. There are eight girls in the first cage my flashlight hits. They are clustered in a group near the middle of the cage, which is crudely fashioned from chain links, like a low-rent dog kennel. The girls are wearing flimsy cotton dresses, far too light for the cool autumn Conestoga weather and they are obviously dehydrated. I can smell perspiration and human excrement. And as I've seen while surveying the warehouse, they are children – all of them. The oldest can barely be eleven years old, the youngest no more than six. I have a flashback to a moment in a village in the Sudan where I'd been sent in to record proof of the genocide in Darfur and found house after house full of slaughtered families. What has happened to these girls seems no less awful.

I move from cage to cage with my flashlight. In the fourth cage, backed in a corner, sweaty and trembling, I see Veronica. A weight I didn't know I was carrying lifts. I shout to the men, asking who has the keys. One of them grunts and I walk over and fish through his pockets until I find a ring of keys. It takes too long to find the key and open the lock. The young girls shrink away from me as I point to Veronica. She doesn't know me at first, and I bring a finger to my lips as I see hope blossom in her eyes. She catches on quickly, remaining silent as I release her. After a second's consideration, I re-lock the cage and leave the keys on the floor a few feet away. One of the girls still inside makes pleading eye contact with me, a bedraggled, stick-thin waif with stringy, elbow-length blonde hair who looks all of eight. I address her in Russian, raising my voice so all of the girls will hear me, "The American police will be here soon. The men wearing black will help get you back to your families. You can trust them."

I consider releasing all of the girls and decide against it. It is infuriating to see children treated like animals, but I have only moments before I risk being detained. It's also better that the FBI witness exactly what has happened here. Besides, there is no telling what kind of power the Russian men have over these children and I don't want the girls freeing them.

Keeping an eye on the bound men, I lead Veronica to the door near the exit bay. I peer outside and see that the parking lot is still clear. The panel van has been reduced to a smoldering skeleton of scorched steel. My watch tells me that FBI helos will be overhead any second. I pause for a moment on the threshold of the doorway, thinking about the story I want to paint for the crime scene investigators. Reaching a decision, I gently remove the Vintorez from my shoulder, laying it down on the ground near the door. I've never handled it without gloves on, but I wipe it down quickly with a soft cloth. Then, pulling Veronica along behind me, I sprint out of the parking lot and down the block where we duck onto a side street. In the dumpster behind the abandoned office building I recover our bags and a gear bag I've expropriated from Stokeley's. I have another pang of guilt before reassuring myself that I have just returned sole ownership of the business back to Don Miller. I take the P90 off my back, strip off my molle vest and drop the bags into the trunk of the Crown Victoria. A few seconds later we peel away, passing three fire trucks and a series of sherriff's cars streaming toward the warehouse on the two-lane road. Three minutes later, as we pull the blue Ford onto the freeway, I hear the unmistakable sound of UH-60 Black Hawk helicopters overhead.

Veronica is still in shock. Her face is ashen white and she looks like she's thrown up recently. I keep the Crown Victoria riding smoothly on the Thruway, heading south toward Kingston where abundant cheap motels near the thruway exit will allow us to get some sleep anonymously. Neither of us talks. Finally, she stirs, seems to come out of the trance, and looks at me as if seeing me for the first time.

"Who are you?" she asks. "That, in the warehouse – and what you did to George – I have never seen anything like that before."

I consider this for a moment. She deserves some kind of answer and I really want her to understand. "I'm – I was – a professional, an operator. This is what I was trained for." It doesn't register with her. She lives in the same world that most nice kids from wealthy families inhabit. That world doesn't have room for men like me.

"I think I understand." She says, but she doesn't. I can see her struggling with shock, starting to lose control. She takes a sharp breath in and pulls it back together. Tough girl.

"So you speak Russian?" she asks off-handedly.

"Yeah, small world," I answer.

Chapter Six –

Wednesday

"**G**ood morning, this is CNN. In the news this morning – explosions and a dramatic gunfight in upstate New York last night as a major sex trafficking ring crumbles. We take you live to CNN correspondent Joanne Meeker in Conestoga, New York."

"Good Morning, Robyn. This sleepy town in the Catskills region erupted last night in explosions and gunfire as the FBI raided a warehouse here just after 7pm. Federal agents rescued nearly four-dozen underage girls from this warehouse behind me, some reportedly as young as five years old. While they have no official comment on the investigation that led to this confrontation, some locals are comparing this to Ruby Ridge. What we do know is this, however: at least twenty-one men are dead and most of them are Russian citizens. These men appear to be members of a Russian criminal syndicate. The good news, Robyn, is that it appears that none of the hostages, none of these young girls, were injured. Although they will not comment on the record, sources tell me that the FBI's elite Hostage Rescue Team conducted the operation in cooperation with local law enforcement authorities based on information from a confidential informant. Local residents here in Conestoga were shocked to learn that this type of criminal enterprise was operating right in their town. The FBI is continuing this investigation, which has expanded to include raids on locations throughout the town this morning. We understand from the Conestoga sheriff's office that they are seeking two people for questioning related to this incident and the murder of a New York City banker just three days ago. One is Michael Herne, a decorated U.S. Army Sergeant and Afghanistan war veteran. The second is Veronica Ryan, a reporter for the White Plains Gazette. We have no idea what part either of them played in these events …"

My mind reels as the *Stars & Stripes* photo of me receiving the Silver Star flashes on the screen. I look at Veronica. "Was there a TV behind the desk when you got the room last night?" We'd checked into the motel, a Super 8, just before nine in the evening, after I'd showered and changed in a truck stop, scrubbing most of the blood off of me and dropping the clothes I'd worn into a dumpster. Veronica got the room, paying cash and registering as Jean Smith, playing the part of a married woman only planning to use the room for a few hours.

"No, I didn't see one. The woman on duty didn't look at me twice."

I look at my watch. It's 6am. "We need to have a serious conversation," I say to Veronica. "The Russians were all from a gang operating out of St. Petersburg." I let that stand for a moment. "You have to tell me what you know." She sits down heavily on the bed and nods. Drawing her knees to her chest, she begins to talk. She doesn't look at me.

"I fell in love, that's how it all started. I had only been in St. Petersburg for a few months. The mother of one of the children I was teaching at the school hired me to give private English lessons to her daughter. Her husband was there in the evenings when I came to tutor the girl. He would joke around with me. He was funny. One day the girl and the mother weren't there when I arrived. She'd had to leave town for a funeral and took the daughter with her but forgot to ring me. The husband took pity on me and bought me dinner. After that…well after awhile…I became his mistress. At first it was like…it was amazing. He took me places I had never seen, to restaurants that weren't in any guidebook and fantastic clubs. He made me feel special. And I met amazing, powerful people. He knew everyone. We grew closer and he started to talk about leaving his wife. His name was Constantine.

"And then one day Constantine told me that he was in a difficult situation. He said that he wouldn't be able to leave his wife unless he resolved his issues at work. He used to have a big job in Moscow but he'd been out-maneuvered politically and sent to St. Petersburg. He had an opportunity to revive his career, to get a big new promotion, but he needed to come up with a plan to impress his superiors. I never really understood what he did other than the fact that he worked for the government.

"That topic never really came up again, but it was always in the back of my mind. I don't know if it was the way he said it, but it was the first time I got a feeling about Constantine that something wasn't quite right." She stops and laughs harshly at herself, "As if the infidelity didn't already tell me that. Anyway, there was this one time that he was over at the apartment. He knew Mel by then and the three of us were watching TV. There was this American show on called 'To Catch a Predator' – you know the one, where a reporter goes online pretending to be an underage girl and arranges to meet some pedophile, then confronts him? Well, he thought it was just brilliant and I remember him asking a bunch of questions about American attitudes towards that stuff. How strong is the social embarrassment, are the laws really enforced, that kind of thing. It was really weird, like he wanted to know everything about being a child molester. Then he started joking that there had to be a pretty good business in trapping perverts. The way he said it was really odd. Mel felt the same way.

"Of course, Mel didn't like Constantine much, anyway, but she was hardly in a position to judge me, given how George was treating her. Anyway, the subject of sexual predators never really came up again, but there was this one other conversation we had in St. Petersburg that I keep remembering. This was just after Constantine got the big promotion and I found out that he was moving to New York City. We were out for dinner with Mel and George. This was the beginning of the mortgage crisis and Mel started talking about how she got a letter from her parents about how many people in Conestoga were losing their houses and how many vacant homes there were. Then all of a sudden, Constantine starts asking Mel all of these random questions: how far is Conestoga from New York, do rich people have their vacation houses nearby, what are the neighborhoods in Conestoga like, how far is it from the interstate? It was really specific stuff, very strange. But it was just after that when Mel got that black eye and…it was Constantine who got me photos of George with the other women. Then he left Russia and took his wife with him and I thought that was the end of it."

"But he started calling after he got to New York, telling me that he missed me and that he made a mistake not leaving his wife. He pressured me to come back home and eventually I did. I had vowed that I wasn't going to see him again, that I was never going to be that other woman ever again, but I folded like a house of cards when he sent for me. At first, it was wonderful in New York. He set me up in an apartment near the consulate on the Upper East Side. He brought me to a lot of cocktail parties, a lot of social functions. After a while, I realized he was never going to leave his wife. I ended it about a year ago."

I start to say something but Veronica shakes her head and I close my mouth. "There's more. It may not mean anything, but I…I have a feeling. This one time we were at a U.N. event, a family day thing and I'm talking with this woman, an American woman. Her daughter is there with her as she's talking to me, a cute little girl with red hair and freckles, maybe seven, eight years old. This guy comes up to us, another American, and says hello, and pats the little girl on the head, then talks to her for a moment. You know, typical kid stuff. There was nothing really wrong with it, but there was something about how he looked at that girl that really creeped me out. The mother must have had the same reaction because as soon as he walked away she knelt down in front of that little girl and started talking to her. I couldn't hear what she was saying, but you could tell she was lecturing that girl, telling her to stay away from strange men. I mentioned it to Constantine in passing because it freaked me out. He asked me to point out the guy. When I did he seemed really shocked, but somehow excited, too. 'Do you know who that is?' he asked me. I didn't. He named a name – I can't remember it, but apparently it was somebody important. I didn't think anything about it at the time. Anyway, that was right before the end. When I broke it off with Constantine, I moved back in with my parents."

The hairs on the back of my neck are tingling and for the first time in twenty-four hours, I feel as if we might have caught a break. But this time I wait for Veronica and after a moment she starts talking again. "About six months ago, I was in Conestoga visiting Mel. It was a sunny Saturday afternoon and we'd just eaten lunch at the diner. As I was driving away I saw his car, or thought I did. I could have sworn I caught a glimpse of him, but I wasn't sure. It was odd."

"What is Constantine's last name?" I ask as neutrally as I am able.

"Drubich. Constantine Drubich. He's the first cultural attaché at the Russian Consulate."

I lean back and take a moment to absorb this. The cultural attaché position is almost exclusively reserved for top case officers – spymasters. The promotion that Constantine was fretting about had to be leading the *Sluzhba Vneshney Razvedki* office in New York. When the cold war ended, the KGB split into a domestic and foreign branch. The FSB took over domestic intelligence duties while the SVR became the foreign intelligence service for Russia. If Constantine is actually responsible for bringing the Tambov Gang to Conestoga, it's big news. But my second question is bigger. I tense as I ask it, knowing it's the bargaining chip I've been looking for.

"Do you remember the name of the man you pointed out to Constantine? The one you saw at the U.N. reception?"

Veronica shakes her head. "I was introduced, but I don't remember his name."

"What did he look like?" I ask.

"At least as tall as you. On the thin side. Red hair."

"Orion here, Sir."

"I wondered if I might hear from you. It seems that you've been busy." An understatement. I've called the Tactical Operations Center at the Activity and asked for Alpha. They put me directly through to him, which surprises me. It's just after seven in the morning. I'm sure that Alpha must sleep occasionally, but nobody I know has ever caught him at it. I've sent Veronica to the Wal-Mart for hair dye and new clothes, thinking that she's less likely to run into someone she knows than I am in these parts. And she's also less likely to be identified, as her photo has not been running on national television in a continuous loop for the last ten hours.

"Yes, sir, that would be correct." Even though I no longer work for Alpha, he is making me sweat. On the occasions in the past where I've been involved in ops that went south, Alpha has reminded me of a junior high school vice principal. He may be soft spoken, but he has a bite.

"And what can I do for you, Orion?" He's enjoying this, drawing it out. Our last conversation was under very different circumstances.

"I have some information about the…current events, which I believe will be of interest to you, sir."

Alpha takes a moment to chew on this. In truth, it would be more appropriate for me to talk to the FBI. They run counterespionage in the United States in coordination with Homeland Security, and they're already knee deep in the middle of investigating the Tambov Gang in Conestoga. The Activity is not supposed to even operate on U.S. soil. But things are not so simple in Washington anymore. During the last administration, the balance of power between civilian and military agencies shifted in some important ways. After the invasion of Iraq, the military ended up responsible for a bunch of jobs that had previously been reserved for other agencies like the State Department and the CIA. That's how you end up with civilian contractors hired by the Defense Department running intelligence networks in Afghanistan and getting mired in a host of other shenanigans that cut across once-clear lines of responsibility.

Guys like Alpha, those who command the most elite and secret units in the military, have their own power base outside the chain of command. Alpha briefs the select committees on Intelligence in both the Senate and the House personally. He is on the phone with top people in the West Wing of the White House any time there's a crisis. I've heard that he has briefed every President since Reagan. So he has the kind of leverage you need to go to the FBI and say "this is my guy, look what he's giving us, you need to keep him out of this." He has the juice to make something like that happen. Without his intervention, it's hard to see how the FBI will view what I've done as anything other than vigilantism. I've told Alpha that I can give him a good reason to intervene. But there will be a price, more than I want to pay. He's thinking about just exactly what he wants from me.

"What type of information?" Alpha asks, weighing his words. We're on an unsecure line.

"There may be a connection between recent events and the activities of a foreign government." That's as much as I dare say, and about as much as I want to say without some more assurances from the man.

Alpha considers this for a moment. "We should discuss this further."

"I'm not near a secure line, sir, but I can drive into New York or get to your office by the end of the day." I offer. There are federal offices in Manhattan, Brooklyn and various towns in New Jersey on the encrypted government network.

"No, I'll come to you. Let's say noon. Call the TOC watch commander in an hour for the location. Use another phone. And bring the girl."

At three minutes before noon, I ease the Crown Victoria to a halt in front of a hardware store on Main Street in Phoenicia. It is a postcard-quaint village nestled in a valley created by glacial retreat. Sheridan, Garfield and Romer Mountains butt heads here like monumental NFL linesmen, leaving just enough space between them for the small town. Main Street completes the triangle formed by the meeting of the Stony Clove and Esopus Creeks as the Esopus twists southwards toward the Ashokan Reservoir a dozen miles downstream. Whereas Conestoga sits on the edge of the Catskills, pressed between the mountains and the Hudson River like mud between a boot and a doormat, Phoenicia is in the heart of Catskill National Park, northwest of Woodstock. The mountains are more immediate here, their peaks visible from Main Street. The morning is clear and for the first time since my arrival upstate, the air is dry.

The summer high season is over in Phoenicia and the town has shrunk to its offseason size of half the residents and a tenth of the tourists it will accommodate in July or August. Many of the tourist-dependent businesses in town are closed for the season. A handmade ice-cream shop and several restaurants with large outdoor seating areas sit lifeless on Main.

As I open the door to the big Ford, I wince. My shoulder is stiff. The body armor I wore last night saved me from the worst damage that might have been caused by the 7.62mm rifle round, but I have an ugly bruise over a shallow cut and the tissue is swelling.

I was surprised when the sergeant major told me I'd be meeting Alpha in Phoenicia. It's an unusually out-of-the way location, but that is probably the point. There are only three roads out of Phoenicia and you can see the traffic on all of them from a single vantage point – the porch of Sweet Sue's. There is a large "Away Fishing" sign in the window. Alpha has closed the restaurant.

Sweet Sue's occupies the lower level of a two-story boarding house with white clapboard siding and blue-framed windows. Founded by Sue Taylor in the 1980s, it quickly became a Catskills favorite, best known for the ingeniously delicate but Frisbee-sized pancakes it serves. It is the only place I've ever eaten where the waitresses caution new customers that a full stack of pancakes might be too much food for a grown man. Since my last visit more than a dozen years ago, Sweet Sue's has prospered. It is now a two-room diner occupying the entire bottom floor of its building, having pushed out the dress shop that used to stand next door.

There are two alert-looking men dressed in khakis and Northface Windstopper fleece jackets standing on the porch, scanning the road in opposite directions. I recognize them. The Activity is not like other units in the army, particularly for shooters. We tend to deploy alone, working with our intelligence guys, locals and operators from other agencies. We have a high attrition rate and the odds of capture are significant, so the Activity doesn't encourage us to get to know each other personally like the Rangers or the Delta Force guys do. We train individually. But if you stick around long enough, you get to recognize some of the key people. More than that, you can tell the look. Activity operators aren't cocky, and they don't carry the chip on their shoulder that you sometimes see with operators on Tier II or Tier III units who get fewer resources. Like me, most of them served in other elite units before coming to the Activity. Most of all, these are guys that have to blend well into the background, so we have very few hulking monsters in the unit. But there's something about Activity operators, something about their overwhelming competence, that you can just feel if you've seen it before and you get close enough. Under different circumstances, I might exchange a few words with these guys, but not now.

My former commander stands as we enter and walk over to the large round in the original dining room. These are Southern manners and they are for Veronica's benefit, not mine. He's dressed in civvies, jeans and a white button-down oxford shirt under an olive blazer. He extends his hand cordially and introduces himself. He uses a name I don't recognize, one that is not his own. We take a quick look at the menu on the wall and order pancakes. I get them straight up with real maple syrup, Alpha favors blueberry and Veronica orders Blue Monkey pancakes with blueberries and bananas. Veronica is voracious – I don't think she's eaten anything in more than a day. I snuck a few energy bars and a sandwich while I was watching the warehouse. I'm surprised at Alpha's ability to make polite conversation over brunch because I've never heard him engage in small talk before. He quizzes Veronica about her time in Russia without asking her directly about Constantine. Alpha is obsessed with language proficiency, and seems impressed that Veronica reached fluency during her stay there. He asks about my Russian and seems gratified to hear Veronica say that she mistook me for a Russian when she first heard me speak the language yesterday. I think she's exaggerating, but the compliment pleases me as well.

When we've finished eating, the waitress clears our dishes and a moment later two women in blue quilted aprons emerge from the kitchen and leave the restaurant with the server. The three of us are alone. Alpha immediately turns to business, almost instantly becoming the man I remember.

"Ms. Ryan, I am Mr. Herne's former commanding officer in the Army. I may be in a position to help you and Mr. Herne extricate yourselves from your current legal troubles. However to do so, I'll need to hear your story in your own words. I can't guarantee anything, but if you cooperate with me, I will make my best efforts." Alpha pauses significantly here to see if I've told Veronica enough for this offer to have meaning to her. I nod slightly. I've told her that he's a heavy hitter and should be able to sort things out for me. She's not really in any trouble herself in spite of Sheriff Peterson's apparent desire to detain her, so I'm mostly relying on her innate sense of decency to help get me clear of the mess I've made breaking her out of the warehouse. This shames me because I know that nothing comes free, and she'll pay a price for Alpha's help just as surely as I will.

"I'm going to record your statement, and ask you to sign an agreement with the U.S. Government. This agreement stipulates that you may not write or even discuss any details of what you're about to tell me, including the events of the past 36 hours and anything concerning these matters that transpires going forward under penalty of federal criminal law." Alpha emphasizes the word *criminal*. Alpha pulls a sheet of paper from his brief-case, which he slides over to Veronica with a pen. She glances at it and signs it. I warned her that something like this was coming. I see a moment of regret as she realizes that she is handing away the scoop that would transform her career.

After Veronica signs the document, Alpha produces a small handheld voice recorder and turns it on, then starts questioning her. He is polite and patient, but over the course of an hour he manages to extract a more complete story of her relationship with Constantine Drubich than I've heard from her, as well as the details of her captivity. When she relates the story from the U.N. party, he questions her in minute detail about the tall red-haired man. When he is finally satisfied, he stops the recorder and slips it back into his briefcase.

"Thank you very much, Ms. Ryan. I believe we are going to need your help over the next few days, and I hope you will assist Mr. Herne with identifying the men you have described. Would you please allow me to have a word with him alone?" Alpha rises and shakes Veronica's hand, not sitting again until she has stepped outside. He fixes me with a look.

"Yes, sir?"

"You've made quite a mess. Did you consider that your actions would inevitably involve my command? I spent an hour on the phone with CJCS and the Secretary this morning trying to talk them down."

"Sir, I recognize that I probably should not have gotten involved with this business to start. But once these people kidnapped Veronica, there was no way the FBI could have intervened without her ending up dead."

Alpha shakes his head. "Do I need to remind you that the Army spent a small fortune and almost a decade imparting the skills that you used yesterday? The purpose of this expensive education was not for you to conduct your own private wars. By doing so, you not only risked your life and the lives of others, you endangered the very existence of units like ours. Funding will disappear in a heartbeat if some Senator gets it in his head that we're a training ground for freelance assassins. Do you remember what happened to the CIA in the seventies? If you ever – and I mean ever – act on your own again, I assure you that I will personally see you stop-lossed back into the regular army from the reserve to spend the rest of your working life doing low-temperature equipment testing at Fort Greely in Alaska." He pauses for a moment to see if his words have had the desired effect on me. I must look as shaken as I feel, because he softens his approach a little. "I understand that you were trying to do the right thing, Orion, but I thought we had rid you of these romantic notions. It would be a shame to have lost your services only to see you forfeit your life engaged in precisely the same sort of activities for such foolish ends. Before we go any further, I need to hear the whole story from you, beginning to end." This time, Alpha does not pull out the voice recorder. He listens as I tell him everything from the moment I arrived in Conestoga through the events of the past day.

"How deep is my predicament, sir? I was looking for the black Chinook outside..." That's a nervous reference to the helicopter that supposedly appears to spirit you away after you've made one too many mistakes in the Special Ops community. I'm straight with Alpha because there's no point posturing with the man. He holds all the cards and he knows it. He's also a shrewd enough player not to throw his weight around arbitrarily. He will convince me of the rightness of whatever he wants me to do.

"It's a difficult situation. The FBI has nineteen bodies and no suspect in custody. That doesn't count the men in your hotel room. Breaking up the human trafficking ring has gotten them a lot of good publicity, so that weighs in your favor. But they're not inclined to tolerate vigilantism." He lets this sit with me for a moment before continuing.

"On the other hand, they may be willing to accept a convenient alternate theory of the crime. It was wise of you to spare the accountant. He is cooperating, and shedding a great deal of light on the extent of the gang's activities. He also described the attack on the building in vivid terms. He believes that a rival gang, the *Solntsevskaya Bratva*, stormed the building. Several of the other eyewitness accounts bear this out, describing gunfire coming from multiple locations. There was also a weapon used in the attack recovered from the facility. It is undeniably of Russian origin." Here Alpha eyes me for a moment, as if he might discern where I've gotten hold of a Vintorez by looking in my eyes. I keep my mouth shut, figuring that I've gotten Don Miller in enough trouble for one week.

"I believe I can convince the FBI to accept the rival gang theory and focus on the human trafficking ring – particularly the question of whether this was confined to Conestoga or if it's a more widespread issue. I believe they can also be persuaded to accept some outside help investigating the counterintelligence angle, particularly if they receive credit for any arrests or expulsions. Your friend, Supervisory Special Agent Menetti, has already done some good on your behalf. Without him, the FBI might already have picked you up.

"It would be useful if you could confirm Mr. Drubich's connection to the Tambov activities, but the more interesting question is whether Ms. Ryan's instincts are correct about a highly placed, redheaded American man. We'll look at this on our end – but while the hair color narrows the possibilities, it's not enough. You've already pulled the line and found the first fish on the hook. Now you need to follow it the rest of the way. You need to find out who this man is, and whether Drubich has compromised him. Given her connection with Mr. Drubich, I'm sure you'll want Ms. Ryan to assist you to make sure you hook the right fish." This is not a casual suggestion; it's as close as Alpha will come to giving me a direct order. Instead of going back to her life, Veronica will have to help me get information from Drubich and identify the redheaded diplomat. She might have been better off staying with the Tambov thugs than becoming bait. Alpha is already having an effect on me because I find myself agreeing with him, at least in that overdeveloped part of my brain that solves problems with no regard for human consequences.

"Sir, with due respect to the gravity of the situation, I do not plan to rejoin the unit." I'm putting it out there because it needs to be said. All things considered, I'd rather go to Alaska or even Leavenworth than back to the Activity.

"I'm not suggesting that," Alpha replies quickly. "We can help each other informally. I can run interference for you with the FBI and supply you with intelligence and support. You can determine how far the activities of Mr. Drubich and the Tambov Gang extend."

"What about the Conestoga sheriff's department?" I ask. "They're the ones who already named me to the press."

Alpha shakes his head. "I can't help you there. But the FBI raided the Vanderhook offices early this morning and they recovered the journal you described along with a sizable amount of cash. They also have the cooperation of the Tambov accountant, one of the few gang members you did not kill yesterday." He pins me with another significant look. "So I imagine they should be able to connect the dots from the gang to the sheriff's office as you did, but it may take some time." This I translate to mean, *you're on your own.* In case I don't completely grasp that, he makes it explicitly clear: "Please be aware, Orion, that you are completely off the books on this assignment. If you are caught breaking any more federal or state laws, you'll be disavowed." I nod. It's not unexpected. If things work out, the FBI will owe Alpha a few favors. If they don't, he'll feed me to the wolves. At least he can keep the feds off my back in the meantime. That's all I expected.

"In order to proceed, we'll need to take your vehicle and any weapons you fired last night," Alpha says. Without hesitation, I pull two sets of keys from my jacket pocket, laying them in front of me on the table. Then I reach behind my back and withdraw the Kimber custom from the loop holster inside the back of my belt. I eject the clip and clear the .45 ACP round that is chambered, catching it in the air. I lay the gun, clip and round on the table in front of Alpha.

"These are the keys to the Blue Crown Victoria outside. It belonged to one of the Russians," I say, pointing to the Ford keys. "These are for my GTO." I tell him where I've parked it in Conestoga.

"I understand you have some history with this sidearm," Alpha says, nodding at the Kimber. *He remembers the story*, I think, momentarily surprised. Alpha continues, "And I believe we can replace the firing pin and rework the barrel and return it to you. Nobody at the Activity has forgotten your contributions," the older man assures me. Then Alpha picks up the Kimber and its spare clip gently and puts them in a padded gun case. Next he pulls a tan leather Hartmann briefcase from the floor, lays it on the table and slides it over to me. I do not move to open it. "The briefcase contains the usual items," he says.

Then Alpha reaches into the pocket of his olive blazer and fishes out a set of keys. "These are for the black Pontiac G8 parked outside. If at all possible, I would appreciate the return of this vehicle to us intact." He hands me the key ring to me then withdraws a slim Blackberry from another pocket. "This is an encrypted device that will send and receive files securely. There's a second one of these in the briefcase. We've also put fresh clothing and some other items you may need in the trunk of the Pontiac. Is there anything else that you require?"

"No, sir."

"Good luck, Orion," Alpha says, extending a hand. It is only the second time the old man has ever offered me his hand. The first time was when he first persuaded me to join the Activity. We walk out of Sweet Sue's together.

Veronica is chatting with the two Activity men on the porch. She seems to have put them at ease. They straighten up instantly at the sharp look they get from Alpha. He tosses the keys to the Crown Victoria to one of the operators and hands the gun case to the other. I follow the first man, an imposing former Tae Kwon Do instructor whose call sign is Sleeper. As I recall, the man was found fast asleep standing bolt upright in the barracks shower during Ranger school. The nickname stuck and eventually became his call sign at the Activity. I tell Sleeper that I lifted the plates on the Crown Victoria and show him the load-out bag with the P90 and the other items I've taken from the Russians and from Stokeley's. I pull my personal bag from the trunk with Veronica's, and the case with my father's rifle.

"Be careful. Orion. You must be into some h-eav-y shit to bring the old man up here," Sleeper says quietly as I close the trunk to the Crown Vic.

"You don't know the half of it."

I toss the two bags into the back seat of the Pontiac G8 then take a walk around the car. The G8 looks like a family car, but it's not. The plain Jane, four-door Australian-sourced sedan conceals a powerful 8-cylinder engine transplanted from a Corvette. It is a brilliant vehicle that appeared with spectacularly bad timing at the height of the recession just before GM's bankruptcy, and never got a foothold in the US market. It was discontinued when General Motors killed Pontiac but there are still rumors that it may return under the Chevy badge. Alpha must have gotten a huge bargain on G8s and I chuckle to imagine him negotiating with a bunch of auto execs when the company was in government hands. As I make one more circuit around the vehicle, Alpha hops into the passenger seat of a black Chevy Suburban, which immediately peels off with a screech of tires, followed closely by the Crown Victoria. They are undoubtedly headed to a helicopter that will whisk Alpha back to Virginia.

I open the trunk of the G8 and see that in addition to a suitcase of clothes, Alpha has stocked the trunk with enough weapons to get me locked up indefinitely if I am pulled over for speeding. I lay my father's rifle in its padded zip case among them. Climbing into the car behind the wheel, I take a moment to familiarize myself with the black G8, which is the manual transmission-GXP model with an up-rated 415 horsepower V-8 engine. I turn the interior light to the off position so that it will not illuminate when I open the car doors. Then I pop the hood and step out to take a peek underneath. I immediately see that the technicians at the Activity have made some of their usual modifications. Satisfied, I hop into the G8 and we head south, past a closed river rafting shop and over the Esopus creek. Veronica lays her hand on mine for a second as I pull the G8 into third gear.

Sheriff Buddy Peterson awakes to an acrid smell in his nose and he flinches away from the source instinctively. I can see him pull away from the ammonia as I push the broken capsule under his nose again. He regains his senses gradually. First, he feels soft flannel sheets under his palms as his hands suffuse with blood. The comfortable bulk of his wife Dorothy is resting against him and he realizes he's in bed. Then he panics for a moment, unable to see, and wonders if he's having a stroke. His eyelids finally flutter open and his tear ducts begin to work on lubricating his dry eyes. He sees that it's dark outside, but the lamp beside his bed is switched on. Now he knows that it's the middle of the night. Then his ears begin to tingle and he hears breathing in addition to his and his wife's. Mine. He knows he's not alone. His eyes bulge as he strains his neck to scan the room.

Presently, his eyes find me. I've sat back into a rocking chair, which I've pulled beside the bed. My legs are crossed and I'm rocking slowly. When Buddy sees me, a glint of recognition sparks in his eyes, accompanied by more fear. He turns his head painfully toward his wife.

"She's fine," I say before he can ask. "But she won't wake up until morning."

It takes Buddy a moment to compose himself, but he does. He starts to rise, but I hold a hand up, and he sinks back into the bed, sitting a little more upright. "What do you want?" he croaks, his voice not quite working yet.

"I wanted to tell you that your days as Sheriff in this town are over. The FBI has gotten the accountant from the warehouse talking and they have a ledger from Charles Vanderhook's office detailing the places where the Tambov gang operated and the money he received. I'm going to bet he'll be anxious to cut a deal. They're already cross-referencing calls to your office with complaints about those locations. Either way, they have plenty to tie you to the gang. You're going down."

I see the steel in Peterson's eyes as he considers this. "You're a wanted man. You killed that banker. You'll be in jail sooner than I will," he bluffs.

"Perhaps," I agree, "but maybe not. You did me a favor by putting my name out as a person of interest. The FBI will eventually confirm that I put them onto the warehouse location where they unfortunately didn't arrive until after a terrible turf war had played out between two rival Russian gangs. It's well known that I haven't been in town for over a decade, so I obviously have nothing to do with this mess. I stumbled into it when the reporter convinced me that my ex-girlfriend was murdered. And the odds are that a forensic examination will be able to tie George Jeffrey's murder to one of the guns the FBI recovered from the mobsters in the warehouse. When it comes out that you and your department were corrupt, in bed with a gang procuring underage girls for child molesters, I think your credibility will pretty well be shot, don't you?"

I can see the wheels in Peterson's brain turning. He's always been a booster, always anxious to support the winning team. He's trying to find an angle, a way to help himself.

"What do you want from me?" he says gruffly.

"Help," I say. "I know this operation extends past this little town. I'm willing to bet that you know a man named Constantine Drubich."

I see the flicker of recognition in his eyes. He can't hide it, and he knows I've seen it. His shoulders slump.

"Do you have a way to contact him?" I ask. Buddy nods. "How?"

"His cell phone."

"Your going to call him now and tell him that you need to meet him tomorrow in this area. Tell him you'll text him the location in the morning, and that he's to meet you at noon. Tell him it's urgent." Peterson considers this for a moment more, but I can see the fight has gone out of him. He looks to his nightstand. His phone isn't there, but I hand it to him and after a moment of fiddling with it, he dials a number. Constantine doesn't answer, so Buddy leaves the message as I've spelled it out.

I get up to leave but pause just as I reach the inlaid wood frame of his bedroom door. I turn back toward him casually, almost as an afterthought.

"You've let some terrible things happen in this town," I say, enunciating slowly. "Melissa was murdered because of you."

Buddy considers this for a minute and I watch him struggle with it. In his heart, Buddy knows he is going to jail. A part of him wants to come clean and be forgiven. I know what I represent to Buddy, even though I'm not the man he thinks I am. I'm counting on that.

"I've been living with that every day, son," Peterson finally responds, his voice catching.

"How did this start? How did you get involved with these people?"

"How does it ever start? You look the other way on a poker game because one of your buddies plays in it and then he sends you a case of beer. You drink it instead of returning it because it's a thank you, not a bribe. Then you catch some low-level dealer selling pot and you let him do it because he promises to tell you if anyone is selling crack or crystal meth. One day an envelope arrives with 10% and you don't send it back. You find a brothel and let it go because it's clean and they don't cheat their customers. When they start giving freebies to your deputies, you look the other way. It's like cancer: if you don't kill it when it's small, you don't kill it at all."

"What about the Russians?" I press him.

"It started the same way. It just…got out of control," Buddy says reflectively. "I got a call from a friend. He asked me to tell him if we got any complaint calls for a certain address. And he wanted me to let him take care of it before we sent a unit out…" he began.

"Vanderhook?" I ask.

Peterson nods, "He'd done me a few favors and it didn't sound like a big deal, so I said okay. Then he drops by a few weeks later and gives me a case of single malt scotch. Before I know it, he's giving me addresses all over town and I'm getting envelopes full of cash from him. Dorothy's baby sister Annie? Her husband lost his job a few years back and those kids weren't going to be able to go to college. It didn't seem like a big deal to look the other way to help them."

"When did you figure out what was really going on?"

"About a year ago. There was a 9-1-1 call routed to us for a domestic disturbance at one of those addresses. I went over to handle it myself. Had to threaten to bring my deputies with a warrant and shotguns to get those bastards to let me in. Some guy beat the hell out of an eight-year-old girl. She screamed, and it was summer, when folks keep their windows open. I wanted to lock the bastard up, but the Russians threatened me. They told me they'd expose me and hurt my family. They knew where the money had been going – to Annie and the kids. They said there'd be a house fire; they'd all die if I tried to shut them down."

"And Mel?" I ask quietly.

"One of the girls snuck out of a house last week. It's happened before but they don't bring girls here who can speak English, so it's not usually a problem. Only this time, Melissa found this girl and you know Melissa spent that time in Russia, so she understood what the girl was saying. The guy who was running that house, he figured it out, broke into Mel's house and killed her. Michael, in spite of everything I'm telling you, I never would have let that happen if I knew," Buddy says, and I can see that there are tears in his eyes. I stare back at him coldly until the man averts his gaze.

"Do you know who this man is, the one that killed her?" I ask. Buddy starts to answer, starts to speak, and I can see the lie on his lips. I shake my head slowly. Buddy pauses to consider his options. He decides to tell me the truth.

"His name is Yuri. Big blond guy with arms like a wrestler," Buddy says. "Does he have tattoos here?" I ask, pointing to the back of my neck. "Intertwined snakes?" Buddy nods, "He does, but a lot of them do."

"I think I've seen Yuri. He tried to kill me," I say, with no trace of emotion in my voice.

"Then you're lucky to be alive," Buddy says and then reconsiders. "I know that sounds strange, especially after Monday night. It looked like that warehouse was hit by an armored division, but it was just you, wasn't it?" Buddy expects me to answer but I don't. "Still, though, there's something about Yuri. He's not like the others. They're all in it for the money but…it's something else with him. He wasn't among the living or the dead that we counted last night, by the way. If he disappeared, it's just as well. I would steer clear of him if I were you."

I consider this. Part of me would like nothing better than to hunt Yuri down and see just how different he is. But Alpha's words are coming back to me and I don't think I'll get a pass on a private vendetta. So I file the information away as I leave the house. I walk around the corner, where I slip into the passenger seat of a black Chevy Suburban. Dan Menetti is at the wheel, wearing an FBI windbreaker over his suit. I peel open a Velcro flap on my jacket and pull out the recording device concealed beneath it, handing it to him.

"Did he talk?" Menetti asks anxiously. I nod. He smiles, interlaces the fingers of his two hands behind his head and leans back for a moment. "Ah, this makes these late nights in the middle of nowhere worth it."

"I think he'll cooperate when you pick him up," I say. "And I'd appreciate it if you keep this out of a trial if at all possible."

"It's not my call, but I'll see what I can do," Menetti replies as he nods sympathetically. "The accountant gave us eight hours of tape today. It looks like this little ring was the pilot project for a national operation. This is big stuff."

"How far did it go?" I ask.

"The accountant didn't know. I understand you're working on another lead?"

"Yes. It's possible that the SVR may have got the Tambov gang to start this operation to trap high profile men for blackmail: a pedophile's honey trap. I had Sheriff Peterson place a call to the First Cultural Attaché at the Russian Consulate. He looks to be the organizer."

Menetti whistles. His thick black eyebrows rise in an unbroken line. "He would be a great catch if you can help us reel him in. Of course he's got diplomatic immunity, but I'm sure State would love to either expel him or threaten the Russians to reveal his involvement in order to get something else they want." Which means that either way the sonofabitch behind all of this is going to walk away. Which I knew the moment I heard he was a consular guy. I've already figured out that the only way to make Constantine pay is to make him look incompetent with his superiors. Shutting down the Conestoga operation with as much publicity as possible is a good first step.

This gives me another thought. "I disabled Peterson's home phone and cable lines and I've got his cell phone, but it would be good if you could pick him up in the morning before he can get to the office."

Menetti shakes his head. "I need to get this to the SSA in charge of the case and he'll want a transcript before we procure an arrest warrant. I doubt we'll be able to execute the warrant before tomorrow afternoon. Sheriff Peterson is an elected official and the presiding legal authority in this town, so we have to play this by the book."

"Understood," I say, but this unsettles me. The Buddy Peterson I just left was a defeated man, but a lot can change in a few hours. I move to open the door to the Suburban and Menetti grabs my arm.

"You were smart to bring your old boss into this. I understand there won't be any further investigation into the shooters from the other night – all resources are being put into rolling up the Tambov Gang's activities in the U.S. We're accepting the accountant's story that it was a rival gang, even though there are some holes in that theory. I've never seen somebody finesse an FBI investigation that way."

I agree that it's impressive but I wonder what price I'll pay for wriggling off the hook.

Chapter Seven –

Thursday

My eyes snap open as I wake to the unfamiliar buzz of a Blackberry. The vibrating feature is designed to be urgent enough to attract attention through a briefcase or handbag, but on the hard surface of the laminated black nightstand, it yowls like a hungry cat. I extend a hand in time to catch it as it plunges over the side of the nightstand toward the floor. I fumble with the buttons one-handed for a moment before it silences itself. It takes me a few more seconds to remember the key sequence to unlock the device and retrieve the message. It's a data file from Sammie, who lets me know he's been instructed to support my activities. The file is a dossier on Constantine Drubich. It paints a somewhat darker picture than the description I've gotten from Veronica. I turn and look over at her, still sleeping soundly, her face tilted toward me on her pillow, the covers rising slowly with her respiration. I can't quite believe she's there. As I slide off the bed, her fingers, still intertwined with mine, grasp and pull me back toward her. My first instinct is to pull away, but I hold Veronica's hand for a moment before my fingers slide free. This is unfamiliar territory for me. Maybe it shouldn't have been a surprise that we'd fall together after the trauma of the past few days, but it caught me completely off-guard. I shift my focus to the Blackberry.

Drubich is forty-five years old, a child of the Cold War. He was an intelligence officer with the KGB and served briefly in the same section as Vladimir Putin. He progressed to postings in the Baltic States and then the Middle East between the two Gulf Wars. He is Georgian by birth and was in Tblisi when Saakashvili came to office in 2004. He was reprimanded and recalled almost immediately. While the dossier doesn't say why, the implication is that his loyalties to Russia were questioned. He was sent to St. Petersburg, a backwater for the SVR, and spent four years there until his unexpected promotion to the posting in New York. Now he heads the SVR intelligence network in the financial capitol of the world. He's dark, handsome and speaks six languages fluently. And of course he's Veronica's former lover. I can't wait to meet him.

I roll off the bed, grabbing keys and a Sig-Sauer P226 from the night-stand. The keys go into a pocket and the gun slides into a loop holster at the small of my back, between a white oxford shirt and black jeans. I pull on a sturdy pair of Merrill Trail Runners, shrug into black raincoat and glance at my watch. It is seven in the morning. I've slept just three hours.

I spot my contact sitting alone at a deuce in the window of a small pub as I cross Partition Street in Saugerties. It's a clear day, and the pub sits in a line of cheerful businesses near the center of the town. A red sign saying just "Pig" sits above it, and the building itself is highlighted in red over the cream façade. The shop next door has yellow trim and window frames, and the effect of these touches of color on the block is transformative. Saugerties is the good twin of Conestoga. The center of the town has the same pre-war architecture as my hometown, the same rough-at-the-edges Catskills grit. Unlike Conestoga, however, Saugerties been renewed by a flourishing of its downtown area. Restaurants, galleries and shops sit cheek to jowl with other small businesses. Young families move here instead of trying to escape. The gastro-pub I've chosen for the rendezvous with Constantine Drubich is a good example of the changes. In Conestoga it would be a seedy bar where derelicts congregate over bottles of Muscatel and Miller High Life. Here in Saugerties, Pig features artisanal beers and exotic food like a coconut tofu sandwich and jerk chicken. I've spent an hour watching the bar and the street to ensure that Constantine has come alone. Veronica is less than a block away in the G8. There's only one problem. The man who entered the pub ten minutes ago and looks so obviously out of place there, the man sitting at the table in the window of Pig Bar & Grill as instructed, is not Constantine Drubich.

Of course I'm not Buddy Peterson either, so it seems only fair that Drubich has sent a proxy. But I have to wonder if Buddy tipped him off, and whether that means I'm pursuing a dead end or worse. I step inside the pub and the man at the window table immediately rises to greet me. It's clear that he knows my face. That's another bad sign.

The Pig draws a mix of Catskill hipsters and local crowds. The man in the severe black suit who extends his hand is neither. He is tall and fair, near my own age and looks to be exceptionally fit. The suit is not tailored, and I get the sense he's not entirely comfortable in it. I glance down at his shoes.

They look like dress shoes, but they aren't. They have rubber soles with a shallow tread pattern, so he can still run in them. They fit much better than the suit. As I take his hand, I see the calluses, the accumulated wear of real labor. This guy is a soldier, not a diplomat. That's the third bad sign.

"Constantine Vladimirovich Drubich regrets that he is unable to attend today due to pressing consular matters," the man says, bowing slightly. His voice is deeper than his size would suggest. "My name is Kiril Ivanov Dmitriev. It is a pleasure to meet you, Mr. Herne."

I know that he knows it, but hearing Dmitriev use my name makes me flush. Spycraft has never been my strong suit and I've already been out-maneuvered at it. At the end of the day, I'm more of a blunt instrument. I try to remind myself that Dmitriev isn't a spy, either. We sit down. Dmitriev orders a glass of dark microbrew and a bratwurst while I opt for a burger and a Coke. I ask Dmitriev where he's from and he names a small town outside of Kiev.

"You're Ukrainian, then?"

"Yes, I am by birth, although my family has lived in Russia since I was a very small child. Have you visited the Ukraine?"

"Just a few trips to Kiev. It's a beautiful city," I say. There's no point dissembling. This guy has read the dossier the Russians have on me. At least one of those trips will have featured prominently in it.

"It is a very different place these days. You must make a point of visiting again soon," Dmitriev replies. He starts to speak again but just at that moment the bartender steps over to the table with our food. We instinctively revert to small talk while we eat and Dmitriev darts in and out of Russian, obviously testing my command of the language. He has prepared for this meeting, and he even knows something about my current role in the State Department. He also makes more than one passing reference to my military background. I return the favor and he nods in silent acknowledgement. After the plates are removed, I clear my throat.

Dmitriev picks up on the cue without missing a beat. "Indeed, to business. The Russian government was very distressed to learn of the involvement of the Tambov Gang in the prostitution ring. They are a very serious criminal enterprise and they have caused us a good deal of trouble in St. Petersburg. Please accept our apology and convey it to your government. Our Ambassador in Washington will be meeting with your Secretary of State tomorrow to repeat this message. We also understand that a very good friend of yours was killed and this distresses us greatly. Please accept a personal apology from my government," Dmitriev says formally. He is obviously reciting a prepared statement.

"They were certainly criminals, but they were also very useful to your government, weren't they?" I push Dmitriev to measure his ability to stay on script.

"My country admits to no involvement. But perhaps we could speak confidentially? For the ears of you and your direct superiors only?" Dmitriev asks.

"Yes, of course," I reply calmly, letting the Russian steer the conversation. Dmitriev pulls out a small hand-held device that looks like a personal digital assistant with a very small screen. He flicks a button. A man at the bar immediately starts shaking his cell phone, as it dies in the middle of his conversation.

"You stumbled onto what was a very productive operation for us, but an old one. It should have been shut down some time ago. We have no desire for further unpleasantness," Dmitriev says carefully. I watch him closely. He's lying.

"The girls I saw hadn't been alive long enough to make this a very old operation," I say coldly. "Have you ever seen a six-year-old forced into prostitution?"

Dmitriev turns a shade paler and stiffens. That's the military honor I was looking for. This business must sicken him. That's probably why Constantine sent him. "I am certain that you are correct, Mr. Herne. It is extremely distasteful."

I nod, "Yes, it is."

"I am here to assure you that we want no further involvement in these matters, but also to warn you," Dmitriev says. He lifts a briefcase and puts it on the table. With a backwards glance at the bar, he pops the locks and opens it a fraction, withdrawing an envelope. He slides it over to me.

"What this?" I ask, and Dmitriev nods for me to open it. Inside I find a stack of black & white, 8x10 photos. I recognize the man in the top photo. It's Yuri.

"The first man is Yuri Ivanovich Kuznetsov. He is originally from Magnitogorsk, a factory town nine hundred miles east of Moscow. We know that he worked in a steel smelting plant as a child and that his father was a drunk and most likely abusive. He joined the army and attained a sergeant's rank. Then he was selected for the FSB and assigned to a Spetznaz unit called 'Vympel.' He served with distinction in Chechnya. He left the service and was recruited into the Tambov gang six years ago. He is a dangerous man, Mr. Herne."

I agree, wondering where this is going. "The next photo is of his brother, Mikhail Ivanovic Kuznetsov. He also served in the military, although with much less distinction. He followed Yuri Ivanovich to St. Petersburg and into the Tambov Gang. He was killed on Monday night. Yuri Ivanovich was not."

This time it's me who pales a shade. Dmitriev observes and continues, "The other photos are of men connected with the Tambov Gang who we believe are local but were not at the location of the attack on Monday night. Only two of these men have advanced military training but they are all subordinates to Yuri Ivanovich in the Tambov operation. It is very likely they will follow his directions in the aftermath of the deaths of so many of their friends."

I begin to understand. "And you're saying you believe they may cause further trouble?"

Dmitriev chooses his words carefully. "We believe that Yuri Ivanovich is unstable and might seek retribution against anyone he believes responsible for his brother's death. We do not wish to see anyone else harmed by Russian citizens."

"And he's also a problem you'd like to see removed," I conclude. I'm not receiving this information because of the Russian's abiding concern for my well-being. This must be why Dmitriev started out telling me lies about wanting to avoid more violence. Drubich is hoping I'll clean up his mess. We talk for a few minutes more and I leave the bar, making doubly sure that I'm not followed as I do. The hairs on my neck are standing up again.

"I've never been that frightened. When—when you didn't come at first, I thought they would kill me." Veronica is pale and beautiful in the sunlight. This is the first we've talked about what happened to her since I pulled her from the cage in the warehouse. I didn't want to risk being spotted by any of Drubich's men in the vicinity of my lunch meeting with Dmitriev, so we've made the twenty-minute drive to Woodstock. There is a small town green right in the center of Woodstock where Route 212 meets Rock City Road. I send her to get ice cream while I call Alpha and update him. I've got some concerns about both Yuri and Dmitriev, and we talk them through. I ask him for one specific favor, one that will probably cost me down the line. He agrees to my request a little too readily and I am still brooding about that when Veronica returns with two sugar cones, hers filled with chocolate ice cream, mine peanut butter. We sit with the cones in the chill fall air, enjoying the sun, which hasn't appeared for days.

"I'm sorry," I say, remembering how I felt when I stepped into that motel room and realized they'd kidnapped Veronica. I try to explain my actions. "If I'd given myself up to the men in our room, they would have killed both of us. You were only useful to them alive as a tool to get me to talk. They obviously didn't know your connection to Drubich," I say. I hope it's true.

"I didn't tell them anything. I wasn't really sure if my suspicions were right, anyway, and I wasn't sure if it would make things better or worse. After they figured out you weren't coming, they threw me in a cage with those girls. You can't believe what they did to those poor children. I don't think they'd seen the sunlight in months," she shivers. I wait for her to continue, sensing there's something she wants to get out.

"It's just...the whole time I was there, for twelve hours all I could think was that this might not have happened without me. If I hadn't given Constantine the idea for this in the first place..." she stops as her voice starts to quaver and then breaks into sobs, burying her face in my shoulder.

"This is not your fault," I say firmly. "Constantine could have come up with the same idea in a hundred different ways. He obviously has a very twisted mind. Even for a spy, it's beyond the pale. When the FBI picks up Sheriff Peterson, he will connect Drubich to the sex slavery ring. The Russian government is going to have a lot to answer for. This will shame them."

Veronica doesn't respond immediately. She stifles a few more sobs before straightening up and dabbing her eyes. Then suddenly she looks okay again. Her eyes aren't red or puffy and her hair has fallen back into place. I admire her for a moment. She's strong. I've seen soldiers come apart in less difficult circumstances. She kept her cool until she got out of that warehouse, kept her composure for another thirty-six hours before it finally caught up with her.

"How did you...how did you do all that? You were completely alone, weren't you? That place was full of all of those armed men and you still rescued me. That was amazing."

"It was foolish. I was very, very lucky. Some of those men were trained soldiers, but most of them weren't. They weren't working together. The entry technique I used depends on surprise and disorientation," I stop myself short of naming Delta Force as the originator of the technique. Even if The Unit has been all over the media and popular literature, its existence is still officially classified. "If the Tambov guys had trained together, they would have been able to cooperate and pinpoint my location, or use the girls more effectively as human shields. It could have been a disaster."

"Then why did you risk it?" she asks.

"I wasn't sure you would be safe if the FBI showed up before I got you out," I stammer. I should probably tell her a convenient lie, but I don't really know what else to say. Veronica turns a deep shade of red.

"How did you learn to do that? Is that what you did in the Army, for Colonel…?" here she uses the name Alpha has given her.

"I can't really talk about what I did for him. I can say those were some years I'd prefer not to dwell on." I change the topic, briefing her on the meeting with Dmitriev. She is both surprised and relieved to hear that Constantine did not show up. I'm uncomfortable. Sending a diplomat in his place might have made sense, but I'm not at all sure why Constantine would send an operator. Possibly he thought such a man would have more credibility with me because of my own background.

That gets me thinking. Sheriff Peterson is our only definitive connection to Constantine. Veronica makes a good circumstantial case, but she never saw anything that could tie Constantine to the Tambov gang. Buddy Peterson is the critical link, unless the accountant somehow offers more conclusive proof of Russian government involvement. The hardcore Tambov thugs will certainly never talk and if Constantine is competent, he'll have made sure there's no money trail that will lead us back to him. A man like Dmitriev is a special-purpose tool, and that purpose is not diplomacy. Perhaps he's in the area for other reasons. This gives me another thought. I turn to Veronica.

"We need to shake things up a little before Constantine starts feeling secure again. I'd like you to call him." Veronica clearly does not like this idea, but she hears me out. "If you tell him you shared the story about the U.N. with me and I'm convinced Constantine must have trapped that tall, redheaded man with his pedophile sex slavery racket, that might scare him. If you're right about the redheaded man, that is.

"If you warn Constantine, I'm willing to bet he'll try to make contact with the man. I doubt he'd risk a direct call, but we might get them both if they meet." This is one of the things I've discussed with Alpha on the phone. The FBI will establish surveillance of Constantine, and the NSA will be tasked to intercept his communications. There are limits to what they'll be able to find – consular communications are rigorously encrypted – but we agree there's a chance Constantine will lead us to the redheaded man. In the meantime, analysts at the FBI are putting together a book of men who fit the physical description in positions of power in our government for Veronica to review.

Veronica weighs my request and finally says, "If I agree, you have to promise me you'll make sure they get Constantine. Otherwise I'm dead. He'll know I was involved."

"He probably already knows. Besides, as an attaché, he has diplomatic status and immunity to prosecution. The best we'll be able to do is deport him."

"That's not enough," she says forcefully.

"I can't promise a specific outcome, but I can promise Constantine will not go unpunished." As I say this, I wonder what this promise will cost me. But Veronica is satisfied and agrees to call Drubich. I give her his cell number and she stands up to make the call as if that will make it easier to confront him. He doesn't answer his cell and she leaves a message, telling him what we've agreed. Then I call Dan Menetti on the Blackberry. He also doesn't answer, so I leave a message telling him what we're doing with Constantine Drubich and warning him that Sheriff Peterson might be in danger. Then I turn back to Veronica.

"This is the end of the road for you," I say.

"What do you mean?"

"You've stuck your neck far enough out already. I'll drive you back to your car in Conestoga. From there you should go straight to your parents' place. The FBI might stop by to show you some photos in the next day or two. Call in sick to work and stay home through the weekend. I think we'll be able to get this resolved by then."

Veronica argues this point but eventually concedes. We hold hands for a moment longer in the sun before we walk back to the car to face reality.

The little Blackberry buzzes just as I'm starting to get uncomfortable.

Instead of heading directly back east towards Saugerties to catch the Thruway, I've decided to cut though the heart of Catskill State Park. It's a gorgeous drive, a real delight with the G8, and the roads have little traffic. I turn west, planning to use Silver Hollow Road to make the jump north from Route 212 to Route 214, which runs east and west through the park. From 214, I'll catch State Route 23A and wind through Tannersville to the NY State Thruway, then exit north of Saugerties and twenty minutes closer to Conestoga. It is a longer drive, but the G8 pulls superbly as I wind out the motor and I'm able to relax for the first time in days.

Until I spot the tail, that is.

I first take note of the big Caddy while we are still on 212, which is no more than a two-lane local road as we wind away from Woodstock. Veronica is already asleep; her head slumps against the side of the headrest on the passenger seat. Now the red Cadillac is about a half-mile behind me. This wasn't suspicious when we were on 212, but as we turn off 212 to Eighmey Road, I see him slow so that he can make the turn while letting me pull ahead a ways. It's an understandable maneuver, but he's too close to escape my attention.

The Caddy itself stands out like a sore thumb. It's a bright red, brand-spanking-new CTS-V, a four-door sedan sporting a supercharged 556 horsepower V-8 lifted directly from the Corvette ZR-1, the only American supercar. The big Caddy can hit 100 miles per hour from a standing start in just over nine seconds, before a Prius would reach highway speed. Practically speaking, the Cadillac driver has little chance of escaping my notice on the nearly deserted mountain roads. It is a spectacularly bad vehicle for surveillance. The tarted-up $70,000 Caddy would draw stares anywhere in Greene County. In the mountains it looks as out of place as a limo at a pig roast. Now the driver is paying the price for having followed too eagerly. Even a soccer mom would notice that the Caddy is trying very hard not to get too close, and it would take a four-car team to trail us without me noticing.

My subconscious is just starting to break through to my active brain as the intersection with Silver Hollow Road comes into sight. I'm very tired, not having had a full night's sleep since I was in jail three nights ago. The human reaction to a lack of sleep tells a lot about our origins as a species. Human motor skills and even the ability to understand language are immediately affected by sleep deprivation, but the parietal lobe activates to take up the slack left by the decreasing activity in the temporal lobe. This allows people to process simple commands and retain some cognitive functions, but it dramatically decreases creativity and the ability to make intuitive leaps. For this reason, elite military operators are screened to be high functioning when sleep-deprived. At the end of one of the hardest days of Delta Force selection, a weighty reading assignment and a written essay followed our forty-mile hike. The purpose was to see which of us candidates retained the basic ability to reason while bone-tired, having slept less than four hours a night for an entire week and not at all for previous day and a half.

I'm not quite at that point, although I can feel myself approaching it. But something is forcing itself into my conscious brain as the Blackberry starts to buzz. Why did Dmitriev show up at Pig Bar & Grill? Why send a soldier? Then, as I'm raising the phone to my ear and I hear the nearly panicked voice of Dan Menetti on the other end of the line, it occurs to me. Before you send a dog on a hunt, you need to give him something to smell so he can catch the trail of the game you're after. In an instant I am convinced that all of the blather about Yuri and his brother was a distraction – or worse. Maybe those pictures are intended to provide a motive for me to be gunned down on a mountain road.

"Sheriff Peterson is dead," Menetti croaks, out of breath. "He had a heart attack about 11 this morning. We don't have a toxicology report yet, so this could just be a coincidence, or a reaction to stress, but I wouldn't lay odds on that."

As Menetti says this, I'm slowing the G8 down as I approach an intersection. This is the center of a tiny village called Willow. I pass a U.S. Post Office on my left. There's a gas station to my right at the intersection. It's an odd crossing because although four roads meet here – Eighmey, Van Wagner, Jessop and Silver Hollow – Jessop hits Van Wagner about thirty feet before Eighmey does from the opposite direction. I'm effectively approaching a T-shaped crossing where I need to turn either right onto Silver Hollow Road or left to Van Wagner. As I pull up to the intersection, a tall man in an orange striped construction vest and a yellow hardhat steps in front the car with a stop sign.

There's a white Ford F-150 waiting on Van Wagner about thirty feet away, also apparently waiting for the construction worker to flag it through. It is an extended cab-model with windows tinted so dark, I can't see the driver. I flick my eyes back to the Caddy in the rearview mirror. It has approached to within thirty yards and stopped. I'm instantly alert. I notice the Caddy's windows have exactly the same grade of tinting as the F-150, obscuring the passengers. *What are the odds?* I begin to think when a flash of movement from the F-150 catches my eye. A man pops up from the flatbed holding an RPG-7 – a Russian-made rocket propelled grenade, used all over the world against light vehicles and helicopters. The business end of the RPG swings toward the G8 as the bulky, broad-faced man in a black nylon jacket points it at my car. At the same moment the man in the red vest drops the stop sign and starts sprinting away from the intersection.

Dropping the Blackberry, I jam the G8's accelerator, depressing the clutch until the engine reaches 5000 rpms as I wrench the steering wheel around to the right. Then I drop the clutch and the G8's tail swings out – around to the left – as a cloud of smoke rises from the tires. Hopping forward, the G8 powers into the right turn just as the rocket from the RPG screams by, scant inches over the trunk. The rear end of the G8 catches the sprinting construction worker in the back, knocked him off his feet on the side of the road. The man has a silenced Glock in his hands as he goes sprawling forward. As we power through the turn, the heavy Ford pickup smashes into our tail, knocking the back end of the G8 loose. The G8 fishtails and as the stability control kicks in, I see the construction worker jump into the back seat of the F-150, the door having been thrown open for him

I glance in the rearview mirror just in time to see the RPG rocket slam squarely into one of the two pumps at the Yancy Country Store and Gas Station, a ramshackle white building with a green awning. The shaped charge from the RPG explodes as it hits the pump, igniting the gas in the line. A double-concussion followed by a pillar of flame rises like a tsunami over the small store as the bespectacled, white-haired owner runs out, his arms waving and his face a mask of disbelief.

An instant later, another man wearing mirrored sunglasses leans out of the front passenger window of the pickup with a Benelli M4 Super 90 Shotgun, a high performance semi-automatic piece with a folding stock. The man aims the weapon at the backside of the G8 and fires. The heavy buckshot hits the rear window, sprouting a mushroom of opaque glass in the center surrounded by a peppering of small divots.

Veronica, who woke abruptly when the F-150 hit us and was momentarily paralyzed by the explosion at the gas station, finally screams, ducking her head down and covering her ears with her hands. I wrestle with the steering wheel as the stability control fights the fishtailing rear end of the G8. The tail swerves right and left before it falls back into line as the chassis recovers from the destabilizing impact of the heavy truck. Then I stomp on the accelerator and the G8 surges forward, the 415 horsepower V-8 screaming. We immediately begin putting distance on the much slower F-150. Another glance in the rearview mirror shows the CTS-V pulling around the corner behind the truck.

"Grab the phone!" I shout to Veronica, who is already starting to regain her composure. Her arm snakes into the well beside my seat and emerges with the Blackberry after a moment. "Hit the speaker button," I yell. It takes her a moment to find it.

"Dan, are you still there?"

"What in the hell just happened?" It's the first time I've ever heard Menetti – a Catholic altar boy – swear.

"We just came about two inches away from being vaporized by an RPG-7."

"Fired by who?"

"I think it's a team led by the guy I just met for lunch – Karl Ivanov Dmitriev. I pegged him as an operator, maybe the leader of a Spetnaz team for the SVR. I'll bet you a steak dinner they're the same ones who took Buddy Peterson this morning. It means that someone – either Drubich or someone above him in the SVR – is trying to erase all the links between the Russian government and the Tambov Gang."

"Why wouldn't he have one of his guys pick you off on your way out of the restaurant, then?"

"I have a feeling that it's not me they're after. Veronica is the one who made the connection between the gang and the SVR. She's also the only one other than Drubich who's seen the redheaded man we're guessing might have been compromised." I glance over at Veronica as I say this. I did not consider the impact on her before I spoke the words. She starts trembling.

"What can I do?" Menetti asks.

"You should be able to pinpoint our location from the GPS chip in my Blackberry. Get me help as soon as you can." As I ask this I realize that by the time they mobilize they'll be doing cleanup of one sort or another.

"You got it. Good luck," Menetti says and gets off quickly.

Veronica is looking back at the truck and car pursuing us. She notices the damage to the rear windshield.

"Is that some kind of bulletproof glass?" she asks.

"It's a government car. There's no such thing as 'bulletproof,' but the car is lightly armored. The front and rear windshields are reinforced. There's also Kevlar in your seat back."

"Well they should have reinforced it some more. It looks like the rear window is about to fall off," Veronica says. The G8 bounds over a dip in the road, momentarily going airborne at 90 miles an hour.

"It's all a tradeoff," I respond, checking the rearview mirror. We are already a half-mile ahead of the F-150, which will never catch the G8 on a paved road. As I watch, the Cadillac CTS-V pulls around to pass the pickup. Then Silver Mountain Road sweeps right and I briefly lose sight of both vehicles. "If this car was armored well enough to stop high-velocity weapons, it would be a lot heavier and slower. Most pistols wouldn't penetrate the windshield but that Benelli fires a hot load – it'll eventually punch through. We need to make sure he doesn't get another clear shot." Still, I am less worried about the men in the F-150 than the Cadillac. The engine modifications to the G8 add enough horsepower to compensate for the additional weight of the up-armoring, but the CTS-V is a much faster car. Then again, I've seen a trained driver in a Honda Accord pass an amateur driving a Porsche 911 at Willow Springs in California.

As we reach the intersection of Silver Hollow Road and Lang, I whip the G8 into a right turn to stay on Silver Hollow, braking at the last moment, then swinging the car's rear end out intentionally to decrease the radius of the turn while maintain the maximum possible speed. As soon as I completed the maneuver, I'm back on the gas. In the rearview mirror, I see the Cadillac swing through the same intersection, perfectly lining up the rear wheels. It is gaining ground on us. So much for my hopes that an unskilled driver is chasing us. I push the G8 through a sweeping left hand turn followed by a right-hander. As I power through the second wide bend in the road, the outer wheels briefly scrape gravel.

As the CTS-V pulls to within a quarter mile, I see a sign blur by, showing an upcoming turn. I realize that Silver Hollow Road takes yet another turn, this one a full ninety degrees to the left, and that going straight will mean joining Cross Patch Road – a dead-end street that shoots straight up the side of a mountain. I stomp down on the accelerator, briefly gaining yards on the Cadillac. I blow past the intersection, ignoring the turn. After 300 yards, Cross Patch Road takes a dogleg to the left as it starts to ascend Little Rock Mountain. The moment we pass the turn and are temporarily out of sight of the Caddy, I hit the brake pedal full-force. The enormous ventilated disc brakes scrub the G8's momentum quickly as the antilock brakes with brake force distribution trigger, allowing me to keep steering control while braking. The speedometer needle sinks like the mercury on a weather gauge in the face of an approaching hurricane.

When the speed hits thirty, I step off the brakes and wrench the wheel of the G8 around to the left as I pulled the emergency brake. The big sedan pirouettes gracefully, swapping head for tale as it reverses directions on the road. As the G8 turns, I tap the power button on the window to lower it as I draw a 9mm Sig Sauer P226 from the loop holster at the small of my back left-handed. Just as I bring the weapon up and get it pointed out the window, the Cadillac comes screaming around the turn and I empty eight rounds – over half a clip – left-handed into it point-blank as it passes. Then I mash the accelerator on the G8 and speed back towards Silver Hollow Road, making the sharp right turn just as I spot the F-150 approaching from the opposite direction.

Silver Hollow Road gains over a thousand feet in elevation in just under a mile as it tracks the Warner Creek's twisting path through the mountains. We pull away from the F-150 immediately, building up a half-mile lead before the road bends left and starts descending, cutting through Silver Hollow Notch. We have almost pulled out of sight of the heavy-duty Ford when Silver Hollow Road abruptly ends, smacking right into Clove Road. I slam on the brakes as a BMW Mini zooms past at the intersection and the Ford pickup quickly draws closer. Then I take a right on Stony Clove Road, heading north. The road follows the valley between Hunter Mountain and Plateau – two of the thirty-five mountains in the Catskills with peaks above 3500 feet. Unfortunately, the road is dead straight, giving us no way to elude our pursuers. I quickly pull up to the Mini and attempt to pass, but I am forced to swerve back into my lane quickly as a Winnebago steams by in the opposite lane. Just as I pull the wheel left again, the boom of a rifle sounds and I see that a high-caliber rifle round has passed through both the rear and front windshields of the G8, leaving a fist-sized hole in the front windshield. In the same instant, the Mini explodes, its diminutive body flying up into the air.

I swerve left, barely avoiding the Mini careening through the air. I manage to keep the G8 on the road, but the big Ford pickup sees the Mini too late, slamming into it just as it lands. The big pickup starts to spin, almost in slow motion as it leaves the road. It hits a small depression and tips over, spinning on its roof with tremendous momentum through a nearly empty dirt parking lot and into Notch Lake. The two-ton truck crashes into the pond like a destroyer sliding out of drydock, sending a wall of water flying upward as it comes to an abrupt halt. The sniper who fired the big rifle from the pickup bed, the same broad-faced guy who'd handled the RPG earlier, is decapitated when the truck overturns and his headless body is dragged all the way to the pond.

I pick up speed again as we hit a clear patch in the road, but I see the Cadillac again, gaining on us quickly.

"W-what was that?" Veronica stutters, looked at the enormous hole in the front window. "Probably a Barrett M107 – a fifty-caliber sniper rifle. That round will punch through the plating on an armored car. It penetrated both windows and hit the gas tank on that Mini," I tell her as I look back. I have to shout to be heard above the roar of the wind in the car. The hole has created some very funky aerodynamics in the vehicle and even though the Cadillac has a half-dozen holes in its windshield, they can't be creating the same kind of havoc we're experiencing. "We're just lucky he didn't have a gyro stabilizer," I say. Veronica just shakes her head, growing paler by the moment.

"What kind of shape are you in?" I ask.

"I'm okay, I'll be okay."

I shake my head. "I mean what kind of aerobic shape are you in?"

"I run about five miles a day. I'm thinking about running the New York marathon next year."

"Good."

"Why?"

I don't answer immediately. The Cadillac is three quarters of a mile behind us, but it is gaining fast. Stony Clove Road is threading us between two of the taller peaks in the Catskills, and I know I have to do something before the guys in the Cadillac start shooting again. The road curves to the right as we emerge from the mountains and cross a small creek. There's a road leading off to the left and a hundred yards further, one to the right. I slam on the brakes. The G8 immediately starts scrubbing down speed, going from eighty to forty in fifty feet. Then I pull the wheel right and the tires scream as I hang the tail of the Pontiac out, barely making the turn onto Plateau Mountain Road. It's a narrow country lane – packed dirt and gravel with splashes of pavement – that is barely wider than the G8. We make it past the first bend and cross over a creek before I hear the big Caddy roar by. Even from a quarter mile, I can hear him hit his brakes as he sees the rubber

I've laid down and realizes I've turned off the road. But he misses the turn; I've gained a minute on him.

There's a turn off of Plateau Mountain Road to Jaymos Lane, which I'm relieved to see, although I don't take it. Then the road switchbacks and shoots two hundred feet up the side of the mountain before dead-ending. I pull the G8 up at the edge of the woods and pop the truck before I jump out, a stopwatch ticking in my head. I grab the soft case with my father's Winchester from the trunk, slinging it over my shoulder along with a small black bag. Thinking for a second, I scrounge the camouflage jacket that Jeff lent me for the deer hunt from my duffel bag and ditch the black raincoat I'm wearing. I glance at Veronica. It could be worse. She's in stretch casual pants and Nike running shoes, her concession to me in the morning. The Nikes won't give her much traction, but they're not terrible, either. I'm in much better shape with Merrill Trail Runners. I take Veronica's hand and gently pull her into the woods. I figure we have about thirty seconds before the Cadillac finds us.

Veronica strains her head to look upward at the seemingly vertical, 3000-foot climb. "Where are we going?" she asks.

"Straight up," I say. She gives me a look and I shrug. I know what at least one of the guys chasing us is wearing and he's not dressed for hiking. I climbed this particular mountain a dozen times as a kid. There's plenty of cover, even though a lot of the trees have lost their leaves at this time of year. Most importantly, we have a chance to get above our pursuers on higher ground. I'm pretty sure it's the best we'll do under the circumstances. I think about how to explain this to Veronica as we start into the woods.

"That Cadillac is a much faster car than ours and the road runs almost dead straight all the way to the Thruway. There aren't any big cross streets or intersections, either. Their driver knows what he's doing: there's no way we could have lost them. They would have caught us in another three or four miles, tops. Before that, probably one of the guys in that car would have gotten off a good shot and we'd be dead. Those guys are pros – more disciplined than any of those Russian mob guys who kidnapped you, better than any of them except Yuri. The only way to even the odds is with terrain. I grew up here. I know these mountains. It's our only chance."

"Where are we?" she asks as we start to climb the mountain, picking our way through the brush. The terrain slopes up at an improbable angle and Veronica starts slipping on the dense leaves almost immediately. I have to grab her wrist and pull her behind me, physically hauling her up the slope. She starts to make a joke about skiing uphill but I hush her. After we've ascended a hundred yards, we pause as I hear the Cadillac pull to a halt below. Even in October with half the leaves gone from the deciduous trees, the foliage is dense enough to prevent us from seeing the road. I count the sound of doors opening. Four. There are four men. At least we managed to lose the pickup with the RPG and the .50-caliber rifle. As I start moving up the hill, I fish a grenade out of the black bag. Veronica's eyes bug out. I answer the question she's already asked instead of the one written all over her face.

"This is Plateau Mountain – it's 3800 feet tall. That's big for the Catskills but tiny for just about any other range. But what this neck of the woods lacks in vertical elevation, it more than makes up for in terrain. Most people from other places don't quite believe how challenging the combination of wet leaves and smooth, round, muddy stones can make things. If you think you're having trouble with those Nikes, just imagine how those guys behind us are going to feel in Rockports. We're bushwhacking – making our own way up. There's a trail on the other side of this mountain. It's called The Devil's Path." That silences Veronica, who realizes she has to focus to stay on her feet.

We're about a quarter mile up the hill and another five or six hundred feet up in elevation when the grenade detonates. I tied a length of nylon cord at ankle level between two trees along our path and attempted to conceal it under leaves. The grenade was triggered by the rope.

"Do you think it got them?" Veronica asks.

I shake my head. "They may want us to think that, but I doubt it. Those guys are pros; I doubt they'd fall for a simple snare. But it will slow them down a little. They know I have a few tricks and they'll guess I could do something more devious. They'll have to go slower. It may buy us a little time."

We reach the first plateau after another fifteen minutes of hard climbing. I'm exhausted by the effort of dragging Veronica from tree to tree up the side of the mountain at the quickest pace I dared risk. I motion for Veronica to sit behind a big oak as I drop prone behind a downed tree. I pull the Winchester Model 70 from the padded case and feed three of the Holland & Holland .300 Magnum rounds. Then I rest the rifle on the log and look through the site.

I spot Dmitriev first. He's the one tracking me and he's made up some ground. He is doing surprising well on the leaves and muddy rocks although he doesn't look happy in his suit. He is smart enough to realize that he's vulnerable and he's using the trees as cover, trying to leave himself as little exposed upslope as he can while following our tracks. The man with him is not as graceful. He is a bear, standing a full head above Dmitriev. He looks like the type who would be more comfortable in wrestler's gear than the chalk stripe suit, which doesn't fit him well. I watch him slip, nearly twisting his ankle, and recover his balance by pulling himself up on a slender tree, bending it over to the point where it seems close to snapping. I can see the curses on his lips as he struggles on.

That leaves two men unaccounted for. I start a pattern search scanning the woods in grids through a pair of binoculars I pull from the small black case. Time is running perilously short. It takes me about a minute to spot the two operators. Dmitriev has done what I would have, if the situation were reversed – flanked one man out on either side of us. Veronica and I are climbing the spine of the mountain, which broadens out to a plateau at the peak, so we can't be easily out-flanked in a tactical sense. But Dmitriev has sent one man running through the woods along either side of the mountain, not gaining much elevation but attempting to skirt around and summit the peak behind us, which would expose us to crossfire. It's ambitious, but I would have tried it, too.

I admire the progress one of the men is making as I spot him somewhat past our position but five hundred feet lower. He looks like a genuine trail runner, moving gracefully through the foliage. He's not wearing a suit, perhaps that's why. It looks like he's decked out as a fall jogger – good cover if they needed to trail me through Saugerties. I'm sure I never spotted him, though.

The fourth man is a little less elegant. He has a blond buzz cut and is proceeding in a very workmanlike fashion on the old railroad tracks that skirt Plateau Mountain on the West, to my left. Unlike Dmitriev and the runner, however, he's not being particularly careful about his cover. He probably doesn't think he's in any danger.

I make a quick decision and site in on the trail runner to my right first. He's the man most likely to cause us trouble if he manages to get around behind us. It's a tricky shot because my view of him is partly obscured, and he's moving at a good clip. I have to lead him while anticipating the tree cover. I run through the calculations, then still myself and focus on the shot. When I squeeze the trigger, I know I've made the shot. The Winchester booms and I pull the scope back down on him just as he crumples to the ground. Without wasting time, I turn the rifle on the man on the other flank. He has stopped dead and has his hand on his ear, apparently speaking to Dmitriev through a comm device. This is a longer shot, perhaps 500 yards, but considerably easier as he is not moving. I squeeze the trigger again. He hits his knees clutching his throat then topples forward.

I look straight down the mountain for Dmitriev and the last Russian but as expected, they've gone to ground. It should slow them down further, though, and make them nervous. I'm counting on it. But now they're bound to be watching upslope, looking for movement. I flatten myself beneath the tree and slip my hand into the soft black bag, finding a familiar shape. I pull the pin on the grenade and release it in an arc, a shallow toss of just twenty yards or so. Then I toss another grenade just to the right of it. They start streaming smoke after three seconds, and soon there's a thick cloud between Dmitriev and us. I slip the Winchester back into its case and grab Veronica's hand.

"What happened?" she whispers.

"Now there's just two of them," I answer, "so we might just live after all." In truth, I'm still not sure.

We continue upward for a half hour before reaching Devil's Path on the flat top of the mountain, just a couple hundred feet shy of the 3800-foot peak. There's little view from this angle and the trail, as I'd remembered, winds its way through dense woods at the top. Many of these are evergreen, which makes this better ground for my purposes. There are tracks from other hikers on the trail and a few even look fresh. It may confuse Dmitriev, but I don't count on it. It's true that he didn't strike me as a backwoods type – a lot of Spetznaz guys spend their careers in urban combat situations – but he also seems exceptionally competent. Not knowing how to track would be a serious gap in his skill set.

I finally find the spot I'm looking for around a bend in the trail, where a profusion of bushes and a few old knotty pines look promising. I hand Veronica the rifle and the soft case, and zip up the camouflaged jacket. Then I pull a small Beretta from a holster on my leg. I chamber a shell and show her how it operates. She hasn't fired a gun before, so I'm not very hopeful. On the other hand, if she needs to use the gun I'll already be dead, so it's as good a play as any.

"Follow the trail three hundred paces and then step off into the woods and find a place to hide yourself where you can see the trail. If I come to get you I'll say your name before I get too close. Shoot anyone else who steps off that trail in your direction."

"What are you going to do?" she hisses.

"Try to end this," I say. Then I step backwards a dozen paces, careful to place my feet back in the tracks I've already made. I look up and spot a sturdy branch and jump to reach it. In a few moments, I work myself up ten feet. I find a position where I'm well covered but have a clear field of view directly below me. Then I slip an SOG Seal Pup knife from its sheath, which I've attached to my belt at the small of my back next to the Sig. I settle in to wait.

In the end, they're closer to us than I expect, less than five minutes behind. I hear the big Russian first, although he's walking a few feet behind Dmitriev. He seems to drop his feet like sandbags with every step. The hike can't be easy for someone his size. Despite what you'd think, most operators are not built like that – too much of our job is based on moving quickly and unobtrusively in confined spaces. Dmitriev moves like a jungle cat; there's no question in my mind that he's at the top of his class. As I've guessed, he knows how to track. In fact, he steps only a few paces past my hiding spot before he stops, looking puzzled. He has evidently looked ahead and seen that my trail evaporates. The big Russian stops almost directly below me. I drop from the branch. Despite what you might think, hitting a man in the neck with a flat bladed knife between C4 and C5 from a ten-foot drop is not all that routine. It would be impossible to do cleanly if the blade arrived first, so I land on his back, using my momentum to knock him forward off of his feet, and only drive the blade into the back of his neck once we've hit the ground. The moment I do, Dmitriev is turning with a Heckler & Koch M5SD, and I pull the big man over on top of me, praying that the relatively lightweight 9x19mm Parabellum rounds don't pass entirely through the enormous Russian's burly chest. The bullets trace an arc down the corpse, but I don't feel any bee stings. I draw the Sig from the small of my back with some difficulty and fire point-blank over the dead Russian's shoulder. Three of the rounds hit Dmitriev squarely in the chest. The fourth gets him in the neck.

I get up and walk over to Dmitriev, kicking the MP5 away from his hands. Then I lean over him. He's not dead – he's wearing a vest, and only the neck shot has wounded him. It will be enough, though. He stares at me with uncomprehending eyes. Even though I can do nothing for him, I linger for a moment. There's something I want to ask him. I pull a clean cloth from my pocket and hold it over his wound, momentarily staunching the flow of arterial blood.

"How did you track me to Woodstock?" I ask gently. "I didn't see you."

"The envelope," he gasps. There is the dim reflection of professional pride in his eyes. "The envelope I gave you has a radiologic signature… not hazardous," he says. He exhales and the life flows from him with his breath. I look at him and see myself. It's a horrible waste of a good man. I think about the manila envelope with the pictures of Yuri and his associates. I have to appreciate the irony – even Yuri's photograph is radioactive.

It takes me a few minutes to collect Veronica. I'm careful to speak her name repeatedly on the trail, worried that she might shoot me accidentally. She's done well so far, but you can never tell with amateurs. From the rate her hands are trembling when I help pull her from the hollow of a tree, my fear is not misplaced. I don't take her back toward the bodies, but continue forward. In fifteen minutes, we reach the summit of Plateau Mountain. We sit on a rock.

"They're all dead?" she asks after what seems like a decent interval. It's colder on top of the mountain and we huddle together.

"Yes," I say.

"Who were they?" she asks.

"The man who met me in Constantine's place for lunch and his team. I think they were Spetznaz – commandos – in the SVR, the Russian foreign intelligence service."

"Why did they want to kill you?" she asks.

"They were after you, not me. Like I told Menetti, if Dmitriev was trying to kill me, his best play would have been right in Saugerties, outside the restaurant. With Buddy Peterson dead, you're the only link between the Tambov Gang and the Russian government. This whole scandal will be highly embarrassing to the Russians if it points back to them. I don't know whether Constantine sent them to clean up his mess or somebody above him is trying to mop up the entire operation. Either way, this was a very good team they sent after us."

"And they're all dead."

"Well, someone might have survived in the pickup truck." I say and then look at her directly, making contact with those green eyes. They force me to answer the question. "But…I get your point. That's what happens in these situations. A lot of people die. It's not very pretty. I don't miss it." Not this part, anyway.

She just shivers and leans against me. After a while she smiles and laughs. "I guess I can see why you'd leave that life. But now I also totally get why your boss wants you back so badly." I look at her in shock for a second, not sure I'm hearing her right. Then I laugh too. It's an unfamiliar feeling in my throat.

I hear the sound of a helicopter overhead and stand as I scan the horizon. I'm hoping the FBI has managed to track the GPS signal in my Blackberry and that it's our ride.

"We're almost there, Orion. A sworn statement from Ms. Ryan along with our identification of the team that intercepted you this afternoon will be enough for your colleagues in the State Department to sit down with their Russian counterparts in the next twenty-four hours and express our displeasure. I believe we are looking to keep the Russians from vetoing a resolution in the Security Council for stronger sanctions against Iran. If we don't get the answer we want, the whole story will hit the *Washington Post* next week. Ms. Ryan should be safe, but I've asked the FBI to extend in-home protection to her for the next few days."

"Thank you, sir," I reply. I'm glad that Veronica is finally going home and that someone will watch her. And while I should be appalled that all misery of the past week has become a bargaining chip to save some parliamentary maneuver at the United Nations, I'm not. I was in this game for long enough to know that even that trifle is more of a concrete outcome than we usually get. In fact, it would be a big win for both the FBI and the Activity. Still, I can't help feeling a little bitterness that so many lives were lost or ruined – from Mel to all of those little girls and even Dmitriev and his men – because of a bunch of spy games. It may seem like we're all the same people in the intelligence community, but operators go in to do a job and get out. We fix problems. We don't much care for the people who create them.

"You may be interested to know that Kiril Dmitriev was the man's real name. We have a substantial file on him – he was an operator with the Vympel counterterrorist unit for about a dozen years until he was recruited to Zaslon. They're the SVR's counterpart to the Special Activities Division at CIA," Alpha clears his throat. The Special Activities Division is sort of like a Delta Force within the CIA, but both Delta and the Activity have had a notably poor relationship with SAD. But then again, nobody ever trusts the CIA. "Dmitriev's team is – or was – thought to be one of the top elimination teams with Zaslon. They've caused us a lot of trouble over the past few years. There's a good deal of excitement in the big building over their retirement." The big building is the Pentagon – top brass. I sigh. It's hard to imagine that my name is not being connected with all of this at some level. I feel Alpha's tendrils insinuating themselves.

"What's your update?" Alpha asks.

"I'm with Special Agents Holland and Brennan in Oyster Bay. We're on surveillance of Constantine Drubich. Veronica rattled his tree this afternoon by telling him I was sure he'd compromised the red-headed man she met at the U.N. party, and that the FBI is actively searching for the guy. As far as the NSA has been able to tell us, Drubich did not make any unusual calls at work today. It will take more time for his encrypted communications to be analyzed. But we think there's still a chance he'll make a move to warn the man, so we're going to sit on him for a couple of days to see if we get lucky. I'll help you through the weekend if necessary, but I have to be back at work on Monday at the latest."

"Without question, you should get back to work whenever you need to, Orion. What you've already accomplished is greatly appreciated. I have one request of you right now, however. You are better qualified at surveillance than those men you're with," Alpha says, his voice echoing in my ear through the encrypted Bluetooth earpiece wirelessly connected to my government-issued Blackberry. I'm suddenly glad he's not on speakerphone. "I'd ask you to ensure that Mr. Drubich does not suspect he is being watched. My understanding is that they've only devoted a single car to the operation, which is troubling."

"Yes sir, that's correct," I reply. "This afternoon a tracking device was planted on Constantine's car when it was being washed. The device allows us to operate a tail outside of visual range, so I think we're okay, but it's still not an ideal situation. The Russian security people sweep these cars all the time, so they might find it. And when Constantine drives into the city, we always risk losing him if we get too far away and he takes off on foot. I'm here for about six more hours. There's a backup team relieving us after midnight." In truth, I am even more concerned than I let on. Alpha can read between the lines, and the fact that he'd even ask the question tells me he's on the same page. The FBI doesn't seem to be taking Drubich as seriously as I'd have expected. Menetti is enthusiastic about the potential connection, but some of his superiors are suffering from not-invented-here syndrome because the lead has been handed to them from the outside. I don't know why else the FBI would be skimping on resources, but there might be some political maneuvering going on.

All I'm sure of is that I'd much prefer multi-vehicle surveillance of Drubich supported by aerial drones and audio and video monitoring of his house. But you play with the hand you're dealt, so I'm sitting in a black Suburban two blocks away from Drubich's expensive house on Long Island with two Special Agents from the Albany Field Office. They seem like good men, but they're out of their depth with Drubich. He's one of Russia's top spies, and he's bound to spot our amateur level surveillance pretty soon.

Drubich has been home from work for just over an hour, so there's an even chance we'll be spending the evening sitting in the Suburban and hoping that one of Drubich's neighbors doesn't get worried and call the cops on us.

I wrap up the conversation with Alpha, which has been circumspect by necessity. I have mixed feelings about our pursuit of the redheaded man. Part of me says it's a wild goose chase; we are staking out Drubich on the possibility that after seeing a redheaded man one time at a U.N. party several years ago, he managed to compromise and blackmail him and will feel the urgent need to meet him in person in the next day or two. It sounds pretty thin: I-hope-I-win-the-lottery thin. On the other hand, Veronica has pretty good instincts – I don't think I'd bet against her with my Final Four picks given what I've seen in the past couple days. I'm more than willing to spend a little time sitting in an SUV eating cold sandwiches to try to prove her right. I'm curious how these guys plan to follow Drubich in Manhattan tomorrow morning. It's impossible to double-park an SUV on Fifth Avenue near the Russian consulate. We'll need more help to follow the man on foot, that's certain.

I'm only half-surprised when, just a half-hour later, a black Mercedes S550 noses out of the gated driveway to the spymaster's house. Confident of his electronics, Agent Holland allows the big sedan to pull out of sight before flicking the Suburban's headlamps on and pulling away from our parking spot. We're lucky that Drubich doesn't live at one of the toniest addresses in Oyster Bay, as those houses are on private, looping roads with peaceful-sounding names like Sherwood Gate, where a strange SUV with blacked out windows parked on the street couldn't sit for more than thirty minutes without entertaining a visit from the police. The street Drubich lives on is nice enough, but even the houses with high shrubs and gates are low-rent, with price tags in the single-figure millions. I'm sure that it's all worth it to live on the North Shore of Long Island, just a stone's throw from the Long Island Sound.

The Mercedes' position is marked by a moving red dot on the built-in GPS in the Suburban. It replaces the standard navigation system and feeds us road directions that allow us to stay just beyond visual range of the Mercedes. We wind our way through the local roads of the Oyster Bay, then onto Route 106 south toward Jericho, where we pick up the Long Island Expressway headed for Manhattan. Following a car without actually seeing it is new to me and feels more like playing a video game than real surveillance work. While the technology has been around for a while, this is a much slicker implementation than anything that was in the field when I was with the Activity.

By the time we get through the midtown tunnel, Agents Holland, Brennan and I are all convinced that Constantine is heading back to work, but we're wrong. Instead of turning north, Drubich cuts south on Second Avenue, then twenty blocks later turns east on 14th Street. Holland has the good sense to reel him in a little at this point, because if Drubich pulls into a parking garage he could be out of his car and on foot before we can spot him. There's not too much danger in Drubich picking up the tail in Manhattan as long as he's on the major cross streets, though.

Constantine cuts east to west across the entire island, passing the Apple Store on Ninth Avenue into the trendy Meatpacking District, a cobble-stoned neighborhood of exclusive boutiques, outdoor cafés and expensive restaurants. As we close to within three cars of the S550, Constantine makes the turn north into Chelsea and onto Tenth Avenue. He slows the big Benz as he passes the Chelsea Carwash and practically crawls through the intersection at 15th Street.

This block looks like a throwback to an earlier era. An iron viaduct snakes above the eastern side of the street, a sooty python of an elevated trestle that once enabled the great rail companies to transport meat to the markets. After shooting over Ninth Avenue, the viaduct wraps itself around the old Nabisco factory in the enormous Chelsea Market complex, then turns south into the heart of the Meatpacking District. The portion of the viaduct crossing Ninth Avenue between 14th and 15th looks like an iron catheter invading a vital artery, while an art deco pedestrian bridge from the 1930s soars overhead.

Constantine pulls his S550 over at the far the end of the block, in front of a fire hydrant. Agent Holland immediately steers the Suburban toward the opposite curb, cutting off a taxicab, which speeds around us with a belligerent honk of the horn. We are about fifty feet shy of the Mercedes on the opposite side of the street.

"I'll follow him on foot," I say, opening the passenger door of the Suburban. "Once I figure out which direction he's heading you can drop Agent Brennan ahead of him. If he steps into one of these places," I nod at CraftSteak and Del Posto, the restaurant Drubich has pulled in front of, "we're going to need more help, because I'm not dressed for that kind of scene and you two will stand out like a sore thumb." Agents Holland and Brennan are both wearing dated grey suits. The nicest thing I can say is that neither one of them is sporting a clip-on tie. Knowing the high percentage of lawyers among FBI field agents, I'm a little surprised they aren't better dressed. I guess their duties in Albany don't call for expensive suits. I'm wearing a cream-colored button-down shirt over black jeans, both of which I found in the bag from Alpha that we rescued from the bullet-riddled G8 on our way out of the Catskills. I've had to ditch the muddy Merrell trail runners for a pair of black Adidas Sambas. I slip on a pair of clear Persol glasses from a lizard case in the pocket of a black Burberry raincoat as I slip out of the SUV.

I shuffle north on Tenth Avenue, watching Drubich from across the street as he peels a bill from a money clip and hands it to the valet who eagerly hops into the Mercedes and pulls away. Drubich crosses Tenth Avenue like a New Yorker – twenty feet shy of the actual intersection. He's wearing a black cashmere overcoat and walks with a gait very wealthy or very powerful people adopt – slow and commanding, as if challenging anyone to disturb him. I stop and bend over to tie my shoe as his gaze briefly sweeps in my direction. Then he's on my side of the street, stepping in front of the gracefully curved arch and billowing red drapes of the Japanese restaurant

Morimoto. Constantine crosses over 16th Street and turns to the right, out of my line of sight. I reach the intersection a moment later. Peering down 16th, I scan the sidewalks for Drubich, but he has vanished. An eight-story modern brick and glass residential building advertising luxury condominium rentals on multicolored vertical banners covers the entire north side of the street, and I don't see any shops on either side he might have entered. I experience a moment of panic, wondering if I've been out of the game too long and my instincts have gone to seed.

As I calm myself and take a breath, a young couple steps directly in front of me. The man has dark hair, thick and windblown, and sports a soul patch – a square bit of facial hair under the bottom lip that looks like a shaving accident to me. The woman is Asian, with long, lustrous black hair and an engraved silver belly-button ring peaking out from a short white tee shirt underneath an open ankle-length black jacket with a faux fur fringe. They've stepped from an exterior stairway hidden away in the corner of the residential building named The Caledonia on a brass plaque. I turn to the stairway and see that it leads up to the old train trestle.

I sprint up the staircase, which winds around an open elevator shaft. As I reach the railway trestle I've observed from Tenth Avenue, an elevator car carrying an elderly man with a walker passes me going down. I emerge into a different world.

The abandoned train trestle has been converted to an aerial park. A pathway of textured concrete with chunks of embedded granite snakes down its length, winding right and left between beds of wildflowers and native grasses. The vegetation, half of which might be properly called weeds by a fastidious suburban gardener, is carefully landscaped to appear wild, mirroring what must have been the prior condition of the abandoned railways. In places, bushes poke up between sections of the original train tracks. In others, the concrete has been formed into narrow strips of four parallel tracks with grasses peaking through them, in a playful allusion to the old railway. Slender metal poles sprout up waist-high through the flowerbeds, softly bathing the greenery in LED illumination. The section I've stepped into snakes between the Caledonia and an enormous tan brick building on the opposite side of the street. The walkway runs north and south above Tenth Avenue, and a dozen yards from where I stand, the path spears directly through the Chelsea market building.

I suddenly realized that I know where I am – I've read about this place. It is Manhattan's newest park, the High Line, and it only recently opened. The park was created by a concerted private effort to prevent the demolition of the abandoned railway lines that had been overgrown with beds of weeds and flowers – a sea of wild tranquility above the planned chaos of the streets below.

Even on a cool autumn evening, the park is busy. A good smattering of couples walk arm in arm alongside groups of friends and solo travelers. There are benches and chairs dotting the landscape and couples sit, watching the long grasses sway in the evening breeze and admiring elevated views of the city. New Yorkers are a legendarily industrious and commercial people – even the creation of Central Park involved the no-nonsense leveling of a teeming shantytown – and they normally move through their city at a frenetic pace that the rest of us would call a slow jog. The High Line, however, has a sense of serenity about it. Tourists and New Yorkers alike are strolling. It is an odd sensation to see the dramatic tapering of pedestrian velocity even as the raucous sounds of traffic moving on the streets underneath the park intrude.

As I enter the park, I adjust my pace and attitude to fit the crowd around me and consider my options. I don't see Drubich, but he could only have proceeded in two directions: north or south. I choose north, because the terminus of the park is just a couple of blocks in that direction. At the end of the Caledonia, a dozen people sit in comfortable fabric chairs on an elevated lounge connected to the residential building, sipping drinks as they chat and idly watch sightseers. The concrete path briefly gives way to a hundred foot section of cedar planks, like an enormous backyard deck. An outdoor amphitheater has been built into the trestle, stepping down from the main level of the park, penetrating the track bed halfway down to the street. Viewing windows at the bottom of the amphitheater allow rows of benches to observe the street below in an odd, voyeuristic inversion. At this time of the evening, half a dozen pairs of young couples sit quietly on the benches, straining for a moment of privacy.

The path narrows north of 17th Street, and I spot the Chelsea Piers sports complex straddling the Hudson River across from the futuristic, weirdly curved IAC building. The park consists of just a single path here, eight feet wide and flanked by beds of vegetation on both sides. There is another staircase leading down to the street at 18th, and I lean over to take a look at the street on both sides, but I don't spot Drubich. He could have popped up into the park as a way to shake a tail, but he wasn't so far ahead of me that he'd have been able to get back down out of the park this quickly without attracting attention.

The park ends abruptly two blocks further on with a high mesh fence standing between the completed section and new construction. I realize I've guessed wrong and that Constantine must have headed south. I turn around smartly, retracing my steps as fast as I dare. As I pass back over the wide, cedar-planked section of the park I spot the Statue of Liberty in the distance. I stop for a moment, frozen in my tracks by the unexpected view. The statue is illuminated in the darkness of the harbor, her arm extended, the copper flame of the torch bathed in golden light.

The park plunges directly through the enormous Chelsea Market building just south of the stairway where I entered. Inside the building, the walkway is set up as a cafe. A long countertop stretches along one side of the pathway and tables dot the other side. Even on a cool evening, the bar is doing brisk business. As I emerge from the shelter of the Market, I spot my man. The trestle makes a sweeping curve to the left on this stretch, and the park is at its broadest point, divided into two levels. The lower level has a long section of the original train track grown over with vegetation beside a narrow footpath. The upper section is much wider and flanked by a series of wooden benches shaped to resemble beach chairs. They are spacious enough for two and largely occupied by teenagers. This section of the park has an unobstructed view, and the beach chairs look due west over the Hudson River.

A hundred yards down the trestle, the two paths merge, and it is here that I see Constantine. He is standing against the riveted black iron trestle railing, leaning on the slanted aluminum rail that joins the rounded iron bar on the top of the railing at an angle. He has one elbow on the railing and his dark curly hair flaps in the breeze rising off 14th Street. He is casually reading a newspaper, which is folded over several times, in the manner that New Yorkers have adopted to avoid offending each other in the confined space of the subway system. In his elegant cashmere overcoat and sheepskin-lined driving gloves, Drubich looks out of place on the High Line. He reminds me of a character from a Magritte painting, with his unusually erect bearing in this city that seems to perpetually lean forward. I notice that the back of the newspaper Drubich is reading neatly frames an advertisement. We've gotten lucky. Constantine's pose is classic fieldcraft: this is almost certainly a meet.

I stop about twenty yards short of Drubich on the lower section of the walkway and lean over the railing, looking out at the Hudson as a small container ship drifts by. There's a small, flesh-colored communication device in my ear, one that is a lot less noticeable than the jobs Secret Service guys wear, and I casually speak into it, keeping my voice low enough to fade into the blare of the traffic below.

"Are you guys with me?"

"This is Holland, we're still where you left us," he says.

"Drive south and drop Brennan at 14th Street. He should enter the High Line Park and proceed north. Our target is standing right on top of 15th

Street. Tell Brennan that when he spots Drubich, he should stay at least twenty yards away. I think our man is waiting for a meet. If I spot his contact, I'll try to get in close and get a picture. Constantine could be here on unrelated business, but there's a chance we'll get what we came for."

"Okay, I read you – is there anything else?" Special Agent Holland asks.

"Better call for reinforcements. If this doesn't happen quickly and we can get someone into one of the buildings overlooking the park, I'd love to get audio on this." I again get annoyed that we don't have a real surveillance unit on Drubich. Unless we catch Constantine in a face-to-face meeting with the mysterious redheaded diplomat, overhearing any conversation he has is vital. Drubich might be untouchable because of his diplomatic immunity, but anyone he meets is fair game for the FBI.

"Gotcha, I'll see what I can do," Holland says, his voice betraying some excitement. I wonder how long he's been in the field.

I turn south, making a show of watching a blonde in a clinging sweater who is approaching me, and start people watching. If at all possible, I want to spot Constantine's contact as he makes his approach so I can move in while the two are first exchanging countersigns and less likely to notice me.

I reach inside the lining of my raincoat. I've clipped a small remote control to an inside pocket meant for business cards that is sewn in near the waist. I slide a toggle switch on the small remote and a viewfinder appears inside the right lens of the clear Persol glasses. The lenses themselves are flat, as I do not need vision correction, but they make an excellent screen for the tiny camera hidden in the black frame. They also transform my persona, theoretically changing me from a bedraggled slacker into an urban hipster. Or so I guess. I don't trust government-issued wardrobe in a place like New York because "the look" is so specific and changes so quickly. I've never believed the folks in Virginia have a perfect eye for details. In any city in the world I can do better by walking around until I find someone who looks the way I want to and asking him where he shops. I do like the raincoat, though.

After ten minutes of watching, someone catches my eye: a man approaching from the north. He's very conventional-looking, which makes him stand out in the lower Manhattan crowd. He's a six-footer of medium build in a dark raincoat not too different from mine, with a dark suit underneath. His shoes are what catch my eye. They remind me of Dmitriev's – they look like dress shoes on top but as he lifts his feet I can see a sturdy Vibram sole underneath. It's the kind of thing a professional puts on when he needs to wear a suit but must be able to move quickly if necessary. I can also tell from the way he holds himself that he's a military guy. It's one of our weaknesses – those of us who spend most of our lives in the service. We get a certain upright bearing drilled into us and it becomes very hard to slouch like the rest of the world. That's why most of us don't do well at undercover work unless we hide ourselves under a shemagh and a thick wool coat.

The man is less than a dozen feet from me when the Blackberry in my pocket vibrates. I pull it out, which serves as a good way to avoid making eye contact with the stranger. There's sometimes an instinct that operators get about one another, a recognition that occurs when we lock eyes, and I don't want that to happen here. I focus for a second on the Blackberry. The number is my mother's. I frown, but press the red reject button to send the call to voicemail as I return the device to my pocket. When the stranger passes, I follow him, keeping behind an Orthodox Jewish couple, the man in a black fedora, the woman wearing a wig of straight brown hair. As we come within fifteen feet of Drubich – an acceptable range for the tiny camera in my Persol glasses, I briefly swivel to stare directly at Constantine, who doesn't look back at me. Inside my coat pocket, my thumb flicks a toggle switch and a viewfinder appears in the right lens of my glasses. A scroll wheel enlarges the image. Having half of my vision temporarily magnified is an odd sensation and I have to repress the urge to close my left eye. Then I depressed a button on the remote with my thumb and the image freezes for a second. I get a clear shot of Drubich. I relax fractionally, relieved that the unfamiliar device works as advertised. As I draw closer, I look away from him, focusing instead on the soldier a few paces in front of me. I'll have to repeat the process if he's really here to meet Drubich.

Then I notice something. Just as he's getting closer to Drubich, the operator slides his right hand inside his coat pocket. The gesture is efficient and calculated in its smoothness. It's not something you ordinarily do when you're approaching a contact unless your instructions are to light a cigarette or offer a piece of gum – both gestures that would look distinctly odd in this context. You normally want to keep your hands out in the open so the person you're meeting won't think you're planning to shoot him. I instinctively step around the Orthodox couple, moving myself directly behind the operator. His hand emerges from his pocket just before he reaches Drubich and I glimpse the thin tip of a needle barely protruding from his fingers. At the same time, I see another man, larger and more solidly built than the soldier in front of me, approaching Drubich from the opposite direction. As I watch, the bigger man stops and turns towards Constantine, tapping him on the shoulder. Constantine pivots towards the larger man and away from me and the man with the needle. In that instant, the operator in front of me raises his left hand towards his mouth to cough, drawing attention from his other hand like a trained magician. As his right hand rises, I clearly see a palm-push syringe in his grasp. The hand snakes towards the Constantine's neck, and I have a moment of total clarity. Drubich may think this is a meeting, but it's really a hit. And if I'm not mistaken, it's his own guys – another Spetznaz team – that are trying to kill him.

Time slows to a crawl as I react. I see the soldier's hand moving towards Constantine's neck in slow motion, following a graceful arc. Meanwhile, the bigger man has leaned in towards Constantine, talking earnestly to distract him. I grasp the Russian operator's hand at the last instant, just before the needle penetrates the skin on Drubich's neck. I swiftly lock the wrist and bend it back on itself. With my other hand I immobilize his arm, which spasms as he loses control of it. Before he can react, I bend the arm back on itself, and the needle in his hand plunges into his own neck. I have a sudden feeling of awareness, like a flashbulb going off in front of me, and I dart sideways, letting go of the soldier. Just at that moment, I hear a scream as the Orthodox man behind me collapses in a heap, followed by the crack of a high-velocity rifle. I realize that a sniper is covering the Russian team on the ground.

The operator I've forced to inject himself collapses immediately, folding like a stuffed doll to the ground. As he drops, I catch the eyes of the big Russian who is chatting with Drubich and see him pulling a small pistol, an SR-1 Vector from his coat. Taking a step forward, I push Constantine Drubich to the side with two fingers and step into the space between him and the big Russian. As Drubich stumbles backwards, a splash of blood erupts from his shoulder, and he hits the railing hard and slides down to a sitting position. There's another crack of that high-velocity rifle. I step towards the big Russian who has his Vector almost in firing position and see that there is another man drawing a weapon five paces behind him. It's a team of four, then – three on the ground and one with a sniper rifle. Accelerating, I step almost past the big Russian, to the left. My left arm sweeps up under his right, hitting it at the nexus of a dozen nerves on the inside of the tricep and forcing the arm and the gun straight up in the air. Then as I straddle the man with my hips perpendicular to his, my right hand sweeps under his neck and I catch his Adam's apple in the crook of my sweeping arm, reversing his momentum just at his point of balance. I point my outstretched right hand towards the ground and his head follows. At the same time, with my left hand, I've gripped his paralyzed right at the forearm, bending it backwards so that it points towards the third Russian, who is frozen in mid-stride, his weapon aimed at me. I dig my thumb and forefingers into the bundle of tendons in the middle of the big Russians forearm and the automatic in his hand explodes once, twice as he pulls the trigger involuntarily, hitting the third man in the middle of the chest, collapsing him instantly. Then I step my left foot back quickly like a matador and turn my extended right arm over, catching the big Russian's neck under my elbow. Arching my back, I wrenched my elbow and feel a snap as I sever the man's spinal cord. I look up. There's an unfinished twelve-story building almost directly in front of me, one that the High Line runs directly through. It's the ideal spot for the Russian sniper, and my eyes fix on it as I finish off the big Russian. Just as he starts to slide from my grasp, I see a flash from one of the unfinished floors in the middle of the building.

I'm already moving, and the shot misses me. In a fluid motion, I draw the Sig-Sauer from a holster on my hip I've rigged underneath the raincoat and put six rounds high into a wall-to-ceiling window on a finished floor just above the sniper. The glass shatters and I hear screams as I bend down over Drubich. I know without looking that everyone in this section of the park, even those who've seen the Orthodox man and Drubich get shot, are now looking up at the hotel, more or less at the spot the sniper is firing from. I'm hoping that this attention will force the sniper to move, if he doesn't want his muzzle flash to be witnessed by a hundred onlookers. It may give me a few precious seconds with Drubich. It's a long shot, but I have to take the chance.

Constantine Drubich is in shock, and he's losing blood quickly. I grab him by the collar of his beautiful overcoat and bring my face to within a few inches of his. Speaking Russian, I say, "You've been sold out. Your own people are murdering you. This is your only chance to get even. Tell me the name of the redheaded American."

He looks into my eyes and he smiles for a moment. Then the cloud starts to come back over his eyes and I can see that he's scared. His mortality is confronting him, but he just shakes his head and smiles. I know that I won't get anything from him. A mental timer goes off in my head and I jump to the side upright just as a high-velocity round smashes into Constantine's chest, ending his life instantly. I jump onto the railing, take three steps along it and then leap off of the viaduct, hitting the roof of a city bus emerging from under the bridge on 14th Street, heading toward the West Side Highway. I roll sideways and regain my feet. Then I make a six-foot leap to the roof of a second bus, going the other way into Manhattan. I have to drop down immediately to avoid being knocked over by the trestle. When I'm under the High Line and out of sight of the sniper, I slide off the side of the bus.

"What the fuck just happened?!" I hear in the earpiece. I can't tell if it's Holland or Brennan, but I ignore them both. I suddenly have a very bad feeling. I pull out the Blackberry and dial into voicemail. I hear my mother's voice on the message. It sounds strained.

"Michael, this is your mother. There are some men in the house waiting for you, some foreigners. I told them you've gone home to Washington D.C.

but they are insisting on waiting and it's already almost eight now. Virginia is here and Amelia is supposed to stop by as well. I don't like the look of..." and here her voice cuts out abruptly as the line goes dead. I suddenly realize that I'm sweating.

A red Toyota 4Runner with tinted windows is parked in the driveway of my mother's house. The porch lights are on, and pale yellow light leaks from a narrow slit in the door. As I unlatch the gate on the white picket fence and tread along the slate path to the house, I notice details that didn't catch my eye on Saturday. The shutters are painted blue, a light robin's egg color that makes the house look a little like a bed and breakfast. Someone has put new stairs up to the porch, but the off-white paint on the wood planks doesn't quite match the rest of the porch. There is a bike with a triangular saddle, twist gearshifts and old-fashioned candy-colored streamers spouting from the handlebars leaning against a column on the porch, probably Ginny's. I remember teaching her to ride on a spring afternoon when my father was passed out on the couch after a bender. As I step up to the porch, I see a little hole in the screen that I made as a nine-year-old when I slipped the hook lock with a pen. I got five smacks with a leather belt for that one.

I pull open the screen door and knock.

The door swings open and I'm greeted by the business end of a Ruger .44 Magnum revolver, a very serious piece of iron. The man connected to the gun is has shoulder-length dark hair, a scruffy beard and familiar tattoos creeping up his neck. I recognize his face from one of the photos that Dmitriev handed me at lunch. His name is Maxim Petrov and he's a goon from Kyzyl, a frozen little Russian town about a thousand miles from anywhere. He linked up with the Tambov Gang after spending a decade in Kresty prison on drug charges. Like the rest of the Tambov thugs, he's in the U.S. on an H1-B visa.

With the gun planted firmly in my cheek, Petrov grabs a handful of jacket and yanks me into the foyer. As he shoves me over the banister to frisk me, I inventory the room. The staircase in my mother's house divides the living and dining areas on the left side of the house from the family room and kitchen on the right. The left side of the house is open but on the right, doors separate the kitchen from the dining room and the family room from the entry foyer. The door to the family room is open, however, and there's a man with an MP5 lurking in the doorway. He's in the shadow but his face and background are familiar to me; Arkady Tchayka is a step up the Tambov food chain from Petrov. This guy is the only one of the remaining mobsters with any military training other than Yuri. Arkady served as a sergeant in the Russian Army and did a tour in Chechnya. He was just regular army, but the guy has seen combat. I can tell by his bearing, even from the millisecond glimpse I get while I'm being spun around. I won't underestimate him.

As hands probe my pockets, I get a better look at the living room. The blinds are all pulled down tightly and the room itself has been rearranged. The couch has found a new home against the living room window that overlooks the porch, far from the fireplace, and the stuffed chairs are parked up against the wall next to the TV. Two plain wooden chairs have been dragged from the dining room. My mother and Ginny are in the chairs, sitting in the middle of the bare living room, their hands bound behind them with duct tape. My mother eyes me coldly as Petrov slides his hands down my legs. Tellingly, she is gagged, while Ginny is not. There are marks on my mother's face, including a fading handprint where she has recently been slapped. She has that effect on people.

She must also feel the imprint of the double-barreled, sawed-off shotgun stuck in the small of her neck for my benefit. A giant, an albino with straight long gray hair and cold eyes, handles the shotgun. He's the real degenerate of the group – his name is Oleg Golovkin. Until three years ago, Oleg was imprisoned in the infamous Ognenny Ostrov, an island prison like Alcatraz on Lake Novozero, 400 miles north of Moscow. Ognenny Ostrov was exclusively reserved for death row inmates until Russia instituted a moratorium on the death penalty in 1996. His crime was the rape, torture and murder of a dozen little girls, which makes him notorious even for the Tambov gang. Neither the FBI nor the CIA had any word of his escape before they ran the stack of photos through a database search. He must have come into the country with forged papers.

The fourth man I spot is bald on top, but compensates for the lack of hair on his scalp with muttonchops and a piratical earring. He's holding an even bigger handgun than the Ruger sticking in my back – a Desert Eagle .45 Magnum automag. That gun can blow a softball-sized hole in you at close range and do something much worse at twenty or thirty yards. It's absurdly hard to control the recoil, however, so the only shot that really counts is the first. Not that you'd need more than one. His name is Valery Pichushkin and he's holding that very big handgun to the head of my sister Ginny. Her eyes are red and her cheeks are faintly streaked with mascara.

The main thing I notice in my glance around the living room is who is not there. There's one person missing from this picture, which changes the entire situation. I don't see Yuri. He may be lurking in the kitchen, waiting to make a dramatic entrance, but he doesn't strike me as the type. The wheels in my head start spinning, trying to figure out why he's not here. Then Petrov stands me up, apparently satisfied that I am weaponless and therefore defenseless.

Arkady attempts to address me in English and I cut him off sharply in Russian. "Speak Russian please, Arkady Sergeivich," I say. He looks for a second as if I've slapped him and I see Pichushkin and Petrov quickly exchange startled glances. This confirms my first suspicion. These guys don't know my background. Yuri is too much of a professional not to have checked me out after our run-in at the steel mill, so that means he's kept them in the dark for a reason. That's assuming he's behind this little hostage situation, but I am convinced that he is. Arkady blanches a little more as he realizes that not only have I spoken Russian, I've addressed him by his name and his patronymic – an archaic form that he's probably only heard his grandmother use. The men look visibly uncomfortable, even the giant Golovkin. They are wondering what else I know. I need to keep them off-balance. I step away from Petrov, gently pushing the .44 away from my cheek while keeping my eyes on Arkady. I lift my left hand and hold it out straight with my finger extended like an accusation and point to my mother, raising my voice a notch as I do, "That's my mother sitting there next to my sister. That's my mother that someone has slapped, gagged and tied to a chair. You have a mother, don't you Arkady Sergeivich? A sister too, if I'm right. Her name is Natalia and she lives in Komarovo with her husband, and a baby boy, your nephew Anatoly. They live in a little wood house with red shutters, do they not? How would you feel if someone were to treat them with this same lack of respect you've shown to my family?" Arkady steps back as if I've slapped him. It's a huge gambit challenging Arkady in this roomful of armed gangsters. Threatening the Slav's mother and sister is especially dangerous, even while they're holding my own mother and sister at gunpoint. But my audacity is also what is holding them back. These gangsters have been conditioned to respect power and I'm throwing around information and threats like a serious player. Before they can regroup I press my advantage.

"Where is Yuri?" I ask, shifting my attention to Golovkin, whom I peg as the dimmest bulb in the group. His eyes dart towards the front door, confirming my intuition. I don't wait for an answer from Arkady. "He's not here, is he?" I spit on the floor, trying not to make eye contact with my mother as I do. "He ordered you to hold my mother and sister as hostage then left? And I suppose he told you I'd come alone without involving the authorities?" I ask, showing outrage. There's more shifting around from the three goons, especially Petrov, who grabs me again and sticks the .44 Magnum I've brushed aside right into the back of my neck. Then I notice Golovkin frowning at Arkady. These men cannot have failed to notice the roadblocks at either end of Green Farms Hollow or the multiple FBI vehicles with flashing lights manning them. Arkady himself has kept his poker face after his initial reaction and is standing stock-still and staring at me.

"You know that I'm unarmed," I say, addressing my comments only to Arkady, the leader. "I'm taking an ice pack out of my pocket," I stick two fingers into my jacket pocket and slowly remove a chemical ice pack. "Let me look at my mother and my sister and then we can talk." The stunned silence in the room stretches on as I pull my arm free of Petrov and calmly walk over to my mother. With a twist I break the pack and dab it on her cheek. She looks like she wants to spit in my face and I'm actually relieved that the Russians have gagged her. When I've gotten both of her cheeks good and cold, I move on to Ginny.

"Just stay calm and don't move," I whisper to Ginny without moving my lips as I rub the pack on her cheeks. Then I straighten up.

"So is this a hostage trade – me for them?" I ask. Seeing Arkady's expression I try again, "Or perhaps you're supposed to kill me in front of them?" Still no reaction. "Or is it kill them in front of me?" and here Arkady involuntarily arches an eyebrow.

"Don't you think the situation has changed? If you fire a gun in here, the FBI will knock down the door and we'll all be dead in minutes. An American prison is still better than getting planted in an unmarked grave," I say.

"Let's kill them all and be done with this," Petrov growls impatiently. Arkady steps past me and, leaning into Petrov, hisses furiously into his ear. When Arkady steps back in front of me, he's flushed. I've managed to cause a little dissension in the ranks, at least.

"You will have the police withdraw immediately or we will kill your mother," Arkady pronounces calmly.

"If the FBI pulls back they'll move just outside of your sight range and you know it. You're bluffing. Yuri ordered you to kill my mother and sister in front of me and then bring me to him so he could finish the job personally. But Yuri was smart enough to know that I'd never walk into this kind of situation alone, so that means he set you up. He put you in a position where you'll certainly be killed. Then there will be nobody left to tie him back to everything he's done in this town. Do you really want to die today? Because if you touch my mother or my sister again, I can guarantee that not one of you will leave this house alive." I stop talking to catch a breath and let the four Russians think about what I've said. I'm having some effect on Arkady because he doesn't speak.

"On the other hand, if you put down your arms and walk out of this house with me right now, I can promise that you will live and that you'll be treated fairly. If you deliver Yuri, you might even escape with something less than a life sentence." In fact I have no idea what the penalties are for the multiple crimes that these men have committed but I suspect they'll never see daylight if they surrender.

For a second – a moment that stretches to eternity – I see that I have him. Arkady knows the score. Maybe he was already wondering why there hasn't been any traffic on the street for the last hour, or why the neighboring houses have all gone dark. Possibly he doesn't completely trust Yuri anyway. Maybe, like me, he's learned somewhere along the way to recognize the truth when it is spoken to him. But then, just as he seems to decide, just as I think he's going to tell his men to put down their weapons, Oleg Golovkin, the serial killer, interrupts.

"Don't listen to him, Arkady! He's just trying to save his precious little family. You know what we have to do."

"Oleg," I turn to address him, keeping my tone even, "I was surprised to learn that you were in the United States. I was under the impression that recreation time at Ognenny Ostrov was limited to the prison yard."

"You're not going to mind-fuck me, American soldier!" Golovkin snarls, and he reaches to pull back the dual hammers on his shotgun.

"Go, go, go!" I yell, hoping my wire is still working, and immediately jerk my head to the left as Petrov's .44 Magnum erupts in my ear, the bullet missing me by millimeters. Before anyone else can react, Golovkin is flung back a half dozen feet away from my mother, the tops of his legs finally hitting the dining room table as he slams back onto it with his arms spread wide. His shotgun drops uselessly to the ground, the hammers never striking. At the same instant, Pichushkin is spun around to the left, his Desert Eagle flying away from Ginny's forehead, and his body jerks like a marionette as a .50-caliber slug tears through his heart. I assume that the boom of sniper rifles has accompanied this but I can't hear a thing: the .44 Ruger has left me deaf for the moment. Before Petrov can fire the big revolver again, I step back and jab him in the throat with the back of my elbow. While he chokes I grab his wrist and using a pressure point, relieve him of the Ruger. Then I have a hand on top of Arkady's MP5, pushing it away from me as I step towards him. Before Arkady can make his mind up whether to fire, I have the Ruger planted in his chest. After a tense moment of silence, he relents and releases the MP5. Without looking back, I plant an elbow in Petrov's face as he lunges towards me from behind and he drops like a stone. Then I lock eyes with Arkady, the only other man left standing in the room.

"Where is Yuri?" I ask. He takes a moment to register the question. He is trembling and he looks like he's seen a ghost. Then, slowly, he composes himself. His fingers spread wide and he reaches slowly into his pants pocket.

* * *

I'm loitering on the porch, waiting for Alpha to call on the Blackberry. Amelia rushed in as soon as the FBI let her through and promptly kicked me out of the house. "You should be ashamed!" she said to me. I told her that the men who invaded the house were criminals, and that our mother was not harmed. "But you brought them here! Look what they did to the house!" she responded. So I told her the government would pay to clean up the mess, although I'm not at all sure if that's true. She scoffed, "Mother will never take a handout, but that's not the point. She's covered in blood! How long do you think it's taken her to get over the last time?" I thought about that for a moment and it shook me up a little. My mother is not a very sympathetic figure, so it's always been hard for me to know what effect my dad's suicide had on her. When I peeled the tape off her mouth as the FBI rushed in to secure the two Tambov gang members still breathing, she refused to speak to me, didn't even make eye contact. I thought she was in shock. But I guess she wasn't. Our reconciliation was short-lived, it seems. Mercifully, Ginny's attitude was different; she hugged me fiercely while weeping openly. Then again, Ginny never blamed me for anything.

Dan Menetti steps onto the porch. I don't know if he was ever a field agent, but he looks a little out of place wearing body armor and a helmet. He takes off the helmet and runs a hand through thinning hair, then sits down on the porch swing opposite me as I lean against the railing.

"How are you holding up?" he asks.

"I think my mother is disowning me."

"Damn straight she is. You should have gotten her out of Dodge a couple of days ago," he says, smiling.

"She hasn't left this town for more than twenty years. Nothing short of a nuclear warhead could dislodge her."

Dan looks over his shoulder at the shattered window and the .50-caliber holes in the wall. "At least you gave it your best shot. Those snipers your boss loaned us are damned impressive. Our guys say they wouldn't have dared make that shot through a wall."

The snipers were Sleeper and Tweetie, the two Activity operators Alpha brought with him to Sweet Sue's yesterday. After Dmitriev passed me photos of Yuri and his men at lunch today, I asked Alpha to have them watch my mother's place. As I suspected, they were still in town.

"They were firing the Barrett XM-500 with thermal imaging sights. That's a very special weapons package your guys probably don't have yet," I point out. FBI snipers are no slouches; I've shot alongside them at Quantico.

"I dunno. That was a neat trick with the icepack, by the way."

I shrug, "I needed to be sure we could tell the good guys from the bad guys." When I dabbed my mother and sister's cheeks with the icepack, I was marking them for Sleeper and Tweetie. The whole plan was probably a crazy gambit. But I wasn't confident that a hostage standoff with the FBI would end up with my family intact and I also wanted to get at least one of the Tambov guys out alive. Don't get me wrong, the FBI Hostage Rescue Team guys are top-shelf – they had a liaison assigned to the Activity and I had a chance to work with him. But when it came down to my own family, I wanted to handle things personally.

Menetti's mobile rings and he steps off the porch for a moment. When he comes back his face is grim.

"I have bad news for you. The two agents we sent to take Miss Ryan home have not checked in. We called Miss Ryan's parents and she did not arrive there. We have a GPS location on their vehicle and there's a team en route right now. Miss Ryan's mobile phone is not transmitting at the moment. We have a BOLO out on her for the tri-state area."

My stomach drops as the pieces of the puzzle start to fit together. Menetti makes the same connection I do and asks, "Did one of those goons give you a note from Kuznetsov?" It takes me a moment to remember that's Yuri's last name before I nod.

"What was the message?"

I hand the note to Menetti, It has a phone number scrawled on it. "The message was to call this number."

"Have you?"

"No," I shake my head. "I'm waiting for a call back from Alpha."

"If he's taken Miss Ryan, it's probably not the worst thing in the world to let Mr. Kuznetsov cool his heels a little. That might get him wondering how you'll react," Menetti observes. He doesn't miss much. "But you have to understand that kidnapping is a federal offense. This is our show." I nod, thinking *one thing at a time*.

Then Sleeper and Tweetie appear, having stowed their gear. We chat for a few moments. It's an odd, awkward situation. I'm glad that Alpha was willing to part with them for an extra day. I'm grateful they were as good as I remember at the critical moment. But I'm still uncomfortable. When I was in the Activity, we almost never got glimpses of each other's private lives. They've seen more of mine than I want anyone to. I'm relieved when the Blackberry vibrates and it's Alpha.

"Sorry to keep you waiting, Orion. I'm looking at an FBI flash report on the incident at your mother's house right now, but why don't you take me through it," he says. I step off the porch into the front yard and walk him through events slowly, taking pains to praise Tweetie and Sleeper for the difficult shots they made that spared my mother and Ginny's lives. Then I tell him about the note and Veronica's disappearance.

"This sounds like it's personal for Mr. Kuznetsov," he observes.

"I think so, sir. What else could Yuri hope to gain? He must know the Tambov operation is finished and that Constantine Drubich is dead. He set up his own guys to get killed by us. I think he wants revenge for his brother, and then he wants to disappear with no loose ends."

"The only way to know is to make contact. Give me the number you received. We'll set up the call and ring your phone when it's ready. We'll be able to trace Mr. Kuznetsov's phone even before you connect."

I read Alpha the number and hang up. A moment later, the Blackberry buzzes again. It's Sammie, who initiates the call. Yuri answers on the second ring.

"Herne?" he asks, his voice raw like a wolf that's lost a patch of fur.

"That's right," I say. "I got your message."

"And your family. How are they?" His tone raises the small hairs on my neck. This guy may have the same training I do, but he enjoys his work in a way I never did.

"They're fine."

"Did any of my men survive?" We both know his men were lambs before the altar.

"Arkady Tchayka and Maxim Petrov are alive. The other two are dead. I'm surprised Oleg Golovkin was one of yours. I would have though you'd have higher standards."

"You make do with what you're given. But you are right; he was not a good man. Very undisciplined." He's missed my point, of course. Whether on purpose or not, I can't tell. "I have the girl. You know this already, yes?" He fumbles with the phone for a second and I hear a shriek of "Michael!" which is abruptly cut off. It's Veronica.

"Yes, you have the girl," I sigh and don't bother disguising it from Yuri. "What do you want?" There can only be one thing. Yuri knows exactly what happened when his associates kidnapped Veronica and he won't make the same mistake.

"If you come to me, I'll let her go."

"So you can shoot me instead? You must think I'm a romantic."

"I know you're a romantic, Mr. Herne. That's why I like you. You'll have a fair chance. More than my brother had."

"More than those little girls had? More than Mel Harris had?" I counter, my blood rising.

"Yes. All the more reason for you to come. Alone. Do you know where the old Overlook Mountain House is?"

"I do." I am surprised that Yuri does.

"Come alone. Leave your guns at home, but bring a knife. If you bring help or a gun, I'll kill the girl. You know I'll see them, don't you?"

"How do I know you won't kill her as soon as you get off this call?"

"You have my word that the girl is alive and I will not touch her from this moment forward if you follow my instructions. I also promise that you will have as much chance to kill me as I will to kill you."

"Okay," I say. It's insane to agree to his terms, of course. Nine of ten professionals would kill Veronica immediately after disconnecting the call and then finish me off as soon as they had a good shot. That's the prudent course of action. But I believe Yuri won't shoot me or hurt the girl because he wants the opportunity to kill me with his bare hands. He's an anachronism, a man who regards his word of honor as inviolate but feels no hesitation abetting pedophiles or murdering innocent women. Or maybe he's a pure psychopath. I don't know. I end the call and a second later the phone buzzes.

"You're going." Alpha says this as a statement of fact. I detect a note of sympathy in his voice.

"Yes, sir. I could use some assistance if you are willing, sir. Would you run interference with the FBI to give me a clear field? The 'house' Yuri is referring to is on the side of a mountain near Woodstock. The weather is good up here right now and the moon is nearly full tonight. If the FBI tries to infiltrate the woods Yuri will spot them from a mile away, and then a lot of people will die. I'd prefer if they limit themselves to sealing off the area with a perimeter at one mile from the Overlook, but no closer."

"Do you really think you'll get the girl out of there alive?"

I pause to consider this. "It seems unlikely, sir, but I have to try."

"I understand," Alpha says. "Hang tight for a few moments while I arrange things for you. And good luck."

The Overlook Mountain House is not a working hotel, not any longer. It's a discarded husk – built on the ruins of two earlier attempts – that sits on the gently sloping face of a mountain just a few minutes' drive north from the town of Woodstock. The first hotel built on the spot was a me-too attempt to capitalize on the success of the Catskill Mountain House, a bigger establishment that wooed affluent domestic travelers beginning in 1827. It was called the Overlook Hotel, and it wasn't actually completed until well after the Civil War, in 1871. It had some early successes, notably a visit by

President Ulysses S. Grant in 1873. Then it burned down in 1875, on April Fools Day. When it was reconstructed in 1878, the new owners called it the Overlook Mountain House. It operated through 1897, although rarely at more than half-capacity. When the owner took his life in the building, it closed for two years and was never fully opened thereafter, but was rented out occasionally to private groups. It was notoriously the site of the birth of the Communist Party of America in 1921. In 1923, just two months after the United Mine Workers revealed the secret of the Overlook House and its connection to the Communists, unknown persons burned the second structure to the ground.

The final attempt to build an Overlook Mountain house re-imagined it as a middle-class refuge. This time, the exterior walls of the structure were constructed not of wood but of reinforced concrete from the Godfrey mill in Conestoga. This third and last incarnation was never completed, the investor having run out of funds. In 1943, a fire tore through the half-finished structure, leaving only the concrete walls standing. In fact, virtually all of the great Catskill resorts of the nineteenth and early twentieth centuries succumbed to fire, including the grand old Catskill Mountain House, burned intentionally in 1963 by the Conservation Department.

I am driving my own car when I reach the trailhead. There's a good-sized parking lot off Mead Mountain Road just across from the Tibetan Buddhist monastery which lets you know that yes, you're near *that* Woodstock. The trail launches off to the east away from the monastery and rises gently by a thousand feet or so over the mile and a half from the trailhead to the ruins. I walk at a moderate pace without a headlamp. It's not hard because the moon is bright in the sky and the forest on this mountain is not dense. I can see why Yuri picked this spot. With a night scope and a good rifle he'll be able to spot anyone moving within a mile of his location. It's another reason why I take an even stride and make no effort to conceal myself on the trail. I'm depending entirely on my reading of Yuri, which is a stretch considering I've only seen him in person the one time, when he was trying to kill me. Since then I've killed a whole bunch of his associates and his baby brother. Coming in unarmed seems like less of a good idea the closer I approach.

The first time I ever ran across the Overlook Mountain House, it was with a couple of high school buddies. We all thought we'd stumbled across the ruins of an insane asylum. There are two concrete structures set caddie-corner to each other in a clearing along the trail. The larger one is a three-story rectangular building, with the narrow end facing the trail. It looks institutional rather than welcoming. These are only the bleached bones, though. The concrete glows in the moonlight. Since I'm expected, I walk up to it and down the stairs to what might have once been a front door.

The concrete walls are just a façade now. There was never a roof on the structure and a large courtyard takes up most of the interior space. There are a few surviving interior walls at one end, but mostly it's just a grassy open space. Veronica is sitting at the far end from where I enter. She's bound hand and foot and there is a thick piece of duct tape over her mouth. She seems to be okay, but I can't really tell much in the moonlight. I step forward into the open courtyard about twenty yards from her and stop, with my hands out in front of me.

"Take off your coat," the voice rumbles from the darkness. I notice the red pinprick of a laser site on me and as I comply I trace the narrow beam back to its origin in an upper window. Or rather, the place a window should be. From up there, Yuri will have a pretty good view of all of the approaches to the structure. I hold my breath for a second while I wait to see if I've judged him correctly. I peel off my shell jacket and my fleece and drop them on the ground without being shot. I take this as a good sign, although I'm chilly in a long-sleeve UnderArmor compression shirt. Then the laser light flicks off and I hear a faint rustle. After a few moments, Yuri appears at the other end of the courtyard. He's wearing plain, pale green fatigues with the pants legs bloused from a sturdy pair of leather boots. It looks as if it may be his military uniform, and I chew on that for a moment.

Yuri approaches with an MP5 pointed at me and a rifle slung over his back. He's a little taller and a lot thicker than he looked the first time I saw him from a distance, but I'd make a fair-sized bet there's not much fat on him. He moves like a big cat, a panther stalking prey. His hair is blond and shaved down to a flat-top, like the deck of an aircraft carrier. Those tattoos I've seen on the other men wind up his neck, glistening in the moonlight. When he gets within spitting distance, Yuri motions for me to turn around. He pats my jacket and expertly frisks me. I'm not carrying a gun. He leaves the SOG Seal Pup knife in its kydex sheath attached to my belt. Then he backs away, telling me to stay put. I wait a long moment before he says "okay." I turn around.

Yuri has stripped down to a plain khaki t-shirt and there's steam coming off of him in the cold air. I can see that in addition to the snake tattoos on his neck, his arms are covered with a gothic mix of black ink. He's holding a knife as he steps forward. It's a Kizlyar Strella, a wicked, double-bladed weapon with a simple, cord-wrapped handle. He flicks it from hand to hand as he comes face to face with me. I slide the Seal Pup from its sheath and hold it blade downwards in a defensive posture.

"Why are we doing this, Yuri?" I ask. He starts circling me while I talk and I rotate slowly to keep him from flanking me. Yuri moves like a wrestler, with his feet flat on the ground all the time, never crossing each other.

"Why are you asking me questions you know the answer to already?" he responds in Russian. "You killed my brother."

"Your brother was armed, he was shooting at me and he was in a rough business. None of this would have happened if you hadn't tried to kill me first, or if your friends hadn't kidnapped Veronica." I involuntarily look toward her when I mention her name, and just as I make eye contact, Yuri takes advantage of my momentary distraction, feinting forward with the knife, then coming in with a powerful shot from his left arm, a classic kidney punch. I deflect the Strella with the flat of the blade of the Seal Pup and spin away from the punch, but just barely. He's quick.

Yuri shakes his head at me. "It doesn't matter. You don't understand. That boy, I looked out for him for his whole life. I protected him from my father, from the army, from everything." Yuri looks sad, a little weary. I've seen the dossier on his brother, passed along by Sammie. The kid was a screw-up. He tried everything that Yuri did, from the army to the Tambov gang, only with less success and a lot more problems.

"I have a sister like that. One of your guys was holding a gun to her head just an hour ago."

Yuri nods. "It is a bad business. I should never have become involved. But my country is not like yours. When I left the army, there was no private contractor job waiting for me. I could not become a security advisor for a rich corporation. The government would not have wanted me. I could have prostituted myself to one of the oligarchs, but I couldn't face that. At least there is some discipline with the Tambovs. But it all went to shit and cost Seryoza his life. You cost him his life." He corrects himself and launches another attack. The blade flashes in a figure-eight pattern as he feints towards my neck then crouches and comes in low. The knife darts forward past my guard toward the inside of my thigh. He's aiming for my femoral artery – severing it would exsanguinate me in under a minute. I sweep downwards with the Seal Pup at the last second and manage to defect the Strella, which slices through my pants instead.

"I'm sorry about your brother, Yuri, but what's the point? Killing me won't bring him back. The operation here is finished. All of your colleagues are either dead or in prison, Constantine Drubich is dead and the SVR is treating anyone connected with the whole business like a stain on a wedding dress. You're a professional, Yuri. Why would you stick around for vengeance instead of getting the hell out of town? You know they'll be hunting you too, don't you?"

Yuri looks at me and I can feel world-weary disappointment spilling from his lips as he sighs. "You speak my language well, but you don't have a Russian soul. Blood is blood. It's all that matters. You took my brother. The blood debt must be repaid. It's not complicated." Yuri comes in again, and this time I'm ready. Our knives meet two, three, four times as he probes my guard. His lips are set in a grimace and I can tell that he's done talking. He leans in and focuses, then charges me suddenly, trying to block my knife with his free left arm. Then he spins around me, his right arm extended with the intention of planting the Strella in the base of my spine. The razor-sharp blade passes through empty air instead as I lean forward, extending my entire body over my bent right knee, my torso parallel to the ground. As I extend, my right arm windmills upward and my wrist catches him under the armpit of his right arm holding the knife. Constantine is off balance, having braced himself to push the Strella deep into my spine, and I toss him over my hip. He grunts loudly as his body hits the ground but then he rolls back over his shoulder and is upright again before I can press the counterattack.

As soon as he regains his feet, Yuri goes back on the attack, leaping to the right, stabbing out and again forcing me to block inside his arm with the edge of my left hand. With his own left hand he thrusts upward, trying to put the heel of his callused palm through my nose. Instead, we become entwined as I drop the Seal Pup and block his strike from the inside with my forearm, then slide it up and over, wrapping his arm with mine. With both of his arms engaged, Yuri goes for a head butt, slamming his head forward like a soccer star looking for the goal. I'm waiting for this and I dodge my head to the side, causing him to wrench his neck while I use his momentum to carry us backward into a roll, wedging my right knee between us and then using it to fling him over me as I hit the ground. I grab his right wrist with my left on the way over and twist, forcing him to release the Strella. I kip back onto my feet and turn, quickly spotting the black Strella on the ground. I kick it away from us. He looks at me in disgust for a moment until I pick up the Seal Pup and toss it aside as well. It's not a show of bravado on my part, even though Yuri interprets it that way. Yuri is better than me with a knife, and I'm lucky that I haven't been sliced yet. Against a lesser man, I'd counter barehanded and attempt to immobilize him. But where other men have nerve endings, Yuri seems to have solid muscle. I need to wear him down if I'm going to have a chance of beating him.

Absent his knife, Yuri roars like a lion and charges low, going in for a wrestling takedown. I deflect his right arm downwards then plant my left hand on his right shoulder and cartwheel over him as he dives past. The next time he attacks, it's as a boxer, with a solid three-punch combination. I bob away from the first two jabs and then when the solid cross comes, I step in towards it, twist outside of the punch and grab his wrist and the underside of his elbow as he goes by. Then I spin as I work the wrist and elbow over. After a revolution, I force him down and he rolls to escape the lock. He's as strong as a bear and I'm sweating. Before I can plan a strategy, he's back up and leaps into the air feinting a kick, then bringing down his fist like a hammer. I use his momentum to throw him again, forcing him to roll on the twig-covered grass.

Yuri begins to sweat as I counter a half-dozen more moves, several times tossing him into a throw or forcing him to roll. He's getting frustrated and I can see him looking over towards the Strella and then to the spot where I suspect he's stashed his weapons. But when he makes a move in any direction, I corral him with small strikes and slaps that sting and anger him without doing much damage. Instead they make him swear and charge me again. Then I put him down on the ground a little more roughly. He's at least fifteen years older than me and he is finally starting to feel it.

As our fight stretches on, I see a glint of recognition light up in Yuri's eyes. He suddenly understands my strategy. Instead of fighting like gladiators or sumo wrestlers, I've turned our contest into a bullfight. Yuri is better than me with a knife, and too strong for me to best in straight wrestling. I've been wearing him down systematically with safe moves to deplete his strength to the point where I can disable him. He's been fighting madly, just like a bull, not thinking I had a larger strategy. A rueful smile tells me all I need to know. He gathers his remaining energy and comes in flat at me like a Greco Roman or Sumo wrestler. As his left hand latches onto me I jab him sharply in a tiny spot underneath his arm. The hand starts to tremble, and he loses control of it. He starts to panic and brings his big right arm up in a powerful uppercut. I dodge the blow and then jab at the arm on the upswing. His right arm, too, starts to spasm. Before he can regroup, I pull him around and wrap my forearms around his head, one on either side.

"It doesn't have to end like this, Yuri," I say through labored breaths. "Tell me that it's over and I'll let you go."

He laughs. "You *are* a romantic, and a fool. You can't let me live now – I'll never stop hunting you. Finish what you started!" Yuri seems oddly exuberant as he says this. I roll my arms apart, applying more and more torque to his neck until my hands run out of slack and I grip his chin and the back of his head with my palms and twist sharply. I feel his neck snap and he collapses, limp and dead. I sit there with him for a moment panting. *He knew*, I think, *he knew from the beginning he was going to lose*. Our match was like assisted suicide, an honorable way for him to die. But he still felt that he'd won somehow, even at the end…

I pant as I stand over him as my mind races to catch up with my intuition. Then, with a sinking feeling, I rush over to Veronica.

She is an awful shade of white and blue, dappled with bits of ghostly light underneath the hunter's moon. She gasps as I pull the tape off of her mouth and it takes her moments to regain her breath. "He...injected me with something just before you called. He wouldn't tell me what it was... told me you'd know." She has to pause to breathe, as if a heavy weight is sitting on her chest. She fumbles with a zipper on her jacket pocket and withdraws a pharmaceutical vial. I read the label and recognize the drug. It's not good news. She looks at me and I just shake my head.

"I'm sorry." I say, looking down at her head in my lap. I don't cry. I feel numb. I pull a phone out of my pocket and call Menetti – tell him to bring paramedics, but I know it won't help.

We sit there for a few minutes, talking quietly. Veronica tells me things she wants me to say to her parents. Then she tells me a few things I would rather not hear and I respond with some things that I know she needs me to say. But still I feel nothing, like I'm observing all of this from a safe distance. After awhile, she drifts away, still breathing shallowly but no longer conscious. She's still in that state when the FBI guys come crashing through the forest, but I barely perceive them. They won't be able to help her. I am numb, almost insensate. As they take her away, I slide to the ground, my back against a concrete wall, and look up at the sky through grasping branches of oak and sugar maple intruding over the old bones of the hotel. It comes to me then, sinking in slowly like the encroaching chill of winter. I perceive the exact form of Yuri's revenge. It's not that he's taken Veronica's life, not just that. It's that he has completed what he started when he killed Mel. The transformation that began when I first set my foot on the road to uncover Mel's killer is finished. Yuri has robbed me of my new life. I have devolved back to the man I once was: an operator.

Epilogue –
Three Months Later

Jonathan Dunleavy contemplates the delicate bit of Maine Cod on the end of his fork, which he has scooped from its beer-battered crust like an oyster from its shell. The food is solid if not stellar at Old Ebbitt's Grill, but food isn't the attraction of the place. The 154-year-old restaurant just across the street from the Treasury Building is one of a handful of lunch spots that attract the power players in Washington, D.C. At least three days a week, Jonathan hits Ebbitt's, the Willard, the Hyatt Regency, Palms or one of a half-dozen other key power scenes. Dunleavy's assistant, Josh Levin, is excellent at wrangling good tables for these occasions. Levin is also proficient at scheduling lunches with the Washington A-list: prominent policymakers, well-connected lobbyists and high-profile journalists. In his three decades in Washington, Dunleavy has become a master at applying Capitol Hill's cardinal rule: appearance is reality. Appearing powerful, popular and persuasive makes you so. The men and women in Washington, D.C. might rule the world, but it often feels to Dunleavy more like a small company town. Everyone is obsessed with gossip; the chattering classes spend endless energy reading the tea leaves for signs of shifts in power.

Of course, things aren't going well at the moment. Josh is supposed to be sitting in for a rising star, a young Florida congressman who has cancelled lunch at the last minute. Except that Josh isn't sitting at all – he's gotten a phone call and disappeared from the table nearly ten minutes earlier. It is unlike Dunleavy's assistant of over two decades, the man who has followed Jonathan from his job as chief of staff for the senior Senator from West Virginia to a white-shoe D.C. law firm, through several positions of increasing authority during the Clinton administration, back to a lobbying firm, and finally on to this dream job with the current administration. Josh is punctual to a fault and always attentive to Jonathan's moods. Right now, Jonathan is getting restless – he doesn't like sitting alone.

Just as Jonathan is about to signal the waiter for his check, a young man in a tailored suit slips into his booth. This alarms Jonathan for several reasons. For one thing, as Deputy National Security Advisor, Jonathan is one of the most powerful men in Washington. He might carry less weight than a Supreme Court Justice, a Cabinet member, Joint Chief or Senator, but Jonathan certainly outranks any member of the House of Representatives outside of the leadership. The presumption of some staffer to sit down uninvited at Jonathan's table in his aide's seat without first asking permission is galling. Then there is the question of personal safety. Jonathan disdains taking a security detail with him on the Hill. But practically speaking he carries more secrets around in his head than 99% of the employees of the U.S. government. So as he eyes this young man, he has to wonder if he is a threat. Jonathan doesn't think so – more likely an eager West Winger trying to score some points up the food chain. But there's something about the way the man slides into the booth that has pricked an undeveloped area of Dunleavy's subconscious, the part that hasn't seen much use in most humans since we were scurrying to avoid being eaten by saber-tooth tigers.

"You don't recognize me, do you?" the young man asks casually. The nerve of the kid actually intrigues Jonathan. There *is* something familiar about him. The young man is trim and fit but he doesn't have the steroidal look of a bodybuilder. He is perhaps six feet tall with thick, straight black hair cut short. His eyes are large and their color is darker than brown, almost black. He's handsome, but not overwhelmingly so. The only odd thing Jonathan notices is that the young man sitting across from him has unusually thick wrists. Ordinary – that's what you'd have to call him. The good side of ordinary, perhaps, but still ordinary. A nobody in a big sea of somebodies. The face looks vaguely familiar, but Jonathan loathes wasting the mental energy it would take to try and place him. Instead he scans the bar for Josh, who will certainly get rid of this attention-seeker.

"I'm sorry, your assistant won't be coming back. There's been a break-in at his house. He should be calling you just about now to tell you." There is an unseemly level of confidence in the young man's voice. Jonathan resolves on the spot to end the interloper's career. Regardless of who he works for, this process will take no more than three phone calls.

Just as he is considering the appropriate words for a brush-off, Jonathan's Blackberry vibrates in his pocket. He raises it discretely to his ear. A chill runs up his spine as he listens to his aide apologize for disappearing and tell him that his house has been burglarized and his wife badly scared. Jonathan hangs up on Josh in mid-sentence and puts the phone down on the table, staring dumbly at the young man sitting across from him.

"How did you know that?" he asks angrily, recovering after a moment of silence.

"We arranged it." The young man raises his hand before Jonathan can reply. "Please save the threats – I need just two minutes of your time and then you'll never see me again."

"You can't have two seconds of my time," Jonathan retorts angrily. He looks around for a waiter.

The young man pulls an envelope from the inside pocket of his jacket and slides it over to Jonathan. "You'll want to look at these before you make a scene."

Dunleavy eyes the envelope. The smartest course of action would be to ignore it. But he is a man who craves secrets when he knows them and despises them when he doesn't. In five seconds, his curiosity wins out. He slides a manicured finger under the flap of the bond paper and opens the envelope. Inside, a folded, blank piece of stationary is wrapped around a dozen 4x6-inch photographs. Jonathan flips through them with mounting horror. They are shots of him, his face recognizable in some of them, his distinctive red hair with the cowlick near the middle of his widow's peak visible in the rest. Jonathan feels the blood rush to his face. The photos show him with several different girls. Very young girls. They are recent. He feels a hard knot forming in the depths of his stomach.

"You're trying to blackmail me?" he hisses.

"No, I am not. Not at all. But I need you to understand that I'm serious. As I said, I just need two minutes of your time." Dunleavy thinks that the young man sounds entirely too reasonable and with a start he realizes that this interloper is speaking a little slowly to him, as if he is addressing an idiot.

"Two minutes, then," Jonathan says briskly, folding the blank stationary back over the photos and stuffing the envelope into his suit jacket.

"You thought you were in the clear, didn't you? After Constantine Drubich was killed?" The name brings Jonathan's gaze up from the table sharply the men lock eyes for a moment before the intensity of the young man's gaze forces Jonathan to look away. He is now straining to remember how he knows this man – anything that will give him an advantage in this awful conversation.

"Don't be ridiculous." Jonathan scoffs.

"My offer is simple. Tell me the truth and these photos will never be released. Lie to me again and I guarantee you that every politician in this town will have a set by dinnertime." The young man's voice has a band of iron at its center.

Jonathan considers this for a moment.

Whatever he wants, the young man already has him dead to rights with the photos. Dunleavy's career will be over in a heartbeat and he'll spend the rest of his life in prison if the photos become public. He suddenly feels weary, completely exhausted. "What do you want to know?"

"You thought you were in the clear because the FBI closed the investigation into the Tambov Gang's activities outside of New York State, correct? "

"Yes."

"And you applied the political pressure that got the FBI to stop looking?" Jonathan nods.

As Jonathan Dunleavy stares at the young man, his name, his whole identity comes to him in a flash: Michael Herne. The one who caused all of the trouble in the first place. A dead chill runs up Jonathan's neck and his chest begins to pound as he remembers reading the man's file. The real file, that is, the codeword-compartmented one that Dunleavy had to threaten the Army Chief of Staff to get read in on. The kid in the expensive suit sitting across from him was one of the deadliest men in the army. His classified file is laced with superlatives, many of them from men in the special ops community who rarely write about other soldiers in these terms. Herne had a string of spectacular successes in Afghanistan in the first few years of the war. Then there was that disaster, the CIA fuck-up that had almost gotten him killed, what was that? Jonathan struggles to remember the details. He starts to sweat. The kid sitting across from him should be dead by all rights. Several times over. Instead, he single-handedly took out two of the Russian Federation's top assassination teams. Dunleavy decides he will cooperate.

"There's one thing that didn't make sense to me. I couldn't figure out why the SVR acted so aggressively to shut down the Tambov ring. Why did they kill Sherriff Peterson and Constantine Drubich? Acting on U.S. soil was a huge risk and it backfired on them. The consequences were far worse than they would have been if they'd left things alone and just taken the hit for their part in setting up the child sex ring. They surely knew the risks."

Jonathan stays silent. He's been a lawyer for too many years to speak in the absence of a direct question.

"I'm guessing that when you first heard the story about the redheaded man, you put pressure on the FBI to focus on Conestoga and nothing else. Which is why I found myself in a Suburban with two B-list special agents from the Albany field office tailing the top Russian spy in America. Is that right?"

"I couldn't interfere with the FBI directly, obviously," he said, pointing to his red hair. "But yes, I pressured the right people to ensure that the focus of the investigation was confined to the New York operation, and eventually I was able to get the investigation closed. But I couldn't influence your boss."

"Former boss," Herne corrects.

Jonathan raises an eyebrow that says, *so what are you doing here now, then?* "How did you find me?" he asks.

"I couldn't let it go. I just couldn't understand why the SVR would risk two of its top Spetznaz teams in operations on U.S. soil just to cover up a little honey trap. If they hadn't tried, we might have stopped looking for you. I doubt that Veronica would have recognized your face from a scrapbook of two hundred redheaded men. That's how many redheads there are in positions of responsibility in the U.S. government, by the way. Once we eliminated the three redheaded men who'd served on the U.S. mission to the U.N., we realized you must have been visiting New York for some reason and just happened to attend that party. It made the going tough – there were just too many suspects. Then the FBI dropped the investigation entirely. Only my old boss and me thought you must still be out there somewhere.

"It was tricky to find you because we spent a lot of time looking for people who had a connection to upstate New York. Then we realized that wasn't it at all. The Tambov ring in Conestoga didn't turn you. That was just a pilot project, a proof of concept for the really high-stakes games the SVR wanted to play in New York and D.C. Constantine wanted to run the test because he couldn't afford to make any mistakes when he was trying to snag you and turn you. So after the Conestoga operation started to operate smoothly, he copied it in Maryland. You were the target. You know what gave you away?"

Jonathan shakes his head automatically, drawn in by the narrative.

"I realized that our redheaded man had to have been have been sitting in on the National Security Council meetings that took place after the Tambov sex ring in Conestoga was exposed. Someone who'd just seen the top-level intel reports wouldn't have known about the connection between Veronica and Constantine Drubich and would never have wanted her to be killed. But a traitor on the NSC would have known the FBI would be hungry to discover whether the Tambov operation had other tentacles. Once we figured that out, we found you immediately. You're the only principal on the NSC with red hair and there are only two redheaded staffers." Herne pauses for a moment to let this sink in. "Do you want to know the most ironic part?"

Jonathan nods reluctantly.

"If you'd just laid off abusing children for six months, we'd never have nailed you. I mean, we would have had our suspicions, but without hard proof we never could have touched you. But you couldn't stop, could you?"

"So what happens now?" Jonathan asks impatiently, ignoring the insult. He is nothing if not practical. He knows that the administration will want to avoid embarrassment. They certainly will not want this kind of scandal breaking while they are still reeling from the aftereffects of the Great Recession and trying to get through an election. The scandal could cost them control of the White House. They'll have to offer him a way out, Jonathan realizes. Maybe the revelation of a previously undiagnosed melanoma will be enough. Jonathan relaxes a little. He still has some leverage.

Herne fixes him with a look, a stare that makes him feel colder. Jonathan is starting to have trouble breathing. The weight on his chest is increasing. *Calm your nerves, it's almost over*, he tells himself.

"There's no place in the legal system for you, I'm sure you know that."

Jonathan is impatient to be rid of this man and this uncomfortable topic. He has plenty of money stashed away. Retirement isn't such a bad option. He doesn't understand why Herne doesn't just tell him how it's going to go down.

"So what are you offering me?" Dunleavy asks, his annoyance showing.

Herne slides from the booth and rises smoothly to his feet. Jonathan watches, transfixed by this deadly man's movement even as his own discomfort increases. Herne leans over him and before he can react, plucks the envelope with the photos from Jonathan's jacket pocket. As Dunleavy starts to protest, Herne lays a hand on his shoulder. It looks like a friendly gesture, but suddenly Jonathan's voice doesn't work. His vocal cords are stilled. His heart slams in his chest and the weight crushing down on him doubles. Jonathan realizes in a final moment of clarity that he is having a heart attack. As Deputy National Security Advisor Jonathan Dunleavy stares at Herne, the younger man whispers a single word into his ear.

"Justice."

Sources

Bits and pieces of this novel come from my own experience, but for the rest I've relied on copious research and the wisdom of others.

Thanks to Douglas Burdett of Artillery Marketing for his wisdom on deer hunting and Army life and his many contacts.

Many thanks go to Mike Noell, Terry Naughton, Tom O'Sullivan and the rest of the guys at Blackhawk (now ATK) in Norfolk, VA. They introduced me to the real world of operators and nearly killed me on the Naval Special Warfare obstacle course.

Thanks also to my former Army classmates at Fletcher who can't have known that they were contributing to a mosaic that would take so long to develop.

The description of Michael Herne's Silver Star action is roughly based on the actual experience of Silver Star recipient Master Sergeant Anthony S. Prior with the 5th Special Forces Group.

For any readers intimately familiar with the geography of the Catskills, you will know that I've taken a few liberties, particularly during the car chase where one of the roads I describe exists on the map but actually ends in someone's back yard.

Thanks to those others who contributed but cannot be named.

Anything that is real in this book is the contribution of the folks above, but the mistakes are all mine.

In addition to the humint above, I found the following books especially useful:

Couch, Dick. *Chosen Soldier: The Making of a Special Forces Warrior*. New York: Crown, 2007. Print.

Fury, Dalton. *Kill Bin Laden: A Delta Force Commander's Account of the Hunt for the World's Most Wanted Man*. New York: St. Martin's, 2008. Print.

Haney, Eric L. *Inside Delta Force: The Story of America's Elite Counterterrorist Unit*. New York: Delacorte, 2002. Print.

Luttrell, Marcus, and Patrick Robinson. *Lone Survivor: The Eyewitness Account of Operation Redwing and the Lost Heroes of SEAL Team 10*. New York: Little, Brown, 2007. Print.

Smith, Michael. *Killer Elite: [the inside Story of America's Most Secret Special Operations Team]*. New York: St. Martin's, 2007. Print.

Stanton, Doug. *Horse Soldiers: The Extraordinary Story of a Band of U.S. Soldiers Who Rode to Victory in Afghanistan*. New York: Scribner, 2009. Print.

Acknowledgements

My editor Rebecca Heyman was a marvel. Her command of the language and its rules, her flair for structure and her nuanced sense of character added depth to a story already rewritten six times.

Walter Harris and Matt Greenfield were early readers of this book and they each kept me motivated through the months and years that my manuscript sat in other people's hands.

The cover for this book is the work of one of my favorite graphic artists, Jothan Cashero whose talents are wasted on cereal boxes and corporate packaging.

Thanks to Constance and Stewart Greenfield who have been part of my family since I was twelve. None of my writing would have been possible without you.

My deepest thanks go to my wife Michelle who has lived with this book since the first day and would often gaze into my eyes and realize that I was writing instead of listening. Tolerating a writer is the truest expression of love that I know.

Finally, thanks to the Tier One Operators at JSOC. I hope that I have captured your spirit and dedication as I have witnessed it. It was my greatest desire to write a book respectful of your training and sacrifice, and to showcase the consummate professionalism that you embody.

I finished the first draft of this novel just before my son Spenser arrived in 2009. I completed the final draft weeks after my father S.K. passed in 2012. This book is dedicated to them.

David Vinjamuri, 2012